TIME CATCHERS

WHEN DAYS TILT

PRAISE FOR THIS BOOK

'*When Days Tilt* invites readers into a vibrant and intricate world, full of imagination and mystery. An absorbing debut for fans of Philip Pullman.' *Anna Morgan, author of* Before The Beginning *and* All That Impossible Space

'An atmospheric, visceral read that casts its otherworldly thrall from the first page. The adventure is always underpinned by the emotional growth of the characters, and the mystery is always grounded in the importance of family and human connection. Perfect for readers who love imaginative historical fantasy with a dash of steampunk.' *Sam-Ellen Bound, author of* Seven Wherewithal Way

'Lose yourself in the world of Victorian London, and the world of its sinister twin, as you travel back – and forth – in time. *Time Catchers: When Days Tilt* will show you London as you've never seen it before.' *Lucinda Hawksley, author and great-great-great-granddaughter of Charles Dickens*

TIME CATCHERS

WHEN DAYS TILT

KAREN GINNANE

PENGUIN BOOKS

PENGUIN BOOKS

UK | USA | Canada | Ireland | Australia
India | New Zealand | South Africa | China

Penguin Random House Australia is part of the Penguin Random
House group of companies whose addresses can be found at
global.penguinrandomhouse.com.

First published by Penguin Books, an imprint of
Penguin Random House Australia Pty Ltd, 2021

Design by Tony Palmer © Penguin Random House Australia Pty Ltd
Cover images: Magdelana Russocka/Trevillion, Lee Avison/Trevillion,
Anna Pavlovetc/Shutterstock
Printed and bound in Australia by Griffin Press, part of Ovato,
an accredited ISO AS/NZS 14001
Environmental Management Systems printer

A catalogue record for this
book is available from the
National Library of Australia

ISBN 978 1 76 089503 7 (Paperback)

Penguin Random House Australia uses papers that are natural and
recyclable products, made from wood grown in sustainable forests.
The logging and manufacture processes are expected to conform to the
environmental regulations of the country of origin.

penguin.com.au

For Mum and Dad, who always believed in me.
Your love and support have been the bedrock of my life.
This book is for you.

PROLOGUE

London, September 1858

It is a time of tilting days.

In the sky a huge comet burns bright, day and night. Below it, a river rots and there are too many bodies to fit in the graveyards.

The city's stink is worse than ever. Not just the usual stench of rotting carcasses, overflowing sewers, tons of burning coal and slums full of bodies that never touch water. Or the throat-grabbing pong from the tanneries and slaughterhouses and soapworks, where they boil old fat and bones. Not just the never-ending mud on the streets, which isn't mud but horse and human dung and anything else that gets thrown down: bones, rotting vegetables, dead flesh, filthy water from knackers' yards; all the waste of a city.

This is the stench of a poisoned river.

There have never been so many humans in one place. London bursts at the seams, overwhelming even the

1

mighty Thames. Its dark waters reek and its banks writhe with worms the colour of blood. It is the rotting underbelly of the city, flipped up for all to see.

In 1858, London is galloping into the future. Humans travel at unimaginable speeds and new technologies fling words across the globe in seconds. Vast buildings rear up from the earth every day. A street one day is a huge hole the next, and a railway line the next. The speed of change is dizzying and the ticking clock is the heartbeat of London life. Time is everything and you have to be quick to survive.

There is one thing that even the quickest Londoner can't escape. One that strikes without warning from Knightsbridge to Limehouse. Something as terrifying as the dreaded cholera because this thing cannot be understood and spares no one.

There have been disappearances before, of course. But not like this. Not people fading into thin air in broad daylight. Vanishing like a magic trick, as though taken from the middle of their own life. No one can say how it happens or where it will occur, or when. Or why.

Sometimes, the people return, unfading back into life. It might take days, weeks or longer. When they do, they are changed. Sometimes, indeed, it would be better if they didn't return at all.

Some people say the comet is God's angry hand on the sky. Humans are getting above themselves. Darwin is about to blow open science with his theories of evolution and people will not know where they fit in the universe. The signs are there in the sky, on the streets, in the river. The world is rending before them.

Turmoil thuds in every Londoner's blood. It is the pulse of life here, along with the din of the streets. It rises in a million different ways, bubbling under the skin of even the most dutiful of daughters.

CHAPTER 1
AVA

London, September 1858

The tiny balance wheel shot out of Ava's hand and disappeared from view. She cursed under her breath. Damned snickerty little pieces! She knew how hard a lost watch piece was to find; flyspecks of metal against her monstrous fumbling fingernails. She picked up her tweezers with resignation. Down on her knees again, peering at the floor, tweezers at the ready. How many times had she done this since she started her apprenticeship, years before? At least this time it was a balance wheel, rather than one of the tiny screws she could barely see without her eyeglass screwed into one socket. But she'd been working on that balance wheel for days and it was the best one she'd ever made! The tiny circle of metal looked like nothing but it was to the watch what a pendulum was to a grandfather clock. It had to be weighted just so, along with the delicate hairspring, and even tinier balance staff, roller and jewel, or the watch would never tick.

It was a thankless task, being a watchmaker. Precious hours of life poured into something most people would never see and if they did would dismiss as nothing. So much invisible skill and patience behind every quiet tick! Most of Father's customers took his matter-of-fact brilliance for granted – had no idea of the almost impossible achievement in every miniature masterpiece. Ava glanced at him, crouched at his bench, his whole being focused on something so small she couldn't even see it from here. He was a watchmaker, born and bred. Calm, patient, obsessive about detail. She felt the familiar surge of affection.

There it was! Thank God, she wouldn't have to start from the beginning. She picked it up and carefully got to her feet, willing her hands not to shake, and gently released the scrap of metal onto her bench. The tweezers were damp from her sweaty palms. It was so hot in this studio at the top of the house. The big windows let light in – essential for their work – but also the heat. They were at the end of the hottest summer London had ever known and even now, when they were ready to welcome the cool of autumn, the air was still humid.

It also stank. The smell wafted up from the river as far as their Bishopsgate house, though it was bearable here – unlike the Houses of Parliament overlooking the river, where the delicate noses of the governing classes had been driven out from their sitting. Ava had avoided the Thames all summer.

It wasn't just the smell they had to keep out. The London air blackened everything it touched. And then there was the noise – you couldn't live on a thoroughfare like Bishopsgate without having all of London serenade you, day and night.

'Father, I need to wash my hands. Shall I bring you something to drink?'

He didn't look up for a moment, engrossed in his work, but then laid down his tools and stretched his neck back with a sigh. 'It's hot, indeed,' he said with some surprise. Removing his eyeglass, he peered at Ava's bench. 'How is your balance this time?'

'Better, I think. It's round, at least.'

Last time her balance had bulged like a balloon. Her father was a rare breed among watchmakers – he insisted on making almost all his own pieces, in spite of the thousands of pieceworkers all over Clerkenwell, each one an expert in producing a specific, tiny watch part. Which meant that she had to learn as well. Maybe she should be grateful for the opportunity to learn a disappearing skill, but she boiled with frustration every time her sausage fingers mangled yet another fairy-sized piece of metal. She held her breath as Father went over to her bench and narrowed his eyes at her work.

He gave a grunt and stood up. 'Ah well. Perhaps you need a break, after all. A glass of cordial would be lovely, my dear.'

Ava's relief wrestled with shame. Poor Father. He had quietly and lovingly raised her on his own, with Violet's help, and she knew she was the centre of his world. In turn she adored him – his gentleness, his calm, even his infuriatingly particular ways.

But she would always be a disappointment to him. If only

she had a sister! Not a brother, who would get all the attention. Ava knew her own family wasn't quite typical in such ways, but a sister would be her equal, her ally, her depositor of secrets and worries. As it was, Ava had to carry the whole weight of his expectation. And she knew her father worried about her future. He wanted her to be secure, to be able to make a living. At least he wasn't trying to marry her off.

If her mother had still been alive perhaps there would be other siblings to inherit her father's dexterity and patience – but as it was, Ava was the only option.

It was as though Father had read her mind. 'Are you visiting Mother's grave today?'

Ava nodded. Saturday had been the day they made the trip to Bow Cemetery to lay a posy there ever since she could remember, though nowadays she was old enough to go alone. At fourteen years old she was nearly a woman – only a few years younger than her mother had been when the cholera struck. Ava had no memories of her mother, but she had heard so many stories from Father and Violet, their housekeeper, that she felt she knew her intimately. Her feminine, dainty mother, with her nimble dressmaking fingers and her gracious spirit. She had been an icon of ideal womanhood – gentle, loving, kind, accepting – and as Ava grew yet bigger, clumsier and more impatient, it became harder to live under the shadow of such a paragon.

She pushed the thought away. 'Yes. I should go down and see what Violet needs from the market.'

She always picked up the shopping at Spitalfields on her way back from the cemetery. It was a long trek, but at least Mother had been buried at one of the new garden cemeteries rather than one of the church grounds nearer to home where thousands of bodies lay crushed together under the ground.

Ava wiped her hands on her skirt before putting away all her tools and the pieces she was working on.

Violet strode into the hallway below and stood at the bottom of the stairs, raising one eyebrow at Ava as she clattered down them. A stack of linen needing mending teetered on her sturdy brown arms, bare to the elbows.

'Do you recognise any of this, by chance?'

Ava groaned. 'You know I do, Violet. I'll do it, I promise.' She fanned her face. 'It's so much cooler down here! I have to get Father a drink – it's like a furnace upstairs.' She stepped around Violet to go to the kitchen, but Violet blocked her path.

'When will you do it, Ava? You're not getting away that easily.' Violet's round face had that stubborn look Ava knew so well. She wasn't letting this go.

Ava let out her breath like a horse. Violet knew how much Ava hated sewing. It was just as tedious as watchmaking. Her life was counting out in ticks and stitches.

Why was she born to a dressmaker and a watchmaker, when she wanted to fling aside needles and tweezers and stride out into the world? To devour news of all the changes in the huge city around her? To be part of the energy she could feel every time she stepped into the street? She had the fanciful feeling that Donati's Comet was carving its brilliant path over London to show her the way out of her own life.

She wanted a bigger destiny, one that looked outward and stirred her soul. She wished – oh, she didn't know what she wished, but it wasn't for a life peering at needles and bits of metal!

Violet was watching Ava closely. Her face softened. 'You know it's an essential skill for a woman, Ava, and one your mother was mistress of. I am only doing what she would do – insist that you have the skills any girl your age should have.'

Violet always could read Ava's mind. Ava was lucky that her father had chosen Violet to be their housekeeper. She was like a second mother to Ava and Ava adored her.

Just not the jobs she gave her.

Ava sighed. 'I will do some now before I go to the cemetery. And the market. And before I do my studies for Miss Buss. And go back to the studio.'

Violet snorted. 'You are no busier than any of us, Miss Bailey, so don't play that card with me. Your pertness reminds me of that girl in your class – Phoebe? I hope you are not being influenced by her, of all people.'

Violet's expression made Ava grin. Violet knew very well how much Ava despised her.

'I wouldn't let your father hear you suggest your work-load is too great. You know he was reluctant for you to apply for that scholarship on top of your apprenticeship. Hmm?' The tilt of Violet's head spoke volumes.

Ava sighed. Violet was right. A girl doing a watchmaking apprenticeship was unusual enough. Attending one of the new girls' schools on top of that was unheard of. Her father had told her it would be too much for her – that she would not do either thing justice – but she wouldn't give in. How could she get out of the house without an education? Other than becoming somebody's wife, but she had yet to see a wife living the life she wanted to live.

No, she could not let Father see her struggling now.

Violet went on. 'I think rain is coming this afternoon. You should go now. Your sewing can wait for later. I will leave it in the front room.'

Violet swept off, calling over her shoulder, 'I will take a drink to your father. Go, quickly.'

She disappeared into the front room. A second later her head popped back out. 'Oh, we need potatoes and some good ribs – don't pay too much! And apples are in season now. Some cress, perhaps.' She looked at the ceiling, deep in thought. 'That should do. And Ava?' She was looking at Ava now, her face serious. 'Take the thoroughfares. People tend to be taken from the back streets, they say.'

The disappearances were a fact of life these days. They struck randomly, at all classes, in different parts of London. Ava did her best not to think about them and it was unusual for Violet to say such a thing. She gave Violet a questioning look.

Violet frowned. 'There have been more lately. And also – I met someone recently who came back. He was not right, Ava. His eyes . . .' She forced a smile. 'But we can't stop living our lives and we must not let fear get the better of us. So off you go – but keep watch.'

Ava smiled reassuringly at Violet's worried expression. 'I'll be careful, Violet.'

She put on her bonnet, pulled her cloak off its hook and picked up a basket. Violet's caution was sensible. London was a filthy, brutal place, full of dangers.

But it didn't matter. Every time Ava left the house she felt the same prickle of excitement. This city never failed to surprise, shock and delight. She strode outside and took a deep breath of smoky air under the long streak of comet hanging silently in the sky.

Into the vast vibration of London life.

CHAPTER 2
JACK

Donlon

J ack shouldn't have told the nun he'd take the message. Too late now. It sat, carefully folded, in his waistcoat pocket, burning against his ribs. He couldn't wait to be rid of it. He kept imagining Hammer's reaction if he knew where Jack was going. Could practically see the slow turn of the head until Hammer's coal-black gaze fixed on Jack, burning him on the spot. Smell the singed hair of the great metalsmith – the ends of his black beard giving off a permanent burnt tang – and the sharp sweat of his body under the heavy leather apron.

Jack's heart started thudding faster as though the huge metalsmith was right behind him. He was a man of few words, was Hammer Smith, but by the gods you listened to every word he did utter and a few he didn't as well. He was tough and usually fair, especially to loyal apprentices, but he could blow. He liked a tavern night as much as any hardworking soul and the stories of his temper towards fools and cheats circled far around Donlon. Kids were raised on threats of Hammer coming to beat naughty children – although these days it was more likely to be stories about the Green Witch who sucked your time out of you and sent you to the nightmare Void between death and life.

With or without her, there was no shortage of threats in Donlon, thought Jack wryly. Parents could take their pick of tales. Maybe the mysterious Black Friars would come and whisk you away, burying you in the depths of their great dark friary on the river, where they did gods only knew what. Nobody really knew what their secret rituals were, but he was pretty sure it wasn't a fun day out. Or the Shepherd's gigantic killer ravens could come for you or maybe the Seven Sisters would capture and sell you to someone else who could use a healthy child. The possibilities were endless.

Sister Beatrice had said the message was for Sister Wisetree and he would do anything for her. She was the head of the Foundling Home – the stern-faced, big-hearted, twinkly-eyed matron, who'd been his mother figure as he grew up in the home, which was part of the great White City nunnery. She'd often been away for long stretches of time, but as a child he'd accepted that as normal, as children accept so many strange things about the adult world. He adored her, plain and simple, and whenever she was there the world settled into a safe, warm shape. She had treated all the children kindly but Jack always imagined that there was something special about the way she looked at him; something extra loving in the softness in her voice when she said his name. And he hadn't had much softness, or kindness, in his life before he'd ended up in the Foundling Home. He'd learnt early on to hold other people away; that showing your feelings was weakness. That the world would descend on you like a pack of hungry dogs if you did. Sister Wisetree was the only person in all the worlds that Jack had let into his life.

When he'd gone to visit Sister Wisetree on his day off to find she wasn't there, Sister Beatrice had stopped him.

'Jack, could you do a favour for Sister Wisetree?'

He'd tensed, but said, 'Of course, Sister Beatrice.'

He was always polite to all the sisters, even if there was something about Sister Wisetree's second-in-charge that made his hackles rise. He would never use his gift of seeing on the nuns in the Home – it seemed disrespectful, like reading the private diaries of a family member – but he could sense something dark and grey and sharp surging under the surface with her. Something unrestful. But that was none of his business, so he held his sight in check. Everyone had something secret they kept out of view from the world. That was just being human and he knew that better than anyone.

Sister Beatrice had held out a sealed message to Jack. 'She asked me to have this sent up to Time Palace.'

She couldn't be serious. Asking him to go to the home of Lady Montagu?

'It's not for the Lady, don't worry, Jack.' Sister Beatrice looked amused. 'It's for the attention of a Mr Rupert Buenaventura, who is a scientist and technician who works on the machines. A brilliant man.' Her eyes shone and Jack felt something squirm within him. He didn't like this.

Why would Sister Wisetree be sending a message to a man who worked with Lady Montagu?

There was also the tiny matter of Hammer forbidding all his apprentices to have any contact with Time Palace.

Everyone knew he had lost a favourite apprentice to the Palace – offered a position there when he'd been helping Hammer make a delivery. The boy had jumped at the chance, leaving Hammer in the lurch. From that day on, no other apprentice was permitted to go anywhere near Time Palace. They did service the palace – making and repairing the great gates and the bigger parts for the old time catchers, and the clockmakers and watchmakers took care of the fine pieces for the delicate clockwork inside – but from that day on, only Hammer was permitted in the Palace itself. The time catchers were old machines, beautiful soaring things that had always been at Time Palace, which was how it had got its name. Nobody really knew how or when they'd first been built but their only purpose was to pluck unused time from the air and recycle it into new, fresh time.

Jack hesitated. 'I'm sorry, Sister, but –'

Beatrice interrupted him. 'Sister Wisetree asked that you do this, specifically. She wanted someone she could trust. This message must reach its destination unread.' She held it out, watching him closely. 'There will be a reply. Sister Wisetree has asked that this be brought back as well. It is an important task, Jack.'

Still he hesitated. Sister Beatrice shrugged and withdrew the letter.

'I did say that Sister Wisetree should not trust a child with this. She was determined that you were capable, but she should have listened to me, it seems. No matter.'

'I'll do it.' Jack's tongue leapt ahead of his brain. He held out his hand. 'Give me the letter.'

He took the letter from Sister Beatrice's hand and turned away from the triumph in her face without a word.

She hadn't won anything. Jack chose to do this of his own free will – not for her. He was master of his own ship. Not beholden to anyone, anywhere.

CHAPTER 3
AVA

London, September 1858

It took a long, hot hour to walk to Bow Cemetery. Normally the chaotic streets made Ava's blood fizz with energy, but today her excitement flagged. Even a tipped-over omnibus and its poor, flailing horses warranted no more than a side glance, even though it was as good as theatre for the crowds milling, offering advice. Was it Violet's mention of the disappearances? Was the comet above her really casting some curse on London, as people said?

She tipped an extra halfpenny to the girl selling posies in Mile End Road. The girl scampered off, fierce glee on her face, and Ava turned down the street leading to the cemetery, past the orphan asylum. She walked through the gates, the familiar smell of newly dug earth and damp greenery tangled with her earliest memories, and followed the well-worn path to her mother's headstone.

Ava bent and put down her posy and wished suddenly, fiercely, that she was not her mother's daughter.

A hot flush of shame instantly followed. Her mother had been a saint, working her fingers to the bone as a dressmaker until the cholera hit and she died an awful, stomach-melting death days later. Her last word had been her daughter's name.

Tears of guilt pricked Ava's eyes and she blinked furiously to clear them. She stooped and ran a finger over the familiar words.

IN LOVING MEMORY OF ELSIE JUNE SWINDLETON

BELOVED MOTHER OF AVA AND WIFE OF BILL

WE WILL ALWAYS REMEMBER YOU

RIP 1829–1848

She whispered, 'I'm sorry, Mother.'

Ava would give anything to feel her mother's warm skin under her fingers instead of cold stone; to hear her words in her ears.

It was a good thing her mother was not here to see the creature she'd given birth to. This selfish, prickly girl who lacked grace and gratitude; who did not see that small, daily frustrations were simply part of life as a woman. Who struggled with living the same way that thousands of other girls like her lived.

It was only . . . it didn't seem much to direct a whole life towards.

As she stood in front of the gravestone a vibration hit her stomach. Was that thunder? A crackling charge in the air pimpled her skin with gooseflesh. She blinked. The air was collapsing into separate pinpricks of light and dark. A storm must be coming and playing tricks with the light. It was hard to see properly.

Something *whooshed* past her head and she jumped back with a cry. A hawk alighted on the tombstone next to her mother's and fixed her with one mocking eye. She sighed with relief and dropped her hand from her chest. A hawk! That was a rare sight in the midst of London. Perhaps it had escaped from one of those stores that sold every animal you could imagine, or a menagerie. What a beauty this one was with its proud curved beak and golden sheen!

Then there was a *thwack* and an arrow slammed into the bird's breast. Ava shouted in shock as bloodied feathers exploded around her. The bird fell to the earth, a sprawl of carnage on the ground. Who would do such a thing? A graveyard was a sanctified place – who would hunt here?

She stumbled back between the graves, putting her hand out automatically to feel for the headstone she knew was just there, but her hand groped empty air. She must have misjudged where she had stepped. She turned her head to look for her mother's gravestone.

It wasn't there.

The graveyard had gone. She was in a dark forest, thick with trees, and striding towards her was a tall, pale figure. He was clad in leather, his face matted with brambles and leaves. No, a beard. The dim light played tricks with her eyes. She peered at him. He was man and tree together, a towering figure with eyes that burned. His skin glowed like a silver birch tree in the darkness.

He strode towards Ava and she staggered back, her voice a dry husk in her throat. He glared at her. 'Step back from my wings or I will earthbound you, feebling!'

One pale arm swept her aside as if she was a twig. She

stumbled and fell as he pulled a knife out of a leather scabbard at his side and leaned forward to pick up the bird from where it lay. He held it by the tips of both its glorious wings, golden with dark flecks and so long when stretched out that even the giant man had to hold them high to clear the ground. He slashed once, twice. Two expert blows that released the wings from their bodily burden.

The mangled carcass fell to the ground and the hunter held the two trophy wings aloft, fierce triumph on his face as the bloody stumps swayed above his head.

'I will take back my wings, Malaikah!' he roared.

Ava's stomach twisted in horror. The man grinned at something just above her head and attached the two wings to his belt. Ava saw now that his tunic – which her muddled brain had seen as a smock and belt as he strode towards her – was a skirt of bloodied wings. They swayed and rustled as he moved. Some had bright-pink stumps, fresh kills. Others were dark with dried blood. Just the wings. No bodies, no flesh. What sort of hunter was this? What crazed creature killed birds for their meatless wings? Any butcher worth their salt would take that plump body to sell to London's ever-hungry hordes.

His smile was terrifying; his teeth fox-yellow. He thrust a clenched fist in the air, muscles and sinews rippling in a dance along his bare arm. He whirled, wing skirt spinning, and strode back the way he had come.

Panic knocked in Ava's throat, cutting her breath into short gasps. She had to get out of this place. She pulled herself to her feet, brushing at skirts heavy with dew from the damp ground. Where was she? She looked wildly around at trees so thick that light could only enter as needles. It was deathly still, except for leaves rustling behind her.

But there was no breeze.

And then the forest spoke. 'The winghunger savage-makes. He hides a deeprot in his breasthorde and I am fiercesad in my bloodshare.'

A winged man stepped forward from the trees and held his arms aloft. He was vast, dark-skinned as the hunter had been pale, with tangled white hair and enormous wings spreading beyond his broad shoulders. He towered over Ava for seconds and yet it felt as though he had always been there. His face was calm and sad. Ava saw how she could have mistaken him for a forest – he was something fundamental, of nature itself. Another realm. Yet she had no fear, as she had in the face of the hunter. His great wings beat the air and he took off above Ava's head.

Ava dropped to the ground and covered her head, wind rushing around her. The mossy ground soaked through her skirts and petticoats, reaching her stockinged knees, but she didn't care. Fierce exultation swept through her, lifting her beyond fear and the worries of the everyday world. She was somewhere new and wild, and this time she belonged.

'All right there, love? Catch your death down there, yer will.'

Ava opened her eyes and blinked. A woman peered down at her, her round face cracked like old dough under her tired bonnet.

'Lying wiv the dead, you'll end up wiv 'em. The chill of the grave'll get in your bones, mark my words.'

The woman's voice echoed as if she was far away. Ava's

whole body trembled so hard that her teeth chattered. Where was she now? She turned her head, tensing herself against seeing the hunter striding towards her, but she was back in the graveyard, returned from both the terror and strange joy. She was back in the known, where every step of her path was familiar, and it weighed on her soul. Her relief was spidered through with dull disappointment.

Was she going mad? The fear of that sent cold fingers into her belly. It was a terrible fate to end up in an asylum, shackled with the lunatics and ravers. But there was no madness in her family and they did say it was in the blood.

Had she been taken? Was this what happened to the disappeared people? She had never spoken to anyone who'd returned, but she'd not heard anything about a wild, strange world.

Something cold and hard dug painfully into her hip. She pushed herself upright. Her hands were disgusting – filthy, muddy and scratched as they pressed against the mossy stone. A blood-smeared feather stuck to one. She picked it off, grimacing at the bird blood it left behind. Sudden horror gave her strength and she scrambled to her feet. Had she been lying on a grave?

Thank the Lord! It wasn't a grave, just an abandoned headstone. Some poor neglected soul. She wiped the blood off her hand.

The old woman peered at Ava with currant eyes.

'That your family stone?' She gestured to the headstone Ava had been lying on and squinted at it. '1-8-4-8. Cholera year, that was. Can't make out the rest.'

Ava automatically followed the woman's glance. 'My

mother died in that cholera, but that isn't . . .' She trailed off, staring at the stone. That inscription . . . it couldn't be. She bent down and brushed at the stone, not caring that the old dirt made her hands even worse. It couldn't be.

The inscription on the old headstone read, simply:

IN LOVING MEMORY OF ELSIE JUNE SWINDLETON

BELOVED MOTHER OF JOHN AND WIFE OF SILAS

WE WILL ALWAYS REMEMBER YOU

RIP 1829–1848

CHAPTER 4

AVA

London, September 1858

Ava turned and stumbled out of the cemetery. She walked unseeingly until she reached Mile End Road where the shoe shiners, poets and costermongers thronged among the Saturday market food stalls.

A voice cut through the hubbub. 'Mornin', young lady! No coffee today?'

Ava usually stopped for a cup of Frank's bitter brew and a slab of his wife's fresh bread but today she shook her head.

His voice followed her. 'Break a man's heart, love! Don't go to him over the road, will yer? Bread like dust and coffee like water with a stone in it!'

His rival shouted back, 'Only thing like a stone is yer wife's bread, Frank!'

Both men scowled cheerfully at each other. Usually Ava would pause to enjoy the banter and pretend annoyance at the hordes of urchins vying for the attention and pennies of passers-by, but not today.

She was reeling from her experience in the cemetery. The tremor of being in that strange, dark world still hummed under her skin. And why would there be another, almost identical gravestone to her mother's with the vital details altered? With her name and her father's erased, replaced with those of two strangers: John and Silas. Someone had deliberately changed the story of Elsie Swindleton's life – and along with it, several other lives. What would anybody gain by that? It must be a mistake.

She turned into Bishopsgate and pushed through the crowds to reach her house and fumble the key in the lock.

The smell of carbolic soap and baking bread hit her as the door swung open, and relief swept over her, as though she had just returned from a long, arduous journey, rather than an outing she made every week without incident. Ava pulled off her bonnet and leaned back against the hall wall, closing her eyes.

'Ava? Did you pick up the vegetables and meat from the market?'

Oh no. She hadn't. She opened her eyes to see Violet's round face regarding her with a question in those sharp brown eyes.

'I'm sorry, Violet, I forgot. I'll go back and get them now.'

Ava straightened wearily, but Violet took her arm in a no-nonsense grip. 'Ava, look at me. What happened out there? Did you see something –'

Ava tried a laugh. 'No, nothing, I just forgot. Really.'

'And what made you forget the task that you perform every Saturday without fail?' One sardonic eyebrow shot up on Violet's forehead.

Ava hesitated. A part of her wanted to confide in Violet, as she had when she was a child. Another wanted to pretend the past few hours had never been.

What had happened in the cemetery? Had she hallucinated the hunter and the winged man? And why was there a different gravestone with her mother's name on it? Had Ava been lied to all her life by those she loved and trusted? Or was she losing her mind?

Ava raised her head and looked straight into Violet's brown eyes. She saw the way Violet's wiry black hair was neatly pulled back into two precise halves in front of her white cap. She looked at the smooth brown cheeks, and the querying eyebrow. The familiar, trusted face that looked the same as it did every day.

Ava's next words came in a rush.

'I saw a strange thing at Mother's grave today.' She would not tell Violet about the vision she'd had. There was a juddering in her belly when she thought of that. 'I – tripped – and fell over an old headstone, away from Mother's grave. It had Mother's name on it and the same dates. But the names of her child and her husband . . .' It was hard to finish the sentence. 'They were both different.'

Violet snorted dismissively. 'The stonemason must have made a mistake and cast it aside. It would cost more to polish and correct the names on an existing headstone than to make a new one.' She patted Ava's arm. 'What else could it be?'

Had there been the briefest pause before Violet's reply?

'It was a boy's name in place of mine, Violet. That's quite a mistake.'

'The mason was probably half-cut and mixed up two families. No wonder he never told anyone about it.'

'Violet, is it truly my mother lying there in that grave?' Ava's voice was louder than she intended.

'Ava, is this what Miss Buss teaches you? To shout at Violet like a fishwife?'

Ava whirled to see her father standing in the hallway, peering over his glasses at them. His manner was mild, but a hot flush surged up her neck. Ava could not stop the words tumbling off her tongue. 'The question, Father – in case you missed it – was whether it is truly my mother lying in the grave I have been visiting all my life.'

Father took his glasses off and polished them, blinking rapidly. The silence in the room was a high glass dome. Her father broke it. 'My dear, you are overheated. Perhaps you need to rest. Your agitation is most – unseemly.' His voice was calm, but the jerking tendon in his jaw and the furrow between his brows betrayed him. He was churning on the inside just like she was. She knew every tic, blink and sigh of this adored man who had raised her so carefully. Ava hesitated. Was she simply overwrought? Had she misread what she had seen?

But how else to read it? She fixed Father with a direct gaze and she did not recognise the voice coming out of her own mouth. 'Not as unseemly as being lied to by those you love.'

Violet's gasp was audible.

'I will not be spoken to in that manner by my own daughter. Your behaviour is unacceptable.' Father's voice was as loud as Ava had ever heard it. He had never raised his voice to her before and even in the midst of her new, strange mood, his tone cut her to the quick.

'Mr Bailey, I –'

'Not now, Violet, please.' Father had two points of colour on his cheeks. 'Ava, I think I have been overworking you. You may take the rest of the day off. We will not speak of this again.'

'Mr Bailey. I think you must recognise –'

'Violet, if you please!' There was a quaver in Father's voice. He closed his eyes and took a deep breath before opening them again. 'Ava, you are not yourself. I will not continue this conversation until you are able to compose yourself correctly.'

The silence quivered like a taut bowstring. Violet stepped over to where Father stood and put a gentle hand on his arm, guiding him to stand further up the hallway away from Ava. Violet reached up to whisper in his ear, her voice so low that Ava could not catch the words. Father shook his head but Violet kept speaking, even as his headshake became stronger. His voice rose.

'No, Violet!' Something unintelligible, and then Ava could hear him say, 'I will not lose my daughter there as well.'

Violet had to raise her voice a fraction to make herself heard. Ava could hear more disjointed words. Their meaning made no sense to her, but it didn't matter. She had heard one word that told her more than any other could.

Violet had said 'Malaikah'.

That was the name the hunter had called out. The name of the great winged man.

With that one word, Ava's life turned, slow and creaking

and unstoppable as a great ship in harbour facing a new journey out to sea. There was no turning back now.

It didn't matter what Violet and Father decided to tell her. Ava knew that what she had seen was true. She was not mad. It was her life that was wrong.

Her story was out there somewhere, and no one else was going to find it for her.

She'd wanted a destiny, and this was hers.

CHAPTER 5
JACK

Donlon

The steam-train station was down the hill from Time Palace. It took Jack a good ten minutes to walk along the river and up to Time Park, where the Palace and Observatory sat. The golden domes of the Palace and the huge pale orb of the Observatory were clearly visible above the pinkstone wall that encircled both buildings.

He stopped. He'd been to Time Palace before, but not for years. He had an early childhood memory of coming here with his dad – up to no good, no doubt – in the days before Jack had been dumped in the Foundling Home. He couldn't remember much except for the extraordinary pink of the stone walls and the gleaming domes – like a magical citadel. He adjusted the collar of his crisp new shirt and pushed his hair carefully into place. Thank the gods he'd made an extra effort with the way he looked today. He did like a nice thread or two, it put a swagger in his steps and it felt as though the world treated him differently.

With a deep breath, Jack approached the palace. The rare pinkstone was from the Montagu estate. Their land covered some two of the richest mines in Donlon – quarrying pinkstone and the even rarer sunstone that the Palace's time catchers were made from.

Near the Palace on the highest point of the hill sat the great Montagu Observatory, the oldest in Donlon. It was here that the path of the stars was tracked – it was the heart of Lady Montagu's domain. She had been their time queen, known as the Time Lady, or simply the Lady, and from here she watched the night sky and contemplated her place at the centre of time and space. For she kept time, of course. Had done long beyond living memory, feeding herself on recycled time from her catchers.

But Donloners had stopped coming to Time Palace, since their time queen had turned dark.

Jack shouldn't be here, but he was. Nothing for it but to keep going and get this done as quick as he could. He stopped in front of the guards at the gate and held up his letter. 'I've a message for Mr Rupert Buenaventura.'

One guard reached out a hand but Jack pulled the letter back. 'I've instructions to deliver this to his hand. Personally.'

The guard ran an eye over Jack and gave a grunt. 'You sure about that, lad?'

Jack's internal warning bell was clanging loud. He cursed Sister Beatrice silently. He drew himself up to his full skinny height, so that all the guard would see was calm determination. 'Yes. I'm sure.'

The guard shrugged. 'If you say so.'

He turned and gestured to another guard in the distance, standing small as a tin soldier outside the Observatory. The other guard responded with a series of quick arm movements.

The guard turned back to Jack. 'Wait here.'

Jack waited until a small figure detached itself from the Observatory and made its way to him. The figure grew larger and became a man with long dark hair, a purple velvet coat and a green cravat around his neck. Jack felt a prickle of unease and the letter he clutched became damp with sweat. He wiped his hand impatiently on his trouser legs. For the love of the gods, Jack! All he needed to do was hand over the letter and leave. He was as jumpy as a cricket in a bottle, and him a man of nearly sixteen years. This was just another man – with a very good opinion of himself, judging by his choice of clothing.

The guard swung one gate open and motioned for Jack to step forward. He did so, holding the letter in front of him, but the man ignored that and held out his own hand to shake.

'Rupert Buenaventura. You have a message for me?'

Reluctantly, Jack extended his other hand. 'This is from Sister Wisetree at the Foundling Home.'

The man's eyes sharpened as he squeezed Jack's hand in his. 'Is that so? Sister *Wisetree*?' He reached for the letter, but held it unopened in his hand. 'But where are my manners? Come up to the Observatory, son. What's your name?'

Jack hesitated. He didn't want to give his name. He didn't want to go anywhere with this man. All he wanted to do was get away without leaving any impression on anyone here at all. But Rupert was looking at him with an easy smile, waiting for Jack's reply, and Jack felt his senses go muddy. He had come here for Sister Wisetree, and she wouldn't ask him to do something that was dangerous or wrong.

'Jack Swindleton,' said Jack.

'Then come with me, Jack, while I read this and prepare a reply. I'm sure she wants a reply?'

Jack was caught. He nodded miserably. Rupert turned and Jack trailed behind. Rupert chatted easily, asking friendly questions which Jack answered as monosyllabically as possible. Every fibre in his body wanted to get out of here. Each breath was an effort and Jack's heart hammered as if he'd been running.

Once they arrived at the Observatory, Rupert told him to wait in an entrance room and then disappeared.

Time turned to treacle around Jack and he felt himself swimming out of his body, as though someone else was sitting on his chair and he was watching himself as a distant figure. He shouldn't be here.

Rupert returned and Jack slammed back into his skin, every instinct screaming at him to run. He was on his feet even as Rupert pulled a small gold machine from his pocket. In one deft move, Rupert flicked its small funnel to face Jack.

But Jack was already lunging away, his body lithe and fast. The machine buzzed and all Jack's strength drained out of him. It was as though he was a puppet and the puppet master had cut his strings. He collapsed, body and soul, as the high-pitched, angry sound filled the room, and everything faded to melting grey.

Jack clawed at the air, but there was nothing to grasp. There was nothing, anywhere. Was this death? But no – death was the end of a cycle. Death came at the end of life.

This was outside of life. Here was pure absence. No light, smell, sound, touch. Stasis.

Jack could see his body, but he could feel nothing. He watched his hands clench so the knuckles went white, and felt nothing. There was no whisper of air on his skin, no warmth or chill. His new shirt collar was not sharp on his neck, nor were his good shoes a little pinched around the toes where they were getting small. There was no gravity pulling his feet to the ground. If he was breathing, there was no sensation of air in his nose and lungs. No puff of breath on his skin; no inhalation or exhalation.

He hadn't realised before this moment that the world itself breathed to a rhythm. He hadn't heard the pulse of the world, until he wasn't in it.

The silence was bleak. This was not the peace of a riverside, or mountain, or forest. It was the utter, brutal deprivation of every sense Jack had.

This was all there was. He remembered words, but they felt heavy in his mind. He couldn't catch their meaning.

What was *where*?

What was *what*?

What was *me*?

Dully, Jack watched hope flee and did not recognise its shape.

CHAPTER 6
AVA

London, September 1858

'Finally! There she is!' Miss Buss waved her umbrella above the mid-afternoon crush at London Bridge train station. A languid hand rose above the crowds in answer. Miss Buss tutted, looking at the railway clock. 'We will only just make the train. Phoebe must improve her timekeeping.'

The crowds near the group of schoolgirls parted and Phoebe arrived like a ship in full sail. Miss Buss's face tightened and Ava groaned silently. The rest of the schoolgirls from Miss Buss's Academy for Young Ladies were dressed appropriately for a train journey in sensible cotton travelling dresses and sturdy leather boots. Phoebe was clad head to toe in a deep lilac silk, puffed out by the fullest crinoline, with matching dainty slippers.

'Phoebe, this is not a garden party,' said Miss Buss sharply. 'That dress is most impractical. You will barely fit through the train door in that skirt! And what are those slippers on your feet? Well, it cannot be helped now. If you cut your feet or ruin the silk, that is not my problem.'

In spite of Miss Buss's disapproval, several of the girls rushed over to Phoebe and were twittering their admiration.

'Phoebe, that colour! Where did you get it?'

Phoebe patted her impeccable bonnet. 'Why, thank you Florence – how sweet of you. This is mauve. Did you know that the queen wore this exact shade to her daughter's wedding this year? The colour is quite new – it's only just been invented. As soon as I saw it, I knew I had to have it! Mama agreed to have our dressmaker make up a little something and finally it arrived yesterday. I simply *had* to wear it!'

Ava's groan was audible this time. Phoebe looked over at her. 'You seem in pain, Ava.'

'It's more of a lingering nausea, Phoebe,' said Ava. 'I'm quite accustomed to it. Please don't trouble yourself.'

She could feel her father watching her like she was a ticking bomb. They had not found an easy way to be together since everything had changed two days ago. Father had withdrawn into a hurt, silent shell while Ava's new, simmering rage bounced off every wall. She was constantly on the verge of either tears or shouting and it did not help matters that she had started to bleed for the first time. Violet had helped her with the practicalities of the cumbersome belt but things between them all were as strained as they had ever been. Ava was no further to finding out the truth of her own life or her experience in the graveyard. Violet shook her head sadly when Ava demanded answers, saying, 'It is for your father to tell you, Ava.' But Father might as well not have been there.

However, this school trip to Greenwich had been long planned. The school had recently received an unexpected invitation from Greenwich Royal Observatory to observe Donati's Comet through one of their great telescopes and had accepted with alacrity. Since Saturday, though, her father had forbidden Ava to go – unless he also came along. He had approached Miss Buss without Ava's knowledge and offered his services as a guest speaker.

Miss Buss had accepted and here they were, together in body but further away in spirit than they had ever been. Also, the strange new headiness was still upon Ava and neither she nor her father knew what might come out of her mouth next. Hence his worried glances.

'We are representing the school, after all,' Phoebe went on. 'I'm sure Miss Buss will forgive me for wanting to look my very best. After all, the scholarship students can't be expected to, can they?'

Ava felt the heat stain her face. The innocent pride she had once felt in her scholarship had long been shredded by Phoebe's scorn, but she could not let her see how her words wounded her.

'I'm sure your motives are entirely selfless, Phoebe,' said Miss Buss with more than a hint of acid. 'Now, here is our carriage. Let's board, girls. Follow me and Mr Bailey will bring up the rear.'

They climbed up the steps onto the train, a minor drama ensuing when Phoebe alighted, as she had to turn sideways and compress her vast skirts to get in. She pressed her cheeks in pretty chagrin and three men leapt to her aid. Ava's grunt of disgust was audible. The girl was everything

Ava couldn't bear. Vain, self-centred, entirely focused on her attire and hair, with conversation that ranged between fashion plates, society gossip and criticism of others. She never took any interest in the lessons and was only there because her wealthy mother had decided that the trend towards educating girls might attract a better class of companions. It was also rumoured that the royal family had a personal interest in the school, which seemed highly tenuous to Ava. However, it was exactly the sort of thing that would attract the attention of social climbers like Phoebe and her mother.

Finally, Phoebe and her skirt were on the train and Miss Buss settled everyone in two adjacent carriages. Propping herself skilfully between them in the swaying corridor, she clapped her hands for attention.

'Young ladies, we are very fortunate to have this appointment with the Royal Observatory to see Donati's Comet. As you all know, this comet with its spectacular curving tail has been visible to the naked eye above London for some weeks. It is the first comet ever to be photographed – and of course it has stimulated all sorts of superstition. However, educated people realise it is not a harbinger of doom or a warning from God, but an astronomical feature explained by science – and it is in that spirit we have the good fortune to observe the comet through the Great Equatorial Telescope.'

Father coughed gently and Miss Buss looked at him questioningly. 'Miss Buss, if I may ask – how exactly did the school receive such an extraordinary honour? The Observatory is never usually accessible to the public.'

For some reason Miss Buss went a little pink. Perhaps it was the excitement of the visit, but she had to clear her throat before she replied. 'I'm not quite sure why our humble little school was chosen. However, we will not look a gift horse in the mouth.'

She went on quickly, gesturing towards Father. 'We are doubly fortunate to have Mr Bailey with us today – a master watchmaker and expert on the history of clockmaking, as well as being Ava's father. Mr Bailey will talk to us about Harrison's four clocks and Greenwich's short history of being the centre of time and space here in England for the past seven years.' She looked sternly around both carriages. 'I expect you all to remember what we have learnt in class when I ask questions later today.'

With that, Miss Buss swung through the door of Ava's carriage and sat down next to Father. 'Now, Mr Bailey, tell me what you think about Mr Bazalgette and his proposals for the new Embankment?'

Ava gazed pointedly out the window, pretending intense interest in the buildings rolling past at dizzying speed. Pretending she couldn't hear the giggles or see the nudges from Phoebe and her disciples in the next carriage. She knew their giggles were directed at Father. He was not the same calibre as the other fathers of girls at Miss Buss's Academy – all wealthy businessmen of some description or another, and gentlemen, while her father was a mere artisan. A highly skilled master artisan, but someone who perched at the top of the working class or at best dangled off the bottom of the middle class. And that classification defined everything. As far as these privileged girls were concerned, Ava and her highly skilled father were, and always would be, an inferior breed. Just as there were deserving and undeserving poor, where you sat in the rigid ladder of class dictated who you spoke to and how, and the manner in which you were regarded. Ava looked at the sneering girls and then at her earnest, courteous father, and wondered how this could be. But it was just the way it was. Nobody questioned it. Society was not about to change, and perhaps it couldn't.

'Papa's in newspapers, of course. They couldn't possibly spare him for a day, even if it wasn't beneath him to attend a schoolgirl outing. I would just die of mortification.'

'And looking like that, too. Doesn't he know that bowler hats are for gamekeepers and road builders?'

The words were in a whisper loud enough to carry clearly to their carriage. Father continued talking as if nothing had happened but Ava saw the set of his jaw and the dull red stain on his neck, even as he laughed at something Miss Buss said. This time, Ava's anger swelled not against him, but for him. Phoebe looked over at Ava, smirking, before turning to admire her reflection again in the train window. 'You don't think this colour drains my complexion, do you?'

Ava leaned forward with a smile. 'Excuse me, Miss Buss. Father.' She got to her feet, steadying herself against the sway of the train as she crossed the corridor, aware of her father's eyes on her. Don't embarrass him any further, Ava. She positioned herself in the doorway of the adjacent carriage, where Phoebe sat with her acolytes.

'Oh, look, it's the grey goose. Like goose, like gander, don't they say?' Phoebe's eyes raked Ava's pale grey cotton dress as titters erupted around her. 'I'd offer you a seat, but we're quite full up.' Phoebe spread her ballooning skirt over the seat next to her before leaning over to the one empty seat on the other side, putting her tiny coin purse on it. She looked up with an innocent smile. 'What a shame.'

Ava kept her voice low and her smile bright. 'Oh, I know. There's no room for anything in here, Phoebe, other than your sense of self-importance, which is as overblown as your ridiculous skirt.' Ava leaned forward and whispered, 'And in answer to your question – yes, that colour does leach all tone from your skin, making it as dull as the contents of your head.'

She gave a tinkling laugh as she stood and turned to go back to the seat next to her father. Leaning forward in the carriage, she fluttered her fingers at Phoebe. Phoebe was too busy pinching her cheeks and scowling at her reflection to notice.

It was a long time before they reached the Observatory, with the trailing gaggle of schoolgirls made slower by Phoebe's globular skirt. It was afternoon on an early autumn day and the comet was clearly visible in the sky, its curving tail almost at right angles to the horizon. In spite of Miss Buss's deprecating comments about superstition, Ava couldn't help but feel a pagan sense of awe as she looked up at the enormous tail silently overhanging London.

Ava knew that it was the combination of the disappearances and the blazing comet that most unsettled people. Nobody really knew how many were taken from the rookeries and streets. It was only the well-to-do disappearances that made the *London Illustrated News*. No wonder Londoners thought the comet was God writing his anger on the skies, punishing humans getting above themselves as He had done since the Garden of Eden and the Tower of Babel.

Finally they reached the top of the hill where the Observatory perched, the black leather Time Ball sitting at the bottom of the mast, waiting for its next daily climb to the top for its drop at 1pm on the dot. The girls straggled behind Miss Buss, reaching the courtyard outside Flamsteed House one by one until finally even Phoebe arrived, cresting the hilltop like a hot air balloon released from its tether. Ava noted with grudging admiration that Phoebe had the merest flush in her cheeks, even though her feet must be aching in those absurd slippers with the effort of dragging pounds of fabric and a crinoline cage up the hill.

Miss Buss stopped just before the gates enclosing the courtyard of Flamsteed House. She turned and clapped her hands for attention.

'Girls, if you please. We are standing outside the gates of the world-famed Royal Observatory of Greenwich. I would impress upon you the great privilege we are being granted here today. Invitations to enter these hallowed halls are very rare indeed, and the opportunity to look through the Great Equatorial Telescope rarer still. I do not need to remind you to make the most of this once in a lifetime opportunity and to represent the school to the best of your ability.' Miss Buss paused and swept a stern glance across the group in front of her. 'I trust that is absolutely clear?'

After a chorus of 'Yes, Miss Buss', their teacher went on.

'You are standing mere feet away from Airy's Meridian Line, which divides the world into east and west and is the point from which time is measured here in England and beyond, thanks to the *Nautical Almanac* first introduced in 1767, which uses Greenwich time as its standard reference. Since the almanac is very widely used, Greenwich time is the standard reference for finding a position at sea.' She pointed to the huge clock that sat in the wall to the right of the iron gates. 'You can see here is the great Shepherd Gate Clock, which has been here for all to see for the last six years. This shows the precise Greenwich time to anyone who passes.'

She turned and gestured gracefully to Father. 'In addition, we are fortunate to have Mr Bailey give us a private talk on the particulars of Harrison's four clocks. Mr Harrison was a humble man who won the prize for developing a clock that could keep accurate time at sea in 1773. Why is knowing the time at sea so important?'

Silence. Ava glanced around. Phoebe was busy adjusting her bonnet but everyone else looked blank. Surely Ava wasn't the only one who knew the answer to this question? She'd grown up with Harrison's clocks, learning their story alongside the alphabet with her father. She couldn't make her sausage fingers into nimble watchmaking devices like her father's, but that didn't stop her marvelling at the intricate, perfect workings of Harrison's masterpieces.

Oh, for heaven's sake. Ava stuck her hand up. 'If they know the time at one point, like Greenwich, and the time wherever they are at sea, they can establish longitude. Then they can work out where they are.'

43

'Precisely. Thank you, Ava. For a seafaring nation like Britain, finding accurate longitude is essential.' Miss Buss paused and shot a stern look at two young men loitering hopefully near Phoebe and her skirt, holding their gaze until they reddened and tipped their hats in farewell.

Miss Buss exchanged some words with the white-bearded gate porter before he pulled open the pedestrian gate and stood back to let them pass. As Ava walked through and thanked him, the gatekeeper looked startled. She followed his gaze to a slight young man crossing the courtyard from the Meridian Building. He was a young dandy with red-gold hair tucked underneath a jaunty top hat, an embroidered green waistcoat, a royal blue cravat and a stiff white collar up to his hairline. A most un-sober smile curved his red lips. Surely this was not one of the dully respectable Observatory staff?

His voice was confident and melodic. 'I will escort these ladies now. Thank you, Arthurton.' The gatekeeper gave a nod and the young man turned to Miss Buss with a smile of welcome. Miss Buss seemed as surprised as anyone, giving a sharp inhalation when the young man tilted his head enquiringly.

'A perfect viewing day, is it not, Miss Buss?' He went on before Miss Buss could gather her words, turning to the girls. 'Welcome to you all. I am Samuel Timeward and I will escort you to the Assistant shortly. May I ask whom I have the pleasure of escorting today?'

Was it Ava's imagination or did Samuel Timeward's limpid green gaze linger on her face for longer than was

44

seemly? She flushed but held her head high. She had nothing to be ashamed of, wherever Mr Timeward might choose to look. And besides, the chagrin that she could make out on Phoebe's face beside her was gratifying.

Miss Buss cleared her throat. 'Thank you, er, Mr Timeward. Allow me to introduce Miss Phoebe Fortescue, Miss Ava Bailey, Miss Hazel Smyth ...' and Miss Buss went around the circle, naming each girl in turn. She turned back to him when she was finished. 'We are all most grateful for this opportunity.'

'At your service.' Mr Timeward bowed gracefully. 'We will proceed into the inner workings of the great Observatory, but first we should admire the excellent view of London and the river that the courtyard affords us.' He offered an arm to Ava. 'If I may have the pleasure?'

Ava put a hand on Mr Timeward's arm – he was a small, fine-boned man, but his assured bearing made this almost unnoticeable. She smiled especially sweetly for Phoebe's benefit and they walked to the railing overlooking Greenwich Park and the river, an eager bustle of skirts behind them. Ava glanced around to see Father in rapid conversation with Miss Buss, a frown on his face. It looked as if Miss Buss was reassuring him.

Mr Timeward was very solicitous in his questions to Ava, asking her politely about her family and life and listening attentively to her answers, before turning to point out the sights of the city and the river below. He was mid-flow when a man's voice sounded behind the group.

'Keep the gate open, Arthurton, there's a good chap. Take a break, why don't you?'

Ava turned her head to see a portly man with big mutton-chop sideburns and a florid face coming across the courtyard, rubbing his hands together in a display of jollity. Ava was interested to see Miss Buss's face tighten with apparent annoyance before she smiled politely at the man. He inclined his head to Miss Buss and Father and approached the group.

'Allow me to introduce myself, young ladies. I am Mr Nathaniel Goodwin, Second Assistant to the Royal Astronomer.' His lips stretched ingratiatingly over yellow teeth.

Mr Timeward turned and fixed the Assistant with a cool look. 'We will be with you shortly, Mr Goodwin,' he said. 'The girls wish to admire the view in the light of the setting sun.' He turned back to Ava as if the matter was settled, but the Assistant bounced on his toes.

'Beg pardon, Mr Timeward, but the optimum viewing time is fast approaching. And we have among you a Miss Ava Bailey, I believe?' His voice was louder than seemed appropriate.

Both Miss Buss and Father stepped forward at the same moment. The identical look of worry on their faces exasperated Ava so much that she raised her head high and smiled. 'I am Miss Bailey.'

'I am told by Miss Buss that you are a most singular student, Miss Bailey,' he said. Miss Buss's expression suggested she had no recollection of such a comment, but the Assistant went on quickly. 'It would be my pleasure to personally show you to the Great Equatorial Telescope so that you may be the first to join the astronomers for the early evening viewing.' He bowed and swept one hand towards the Meridian Building. 'Miss Bailey, after you, if you please. I will briefly leave the rest of you ladies in the very knowledgeable and capable hands of Mr Timeward, and Mr Bailey, of course.'

Ava could not help the delight bubbling up inside her. To be singled out for praise by none other than the Second Assistant of the Royal Observatory in front of all her classmates! And Father.

She pulled her hand away from Mr Timeward's arm – not without some resistance; it seemed he was a rather forward young man – and pushed her way through the other girls' skirts blocking her path. Out of the corner of one eye she saw Father coming towards her. 'I will come with you, Ava.'

Ava felt a flash of anger. Father clearly thought she was still the stupid child he had raised under the shadow of a lie.

'Thank you, Father, but I'm sure I will be perfectly safe with the Second Assistant of the Royal Observatory.' Her words were clear and cold. Without a backward glance she swept towards the Meridian Building.

A scuffle behind her and a cry. 'I simply cannot wait another moment to see the Great Telescope!' exclaimed Phoebe. Ava turned in irritation to see Phoebe pattering behind her, skirts swaying. 'I must accompany Ava,' she said breathily.

Her charms clearly had no effect on Mr Goodwin, who shouted, 'No!' Ava jumped at his bellow. 'I mean – please wait in the courtyard with the others, Miss.'

Phoebe completely ignored his request, her great skirt

reaching the Meridian Building several inches ahead of Ava. 'Ava, you are blocking my way.'

'I don't think it's my presence impeding your progress, Phoebe,' said Ava, looking pointedly at the crinoline, at least two doorways wide. 'Indeed –'

But Ava did not have the opportunity to deliver her next retort before a confusion of movement snatched her attention away. To Ava's startled senses it seemed that Mr Timeward ran to the entrance gate at the same moment as a cloaked figure appeared, holding something like a gold chronometer. There was a buzzing sound, like a swarm of angry bees, and the next moment a gigantic, invisible fist thumped Ava hard in the chest.

The blow hurled Ava backwards and she landed flat on her back on the paving stones. She lay there for a stunned second, sucking air into lungs on fire. She was distantly aware of Father and Miss Buss calling her name. What had happened? She pulled herself awkwardly to a sitting position and squinted. Something was wrong with her eyes. Phoebe was just there, by the doorway, but she looked blurry. Flickering, like a weak flame. Ava blinked. In the next moment Phoebe was gone, as completely as sugar dissolving in hot water.

Gone.

A split second of clarity showed her the scene like a painting. The cloaked man with the gold timepiece and Mr Timeward reaching for him. Father, leaning over her. A space where Phoebe had been. Miss Buss turning from Ava to the gap that had been Phoebe. Girls frozen in shock. Mr Goodwin, oddly silent and watching.

And then the scene disappeared. Everything was formless. There was nothing to see. Nothing to smell, or hear, or feel. She was numb and all around her was a deep absence.

And there was nothing other than this.

Was this before time began? Or after time ended?

Had she been here a second or a century?

Where was she?

Who was she?

CHAPTER 7
AVA

Donlon

A memory, scratching at the edge of her mind. Something she needed to hold onto, something slipping away.

Much easier just to let it go. To sink into the everlasting now.

A sound. What was it? A rushing, filling her head. She opened her eyes and – *Oh!* The glorious, full-colour world flooded back. She remembered! She was Ava, she was on a school excursion, her father was just there and she could feel the warm grass beneath her. Grass? She looked around.

No.

She wasn't back.

This wasn't Greenwich Observatory. She was on a lawn below a beautiful mansion built of stone that glowed salmon-pink in the late sun. It was topped with gleaming golden domes. Another round white building perched nearby at the top of the steep hill. The white building reminded her of the Observatory in Greenwich, with its big orb. Both buildings were encircled by walls made of the same dark-pink stone. Guards flanked the wooden gates that sat like a vast studded buckle in a giant stone belt.

Where was she? She was on a grassy slope under the warm sun and there were trees swaying gently above. A broad river surged at the bottom of the hill, behind her. That was the rushing sound that she'd heard. The river was studded with wooden waterwheels of all sizes, groaning as they turned, and tall spidery windmills flowered on the banks.

Ava watched, mesmerised by the murmuring and creaking. She was strangely calm; being present was enough for now. The grass beneath her hands, the sun on her face and the sound of the water were sensations to cherish.

The sun was sinking, its long rays stalking across the grass and burnishing the apricot-pink walls of the palace deep gold. A shout of laughter rang through the air, followed by the high, mad jibber of a fiddle played at speed. Other instruments rushed to join it in a joyous clatter of guitars, drums, tambourines and banjos, voices weaving in and out and feet and hands clapping time. She turned to find the source of the sound.

On the other side of the great park surrounding the walled buildings, a huge circus tent poured music and light into the deepening dusk. It pulsed with a welcoming warmth. The dancing people had seen her and were smiling and beckoning, reaching out hands as they stamped and swung. It felt familiar, as if she belonged, and she was overcome by the need to be in that tent, with those glowing people. It was very simple to belong, she suddenly realised. Happiness was right there for the taking.

She staggered to her feet and started towards the tent. Her limbs felt clumsy, as though she hadn't used them for days, but she picked up her skirts and pushed herself forward. She started to run. She was nearly there, near the beckoning lights; she could almost reach the outstretched hands to whirl around and around in the wash of that giddying music, when a boy appeared in front of her.

He was crouching on all fours. She hadn't seen him until it was almost too late and she stumbled back. He was as faint as paint in water, then he was thickening, as if someone invisible was colouring him in. He raised a pale, pointed face. His eyes were dead, his face a thick curd colour and he was motionless. Ava took a cautious step forward.

'Hel– hello?'

Still his eyes were as bright and cold as marbles. Why did Ava want to cry? She hesitated, then reached out one hand and touched him gingerly on the cheek. His skin was cold as porcelain under her fingers, but it twitched at her touch. She jumped back. He blinked, once, twice, then turned his head stiffly. He reached up to press his hands to his temples. The ground tilted under her feet and she clutched her own head. Something was pushing at her mind. This boy was? *What* –

He reached out to grab her arm, too hard. His movements were jerky, like a badly built automaton. 'Where are we?' he rasped. He looked past her and she turned to follow his gaze. The music and laughter rushed back to fill her head, and in a flash all thought of the pale boy had gone. She pulled away and strode towards the tents, the music dragging at her like a warm undertow.

'They're Hams!' The boy's voice was harsh. She broke into a run but his words pursued her, jarring as though he hadn't used his voice for a long time. 'But which ones? Pecks, East, West? That's Time Palace – could be any of 'em.'

The boy was gibbering. Why wouldn't he stop? A fizz of fireworks and a shout of laughter dragged her towards them. She was nearly there, a promise of love and life and warmth beyond anything she'd ever felt before beckoning.

'Stop!' the boy shouted. 'They're Hams! Don't go to them!'

He grabbed her arm again and yanked her around. How dare he!

'Let go of me this instant!' She pulled away but his grip was strong.

He pushed his face close to hers. 'Look at me! What are you doing? You never run to the Hams!'

'What are you talking about?' she whispered.

'Every kid knows that you don't never make eye contact with the Hams. They get inside your head. Come away now.'

The boy was stronger than his skinny frame suggested. He pulled at her again and she felt a flicker of fear, but it wasn't because of him – it was the realisation that she might not make it to them. She twisted to look back over her shoulder and saw a beautiful woman coming out of the tent. The woman smiled and held a hand out to Ava. Desperation fizzed in Ava's belly. She was consumed by a need to reach the woman, to take her warm hand in Ava's own.

Ava tried to tear herself free, but the boy hung on. Without thinking, she sank her teeth into his arm. He yelped but held on grimly, fingers sharp in her flesh. In spite of everything, they were stumbling further away.

The night was cooler now, the music a tinny sound in the distance. Ava's face was damp in the cool air. The thread between her and the people in the tent had snapped and a deep, ragged grief swept over her.

The boy peered closely at her before letting go of her arm. He rubbed his own arm while Ava wiped her eyes and nose on her dress sleeve, not caring if anyone saw.

'That was touch and go. You nearly didn't come back.'

Back? Ava took a shaky breath and pressed her hand to her forehead. Her skin pricked hot and cold.

'I'm Jack. I'm sorry I dragged you, but you was in danger.'

'I'm Ava.' Shame swept through her. 'I bit you. I'm so sorry, I don't know what possessed me.'

'I do. The Hams did. Them and their mind games. Powerful mental magicians, that lot.' He rubbed his arm and frowned. 'You couldn't help yourself. But you fell hard and fast. They found something in you they could latch onto.'

'I've lost myself.' The words were out of Ava's mouth before she could stop them. Hearing them said out loud shocked her, but Jack answered as if she'd commented on the weather.

'Well, that makes sense,' he said.

'I didn't mean – that's not really true, you know.' Ava felt the bright shame of self exposure, but Jack didn't seem perturbed by the sudden intimacy. He looked searchingly at her, as if he could read her thoughts.

'They can latch onto anything that's shifting. People between one thing and the other. If you've lost your centre, it makes it easy for them.' The scrawny boy spoke easily, as if losing your very self was an everyday matter. His acceptance loosened her shame, and her tongue.

'I don't know who I am. I don't know where I am. How did I get here? What happened to me?' She frowned. 'And do I – know you?'

What sort of question was that? She regretted it as soon as the words were out of her mouth. But still Jack looked unsurprised, as if a strange girl having conniptions in front of him was nothing out of the ordinary. He looked around at the darkening park and the empty black roads to the edge of it.

'We're at Time Palace in Donlon. And I was taken. That what happened to you?'

'People disappear here, too?' Ava said. 'Where is *here*? And are you – are you all right?'

His face closed like a slammed door. 'It started here. Anyway, I'm back and it's over.' His face was hard. 'So you ain't been snatched?'

Ava shrugged uncertainly.

Jack went on, almost as if musing to himself. 'But you ain't from here. You didn't even know about the Hams. You must be a transient, then, and this must be your first time.'

'Transient?' said Ava.

Jack's expression of incredulity was not flattering. 'Don't they teach you nothin' over there? Transient is someone who can go between here and London. You can live in both places. Can be born like that or you can get it later, like you.'

'Oh.' Ava didn't like his tone. 'Actually, I go to a very good school, thank you. I'm sure there are things I could tell you.' Why was she bothering to justify herself to this rat-faced boy? 'I didn't mean to come. Something knocked me over, and then Phoebe disappeared into thin air and . . .'

'She must'a been taken, then.' Jack's voice was unemotional. He had read her mind again. 'People don't disappear into thin air otherwise, unless she was a transient. And she ain't here, so –' He spread his hands.

Ava couldn't stand Phoebe, but her chest tightened. She wouldn't wish that on anyone.

'Are you a transient?' she asked. Maybe he could show her how to return to London. Not that she wanted to ask this scornful boy for any help.

'Nah.' He glanced around. 'Look, we have to go,' said Jack. 'Can't stay here any longer. South Donlon is a bad place to be and near Time Palace is the worst. The Lady ain't no time queen anymore. And anyway, I have to get back to Hammer's smith. I'm one of his apprentices.' He raised his chin with pride.

'Oh, that's – good. Is Hammer a blacksmith?'

'Only the greatest smith in Donlon!' said Jack. 'He works magic with metal, any metal. Silver, brass, copper, you name it. He's a master locksmith, too, and only takes on a few apprentices every four years. I 'ave to get back and take back my place. He might think I've done a runner.'

It was very dark now and his thin face was full of shadows cast by the pale-yellow street lamps.

'Aren't you going to see your family first? To tell them you're back?'

'Nah.' Jack's voice was brusque. 'Hammer's all the family I need. Coming to the station?'

His face clenched like a fist and Ava bit down on the questions on her tongue. He turned and started walking and Ava hesitated, before glancing around at the dark streets. She shouldn't just walk off with a strange, rough boy.

Did she have any choice? And anyway, somehow she knew she could trust him.

She scuttled after him, catching up as he walked along a road lit dimly by the lamps. Dark shapes hunched in the shadows. They were the size of a small dog, but the wrong shape. Then one lifted its head and Ava saw a long beak as sharp as the hand-bushing tools in her father's studio.

It was a huge bird. A whole group of enormous birds huddled around something on a small green.

'Nasty brutes, them ravens.' Jack spat on the ground. He was just like a London urchin. She moved her shoes out of range.

'Ravens? I've never seen a raven the size of that!' said Ava with a shudder.

'Yeah, they're hunting. They must be hungry, which ain't a good sign. Come on, let's put some distance between us and them.'

They crossed to the other side of the road, where a low brick wall ran in front of a row of houses. 'Ravens aren't hunters,' said Ava. 'They eat carrion. Every child knows that!' She tried for the sarcastic edge that Jack had delivered.

Jack gave a short laugh. 'These birds ain't fussy if a body ain't quite dead. They'll help it along, specially if it's weak or sick. Or a baby. You saw them beaks. Like daggers, they are.'

'You mean they kill? *Human* babies?' Cold horror gripped Ava.

'Of course. But you're a new transient – you don't know.' She couldn't see his face clearly but she could practically hear the eyeroll. Thought he was quite the man, this skinny boy. Probably thought that her brain was inferior, as a mere female. She scowled in the darkness. He went on. 'See, normally the Shepherd feeds 'em. He's a bird shepherd, or used to be. Him and his gold hawk used to hunt for the ravens, get them enough meat to keep them fed. But then he lost his hawk and he's gone a bit mad, and the ravens have gone feral. Now they're out hunting themselves. You don't see anyone out in the streets at this time.' He gestured towards the houses, all with doors and shutters firmly closed.

Jack and Ava watched the birds. They were so still. So silent. Their dark shapes gripped Ava with an ancient dread. Jack's explanation made no sense to her, but a memory rose unbidden of the mad-eyed hunter with bird wings as a skirt. Could that be the shepherd Jack was talking about?

Ava turned to ask and saw that Jack's eyes were huge in his pinched face. She felt a stab of anxiety. 'Jack, what's happening here?'

'Donlon used to be a good place. Lady Montagu was our time queen. We always hoped she'd give you some time – but then she stopped bein' a queen and started time-snatching. Snatching . . .' He trailed off, then tried again.

'It – makes holes in people and other things start to go wrong. Things tip out of balance. The weather gets rough, lakes dry up, animals get violent or die. People are scared. And then –'

He broke off, his face a greenish colour in the wan light. He leaned against the wall, looking as though he was about to collapse. Ava stepped forward instinctively, but he didn't fall. He grunted and struggled on.

'When – when you get snatched, you go to the Void. A grey place where nothing is. It sucks you dry.' His eyes burned too bright in his pale face. 'It's hell. And when you come back – bits of you are missing.' He looked through Ava. 'You're torn.'

The grey place. The Void. So that's where she'd been, for one terrible moment, before she came here.

'Then I was snatched, too,' she whispered. Just for a moment, lingering in the grey for a timeless second, but the thought of being there any longer clutched her stomach with fear. It felt like losing yourself completely.

How could anyone stay there for days, weeks, even months and not go mad?

Maybe they couldn't. Maybe that's what Jack was saying. She looked at his hollow face and felt pity squeeze hard in her chest.

He had slumped further down on the wall. He looked wrecked. He licked his lips and spoke in a low, hoarse voice. 'You lose yourself in there. I was there for too long. Then the world came back, and there you were again.'

He raised his head and his eyes locked onto hers. They were not normal eyes. They saw too much. Something scraped at the bottom of her memory, stirring up inky sediment. She blinked and stepped away.

A scrabbling behind them made her whirl around.

The birds were closer. They'd abandoned whatever it was they'd been pecking at and were squatting on the road, as patient as stones. Waiting. For what? She turned back to Jack and her heart sank. Jack had slid onto the ground and collapsed into a heap. No. *NO*. They were the only living things on this street, apart from the dark shadows on the road.

As if on cue, the hunched shapes hopped closer. Bile rose in her throat. She stamped her foot and flapped her arms at the birds. 'Shoo! Get away!'

The bird nearest to her cocked its head. None of the others moved. They sat as though they had all the time in the world. How much time did they have? She bent down and shook Jack hard.

'Jack! Wake up! We have to move!'

His head lolled as she shook him again. No response. He was out cold.

Every instinct she had screamed at her to run, to leave him there. Get away from the feathered shapes . . . but she couldn't just leave him. They would kill him. And she needed Jack. He was – She didn't know how to finish the thought.

A rustle passed through the birds, as if on signal. They juddered closer in one black mass. The raven closest to Jack hopped forward and stabbed its beak at Jack's foot. Another bounced forward and let out a harsh *caw*, as if on signal. They moved nearer, beaks gleaming black in the dim light.

'No! Get off!' shouted Ava. Blue-ice eyes gleamed and their black beaks stabbed as they hopped. *Thud, shuffle, thud, shuffle.* She kicked out towards the nearest bird and her foot connected with a big feathery body. The bird shrieked and flapped away but another raven landed on Jack's still body, followed by a second and a third.

'*NO!*' shouted Ava.

She kicked out again and threw herself across Jack to shield his eyes and stomach, sobbing in disgust as wings flapped and claws scrambled on her. She squealed as a sharp beak stabbed her shoulder.

It was no good. They couldn't stay here like this. She rose to her feet, flapped at the birds and grabbed Jack under the armpits.

A guttural sound came from her throat as she heaved and her shoulder burned with the effort. Damn him! She couldn't carry him, she should just run . . . But then an old, deep strength was coursing through her like blood. It burst out of her as she roared at the skies as the beaks and claws raked them, stabbing and ripping, tearing . . .

Then there were more wings above. Big wings this time, bigger than any raven. Something else coming down from the skies. She dropped to the ground, hunching down over Jack, making herself as tiny as she could in the ancient instinct of all prey. Even the ravens were scattering, escaping the beast from above.

It landed beside her, great wings flapping dust and leaves into her face. She huddled low, waiting for the claws to rake her flesh, the beak to stab her back – eyes screwed shut against the pain to come.

Nothing happened.

She peered sideways from underneath her arms and what she saw made her sit bolt upright in shock.

It was no bird. She'd seen this wild creature with tousled white hair and ragged clothes before, in a London cemetery. From his back sprouted a pair of enormous, gently moving and somewhat dishevelled wings.

CHAPTER 8
JACK

Donlon

Something touched Jack's face – so soft, so warm. Then like magic, the world came back.

He could hear the waterwheels, smell the grass, feel her light touch. The grey brightened into form and colour and the first thing his eyes focused on was her. Her long dark hair and those strong steady eyes. Blue like deep water. Watchin' him.

He took a breath, and the breath was her. She stepped into his soul without moving a muscle. She was his sister and she was part of him. Always had been.

Who was this girl he knew so well?

'Hello?'

Her voice brought him all the way back to his senses.

He knew her. Because of her, he had – Then the shutters slammed down. He didn't want to remember. The only way he knew how to keep safe was to put up his barriers.

CHAPTER 9
AVA

Donlon

A ragged tunic hung off the winged man's muscled brown shoulders and worn trousers encased his tree-trunk legs. His wings protruded through a tear in the tunic, mounted on thick flesh. He was a gigantic, still presence on the dark street, his wings moving gentle as breath as he looked around, eyes calm through a tangle of bone-white hair.

His wasn't the malevolent stillness of the ravens, stirring inky places inside of you. It was the stillness of an ancient oak tree or a sea glittering quietly under the stars. Ava couldn't tear her gaze away – couldn't move until he looked down at her, eyes bright and sad.

'Torn battleflags take the welcomeplace. You are born for greeting carpets but instead you receive faceknives.' His voice was wind and vibration, the strange words a breeze rustling over the deep drone of the earth. He squatted down and looked Ava in the face and all she could do was gape back.

She could feel his voice in her chest. 'I am Malaikah and I welcomegive to your birthcity. I came flying in a timejump but I nearly didn't get here, before –'

He didn't need to finish the sentence. His eyes were now on Jack. She realised she was still half-lying across him and scrambled to her feet. 'Malaikah.' She remembered Violet saying the name and she held the word like an incantation on her tongue. It belonged there. 'You are Malaikah. My – birthcity? Here?'

'Yes.' He bowed his head, then turned to Jack. He ran light fingers down Jack's body and gently pulled up the bottom of his trousers. Ava flinched at the deep red gashes that sliced his legs. Maybe she was in a strange, shocked state, but she could feel mirroring pain in her own legs. 'Ah. This one is sucked dry. Snatched for overlong, and then facekniffed by ravens.' He looked back at Ava. 'And you? Is there surfacepain?'

His words danced on the very edge of sense, but the code-poems resonated with a deeper meaning. They unlocked something in Ava, releasing a tumble of words. 'No. No, we were on our way – he has to get to Hammer, he's an apprentice and the snatching has hurt him. He collapsed and I thought he, we, were gone. I thought the ravens would, that they would finish him, us . . .'

Her teeth chattered so hard the words couldn't get through. Malaikah reached across and placed a great hand softly on her head. All the pieces of herself gathered into the centre, like iron filings to a magnet, and calm lay blanket-heavy across her. The shaking stopped and she took a deep breath.

'His name is Jack.' Her words were steady now. 'Can you help him?'

Malaikah smiled at her and she sighed deep into her lungs. The smile lit the dark streets, and his rags and tousled hair had the wild beauty of a sea eagle. She felt as she did when she saw a blazing sunset or a dark sky full of stars; felt that savage wanting to disappear into the greater thing before her.

'His fleshpain will heal but I cannot return the lifewind once snatched. For you, I cannot yet seefar. Your heartguide made me come, he is curdled. I have never seen him so butterchurned. But now, we go to the Hammerwitch. She can closefast any wound.'

'My – heartguide?' Picking sense out of Malaikah's words was like sieving weevils out of fine flour.

Malaikah leaned down and picked Jack up gently, one arm under the boy's armpits and around his narrow chest. The other great arm scooped up Ava as if she were no more than a kitten, lifting her easily around her waist. Ava had never had a man's arm embrace her so tightly, not even her father's – and yet not a cell of her being jarred in protest, as though being picked up by a giant winged creature was lodged deep in the memory of her body.

'Your heartguide, Bill-man,' he answered. His breath stirred the hair on the top of her head.

Huge wings juddered behind her, sending dust swirling as they left the ground, but Ava barely noticed as she realised what he'd said. Bill-man. Bill. Malaikah knew her father. This wild, cosmic creature was part of her mild-mannered father's world. How was that even possible?

And Malaikah called this her birth city. Did he mean she had been born here, wherever here was?

She could not order her thoughts before Malaikah thrust high into the sky. Ava's stomach sank to her shoes and she squeezed her eyes tight, digging her fingers into the arm around her. It wasn't possible to go so fast. Even on the thundering railways she had never felt speed like this. Could a body bear it? Would she survive this crush of speed?

When she dared to look again, cold sweat pricked down her back. They were high above Donlon – as high as a hot air balloon. The night city sprawled below, pricked with yellow dots of light that did nothing to push back the velvet dark. The cool night air rushed past her cheeks and the only sound was the wind and the *whoop, whoop* of Malaikah's great wings above. Ava looked over at Jack, who was dangling limply, still out cold. She felt very close to joining him. The backs of her legs were dissolving in tingles and her stomach swooped like a swallow in a midge haze. She forced herself to look straight ahead, not at the far, far earth, all the time clinging to Malaikah until the muscles of her hands ached. She could just make out the shape of the river far below, tiny lights marking its curve.

Then the river was beneath them, impossibly soon. The wind against her face softened and she realised that they had slowed and were hovering in one spot above it. She risked a glance downwards and immediately wished she hadn't. Lights were moving, jostling into each other, and with a jolt she realised the riverbank was thick with people. The lights she had seen were torches and lamps. Ava could hear shouts from below.

'What's happening?' she called upwards.

In answer, Malaikah tightened his grip and swooped without warning, forcing Ava's breath out in an involuntary *oof*. People scattered or crouched, covering their heads as Ava had done at the sound of gigantic wings above. They landed and Malaikah closed his wings with a rustling snap. He lowered Ava to her feet and Jack to the ground and stood towering over the scene.

It was the smell that hit Ava first. It was not the stomach-turning stench of the rancid Thames in London, but a sharper, throat-closing odour. It rose from the forlorn crowds of people on the riverbank. The people looked worn and weary, travel-soiled and ragged. They clutched bundles of meagre possessions, pots and pans, food. The scene was half-lit by flickering gas lamps and fire sticks, leaping flames hissing and spitting above their heads. Malaikah's voice vibrated above it all.

'What happenchance, humblings?'

Voices jabbered indecipherably and then one man stepped forward, his face twisting in the firelight. He pressed a hand to his chest.

'Malaikah, we greet you. The Knights of the Bridge block our passage. We have been walking for days from Mort Lake and now can't cross the river.'

Ava looked at the bridge spanning the river. Sure enough, two figures in full armour sat high on draught horses, swords at the ready. Their armour looked as black as the night around them. A woman's wail broke through the crowd and Malaikah's voice hummed above her head. 'The sickmake is worse in Mort Lake?'

The flickering light carved hollows in the man's face. 'The gas is spreading from the lake. A week ago, the plants within two fields from the lake started to die – leaves withering like autumn and flowers burnt brown. Then birds fell from the trees and the cats died. Two days ago the yellow stink choked our lungs. We took what we could and left. We heard things were better on the other side of the river, but now . . .'

His voice trailed off and he spat towards the knights standing guard, before turning to comfort a woman cradling a baby. The woman and baby were both crying.

Malaikah looked down at Ava, his blue eyes like cold fire in his shadowed face. 'Watchsafe over Jack, Avaguard.'

He straightened and walked to the bridge until he stood in front of the knights. The crowd fell silent and Ava held her breath. Malaikah looked suddenly smaller before the great horses but his voice was strong, carrying back towards them.

'What happenchance, Bridge Knights? Your bridgeguard is a pledge to keepsafe, not passblock.'

One of the knights answered, his voice rough. 'We decide who passes now, Malaikah. Money decides. This lot can't pay and other people are happy to pay us to keep their kind out. They're trouble. We don't want none of their problems our side of the river. They don't belong here.'

Malaikah's voice boomed like a deep bell. 'Your words shamemake you as Names. They are as Donlon as you, Knights. Do not blamecast wrong.'

The other knight gave an ugly laugh. These knights were from no noble class, thought Ava. 'We go where the money is, Malaikah. The people who pay us ain't in the mood to take chances. Dangerous times and the troubles all come from south of the river. Their problem. Let them sort it out.'

'Recall the ancient Namecode? You are to guardsafe the bridges for all. You are wrongNamed, if you do not.'

The one who had spoken first made a scornful sound. 'Malaikah, times have changed. The old words don't mean nothin' these days. Not our fault Donlon is the way it is today. Just doin' what we have to do to survive, see?'

'Stopping weaksmalls does not strongmake you. We must help those who forceflee. Hurl your strongskills at the snatchings, not at these humblings!'

The knight's voice sounded flat and hard. 'You can't stop the Green Witch, Malaikah. Forget it and save yourself. That's all that's left to do.' The two knights raised their swords in unison, as if to say the time for words was over.

A cry rang out from the crowd and a small figure darted out and made a stumbling run towards them. Ava sucked her breath in sharply when she saw it was the mother, still clinging onto her baby as she ran.

'Stop now or we strike!' shouted one of the knights as they raised their swords higher.

Another figure ran out after the woman, still brandishing a burning brazier, and Ava recognised the first man who had spoken to Malaikah. As if at a signal, men surged after him in a solid wave bristling with axes, cudgels and the occasional glinting sword, a roar of pent-up anger and frustration filling the air. The horses reared and the knights slashed with their swords. Ava watched in horror as the woman weaved and ducked underneath the great hooves of the horses. As if in slow motion, Malaikah dived towards the woman and baby, seized them around the waist and with a single great flap of his wings swooped with them to safety.

The crowd fell back before the great horses and the knights' swords. Their momentum lost, they broke away from each other and milled like confused sheep. Malaikah called down, his voice carrying through the night air. 'Groundgive, Mort Lake smalls! You will grindsmash under the hooves and swords. Be still.'

Malaikah dropped to the ground and carefully lowered the woman near her husband. 'Watchsafe her.' He turned back and looked out over the crowd. 'You are far from fightfit.' Malaikah's voice was soft now. 'Stayrest and we will helpbring soon.'

Ava followed his gaze. The adults looked back at them with worn, pale faces and hopeless eyes. Children stood dull with fright and fatigue or clutched adult arms and legs. Hacking coughs racked the crowd, the tearing sounds convulsing bodies in a terrible, heaving dance.

Ava had seen suffering, of course. London poverty was a beast with blood on its lips. The rich and clean mostly lived within a few streets of twisting, filthy lanes where street urchins ran barefoot and desperation rapped at each door. Death was ever-present and poverty clawed the hope and dignity from every soul who smelt its dank breath. You had to harden your heart against the grimness and redouble your efforts to keep want away from the door of your loved ones and those few you could help.

But she had never seen an exodus. Never seen hundreds upon hundreds driven out from their homes, with nowhere to go. She looked at a mother whose arms were entwined with a girl just a bit younger than Ava and her heart surged with sharp pity. They stared into space until the girl coughed and her mother pressed the girl's face to her own chest in a universal reflex. That maternal gesture stirred a strange spasm in Ava's heart. It felt like envy. How could that be? These people knew hardship, far beyond anything Ava had ever experienced. They had nothing, they were ill and poor with nowhere to go ... but the mother and daughter had each other. It was intimacy that came from years of being together. She would never have that. She did not even know who her mother was, now.

Ava spun around. This was not her world. These were not her people. She could not help them, just as she couldn't help the urchins that darted underfoot in the Devil's Acre in London.

'Can you take me home, Malaikah?'

Suddenly she wanted nothing more than to be back in Bishopsgate.

Malaikah looked down at Ava. 'Is this your heartwant straight?'

It took Ava a moment to understand his meaning. 'Yes. Yes, it is.'

'Your father is heartchurned and safefears you. He wants the truegood for you, but does not have the truesight, like Violet. Be listenful with Violet, and let your own wisetree grow. You will need the fruit from it when you homego, Avasmall. Until your time is here again.'

His words sang like wind in the trees and the meaning was as hard to grasp. What was he telling her? To listen to Violet more than her father? They had both lied to her and pulled her world out from underneath her – but at least she knew the taste of that deception. It was familiar and woven into her very life. She had no role here – nothing to anchor her. If she had a centre, it was back there in London. She felt a desperate need to reassemble the shattered pieces of herself, and she had to start there.

She looked past Malaikah. Jack was sitting up, his eyes glinting bright in his pinched face. As if in reflex, her heart clenched with pain – but she had the strangest feeling this was *his* pain, not hers. In that moment, she wondered how she could just leave him. As she caught his eye he jerked his head away. Had she imagined the raw look of pleading on his face? He got to his feet.

'You need to take Ava home, Malaikah.' His voice was flat as cardboard. He put his hands in his pockets and looked over Ava's head at Malaikah. 'This lot ain't goin' anywhere. Hammer's smith is just over that bridge and I can go there and get help for them. Food, blankets, stuff you can carry.'

His words were flat and cold, but she could feel the lie. They hid something huge – something she did not understand. She felt a swell of simple, childlike love for him. As though they belonged together and were family. But how could that be?

'You are a bigheart humbling, Jack, but you cannot yet walkfar. I will wingbear you.' He looked at Ava. 'Yes, Ava must homego. She is a paleweak and only halfdone,

73

when we need a warriorstrong. You must shieldheart and wisegrow, Ava. Come quick, humblings.'

He bent and took them up by the waist, one arm for each, and this time there was no warning as he swept them straight up in the air, stealing Ava's breath from her mouth and Jack's too by the sound of his gasp. Malaikah accelerated so fast that the speed of the last journey felt like a leisurely stagecoach. His wings *whoomped* them across the river and towards a glowing light in the distance. The night air whipped tears from Ava's eyes and it wasn't until Malaikah slowed and she could blink the wet salt out of her eyes that she could see their destination.

The heat of the foundry slapped her face, even from so high. The roar and *whoosh* of flames up furnace chimneys, the echoing clang of metal upon metal, the shouts of workers and the burning smell of hair and metal was like a vision of Hell. She looked over at Jack and saw the flames reflected in his eyes, his mouth curved in a smile. He was home. He knew where he belonged. She felt another stab of longing.

Malaikah dropped to the ground and let Jack down. 'Homego to the Hammerwitch to deepmend. I will fallback soon.'

Jack turned and put one hand on his chest and bowed in the same gesture of the man at the river. 'Thanksgive, Malaikah.'

He came close and put out one hand. Ava could not see if he was looking at her, his face a black silhouette against the flames. He took hold of her arm and held it hard, like he had before, as though the grip was steadying him. As though he was drawing something out of her. She instinctively

74

pressed his hand in return, as if this was the most natural response in the world before Malaikah shot back up into the air and snatched them apart.

Ava felt his sudden absence as a wrench. She pressed one hand to the twinge in her chest as the rhythm of Malaikah's mighty wings formed a chant in Ava's head.

Paleweak, halfdone . . . She had never been expected to be anything but pale or weak – desirable traits for a modern lady – but now the words were a humiliating chant that kept time to Malaikah's wings.

Ava didn't realise what had changed at first. The dark night was pouring like sand and specks of light were puncturing the darkness. The air was breaking up into tiny pieces and a shivering thrill rushed through her, like when you misjudge the number of stairs and stride out into empty air. Her body prickled and every hair stood upright, an animal sensing deep danger in the collapsing space around her.

She shut her eyes tight but the dizziness didn't stop. Dizzy was an inadequate scrap of a word to describe this sensation of compression then expansion, as though her smallest particles were flinging to all corners of the earth. She gripped Malaikah's arm and groaned.

He suddenly released her and her stomach flipped in panic before she realised that her feet were on the ground. Her eyes flew open and she stumbled, but his hand was ready, gripping her arm and pulling her relentlessly along. They were in a vast crowd of people and Malaikah was striding along with them, weaving in and out adroitly while Ava's legs continued to function like milk-soaked bread. She hung grimly onto his arm, concentrating on staying upright.

She didn't need to look around to know they were in London. The smell of the mud and horse dung on the streets, the smoke in the air from thousands of fires and industry told her that. As did the ever-present background tang of the stinking Thames. More specifically, the throat-gripping stench of rotting vegetables and meat told her they were near a market. Glancing up, she saw the familiar spire of a Hawksmoor church and felt the deep, welcome thud of homecoming.

Spitalfields! Never had she been so pleased to see its rubbish-strewn streets and its rancid press of humans. No murderous ravens. No poisoned refugees. No mind-melding con artists. Well, maybe some of those things, but in a familiar form. This was her stinking borough and these were her people. Suddenly the mundane and the squalid glowed with warm welcome.

But why did no one look twice at Malaikah? You saw everything on these streets and Londoners were famously unshockable, but a giant, half-clothed man with wings would surely produce a flicker of interest? Ava looked sideways at Malaikah and blinked. She was clutching the arm of a tall, white-haired hunchback, his wings tucked beneath a ragged tunic that was not out of place here.

Malaikah stopped by the front door of Ava's house. She paused, awkward. She had no social guidelines for this. Did she just say thank you and goodbye? He had saved her life and they had crossed worlds together – it did not seem adequate. But it felt absurd to invite him in for tea.

Malaikah rapped at the door and it opened as if someone had been waiting on the other side. Violet and Father jostled in the doorway, expressions of relief and anxiety chasing over their faces. Violet rushed forward and grabbed Ava in a tight hug, before releasing her to throw her arms around Malaikah. Her sobs mingled with Father's earnest, formal thanks. Both of them ushered Malaikah inside with Ava, but he stepped back, one hand on his heart in the gesture becoming familiar to Ava.

'I heartbrim to see you again, favoured humblings. The youngling is homecome, as wordgifted. Let not her heart stuntygrow, Bill-man. I must fallback to the sicksore humblings.'

He turned to Ava and fixed a blue gaze on her. 'You will return to Donlon, Avasoul. Your mother awaits you there.'

With that, he stepped back into the street, walked into the crowd and disappeared.

CHAPTER 10
AVA

London, September 1858

It was not until Violet had led Ava to her bedroom, stripped her to her shift, exclaimed over her wounds and fussed around her with hot water, soap and a towel that Ava came out of her shock. She glanced at her surroundings in vague surprise. When had they walked up the stairs?

She looked at Violet. 'Did – did Malaikah say my mother was waiting for me, there?' Her voice was a croak. She was not at all sure that she had his meaning right, even now.

'He did,' said Violet.

'He didn't mean . . . that? It must be his way of saying something else?'

Malaikah bent words like wire into new shapes. It was the only explanation. Surely. Ava watched Violet, her heart thudding hard in her throat.

Violet gave a great sigh and stopped her fussing. 'Your father would want me to say it was code for something else, Ava. But I think you deserve some truth now. And anyway, there is no going back to innocence.' She turned to Ava and looked her straight in the eye. 'Malaikah meant that your mother is alive and waiting for you in Donlon.'

'Mother is – *alive*?' The words were no more than breath.

All this time. She could have seen her mother's face all this time. She could have known a mother's touch in the way that poor Mort Lake girl had. Felt her hand in hers, heard her voice, known what her laugh sounded like. The pain of this truth stabbed her like a knife in the chest.

Why? Why had her mother been kept from her all her life?

A thought struck her. Was her mother not whole, in the way Jack had described? 'Is she . . . is she mad?' she whispered. 'Is she torn? She is not in . . .'

Images of a terrible asylum filled her head – of bound women in torn, filthy dresses, chained to the floor with a viewing gallery for the entertainment of the public. Women were thrown into asylums for so many definitions of madness and, once they were there, they hardly ever came out.

'No, Ava. She is not mad – far from it – and she is not in an asylum. And I will tell you just one more thing for now. You will hear things but I want you to hold onto one truth. Your mother loved you then and loves you now – whatever else happened.' She leaned forward, her gaze serious. 'Whatever else you hear. Do you understand?'

No, she didn't understand. She didn't understand anything.

Violet pursed her lips. 'Enough for now. You need to sleep. You've been through too much, too quickly.'

Sleep? Had Violet lost her mind?

Violet gestured towards the nightdress on Ava's bed.

'Violet, I've just discovered I have a mother living in another world. I might never sleep again. There is too much to know! I mean, who is she? And why did she –'

'Good night, Ava,' said Violet. She turned and walked out the door, closing it firmly behind her.

This was absurd. Sleep was unthinkable. Shock still hummed through Ava's body. Her mind was tumbling like an acrobat trying to find footing.

She had so many questions. Too many to focus on.

Her body suddenly felt like lead. Lord, her legs ached. She lifted them onto the bed and pulled her shift up to examine the raven punctures on her legs. She fell back with a groan. She would lie here for a moment; try and gather her thoughts. Two breaths later, she sank deep into a tidal tug of exhaustion.

Ava was pulled back to consciousness by someone shaking her shoulder gently. Violet. She always smelled of lavender water and carbolic soap. Ava squinted upwards. She was now under the bedclothes in her shift, nightdress still folded neatly at the bottom of her bed. Did Violet do that?

'I dropped off to *sh*leep,' she slurred.

With a thud, she remembered that her mother was alive. The shock was a physical jolt. The next second, she thought of Jack and sighed. It was a warm feeling, like the feel of a comfortable old toy.

Violet set down a tray with a bowl and a pile of bread and butter, a cup of coffee on the side. Ava turned away and mumbled, 'Don't want supper.'

'Yesterday's supper and today's breakfast and lunch have been and gone.' Violet was brisk. 'We are now nearly onto the next supper. Your father has not yet finished work but I thought you might like to have something here.' Violet sat on the edge of the bed and patted Ava's arm. 'You have to eat, dear. You have to get your strength back.'

Yesterday? Ava opened her eyes properly now and looked at the curtains. Violet had already opened them and the light was at the same angle as it was when she went to sleep. She'd slept a full day through. She felt like a sponge that had been dipped into water and was still half dry. How could she have slept a whole day and still feel exhausted?

'What – what day is it?' Not that she much cared, but the question was a normal, everyday one. The answer might help pin her to a normal, everyday world.

'Thursday.'

Ava shot upright, all drowsiness gone. Now she cared. 'Thursday? But we were at Greenwich on Monday and I came back the same evening.'

Violet stirred the bowl and picked up the tray impassively. 'No, my dear. You came back on Wednesday. Have some soup.'

Ava obediently arranged herself so that Violet could put the tray on her knee, her mind trying to slot puzzle pieces into mismatched holes. If she'd come back on Wednesday night, where had Tuesday and most of Wednesday gone?

'But – but I was only in that place for a few hours. Wasn't I?'

Violet brought the spoon to Ava's mouth. Was she going to handfeed Ava like a baby bird? Ava sighed but opened her mouth to take the soup. The thick meaty broth burst onto her tastebuds in a dense surge of flavour and for a moment the whole universe stopped to marvel. She was starving. She grabbed the spoon from Violet and started to shovel the soup in.

Violet sat back and looked satisfied. 'Yes and no is your answer. You were active in Donlon for a few hours, but the time stream here moved on further while you were there. Time slips between the two cities and you can never be sure how long you've been away until you get back. It works like that both ways.'

Ava had half-finished the soup while Violet was talking and had started on the bread, using it to mop up the fragrant meat juices pooling at the bottom of the bowl. 'Which is why you're ravenous as a street cat. Your body is back on London time and hasn't been fed for days.'

Ava's stomach was making some very strange gurgling noises. She ignored it and picked up another piece of bread. 'I don't even know what questions to ask, Violet. There is nothing about this I understand.'

'I know, sweetling. You have to get the body functioning again first. Don't try and think just yet.'

Ava chewed the last piece of bread. She had never been this hungry before, proper deprivation that narrowed her focus to the meal in front of her. There were so many people in the streets around her who felt like this every day. Who had to get on with life with a sense of panic that the next meal wouldn't come. She felt strength course through her veins again and understood how close a human body could come to stopping without fuel.

Ava swallowed the last mouthful regretfully. 'Is there more, Violet?'

Violet tutted. 'Not for you, heartlove. Too much too soon is as bad as not enough. There's your coffee – drink that down.'

Ava took the cup. 'Violet?'

'Yes, Ava?'

'Why did you pretend my mother was dead?'

A sigh. 'Your father decided that, my dear. He – well, it's complex. I can't say more without him being here.'

Ava wrapped both hands around the gently steaming cup and raised it to her lips. The knowledge that her mother was alive was still a fact she could not fully absorb. She opened her eyes with a lurch of guilt as the crunch of carriage wheels stopped outside. She had almost forgotten about Phoebe. Was she somewhere in Donlon now? Or drifting in the grey halfworld? The memory of that deathly unplace sent cold threads through Ava and she pushed it away. She could not wish that place on even her worst enemy.

Violet went to the window and looked down into the street. She tutted. 'We spent enough time with those two in Greenwich over the last two days. Your poor father has been frantic every second since you left, talking with police, newspapers, detectives – you will not believe how much attention this had caused, Ava. The disappearance in broad daylight of a society girl at Miss Buss's Academy on the way to see Donati's Comet. Honestly, the tosh that's being talked. And of course we had to talk to the Order, which your father swore he would never do again, after . . . well, never mind.' She glanced at Ava uncomfortably.

'I forget myself. So much has changed in the last few days that –'

'Violet, what happened at the Observatory? I saw a cloaked man with something like a chronometer and Mr Timeward running towards him. Did we – did Phoebe get snatched?' There were so many things Ava didn't understand. Something else suddenly occurred to her. 'And what do you and Father have to do with that other world?'

Violet kept her eyes on the street below. 'Yes, Phoebe was snatched, and you were –'

The doorbell rang and Violet jumped and scurried with what seemed unnecessary haste to the door. 'I need to get that. You rest, heartlove.'

'Who is it?'

'Phoebe's mother. That woman is incorrigible.'

And with that Violet rattled down the stairs, taking more mysteries with her.

Ava put the tray on the bedside table and swung her legs out of bed. The last thing she felt like doing was encountering Phoebe's mother, or even getting out of bed – she was still exhausted – but there was no way she was missing out on what she had to say. It had been a while since she'd been of an age to listen in on conversations from the stairway but every child worth their salt knew that was the best way to glean unguarded adult secrets.

She dressed hurriedly, cursing the strings of her corset under her breath – so many layers! She fantasised about clothing that could be thrown on in a single motion. As soon as she was at a standard that would not get her arrested or thrown into an asylum, she tiptoed to the door and crept down the stairs until she could make out the conversation in the sitting room. She settled down on the lowest step she dared and craned her head.

Phoebe's mother's voice brayed loud and clear. 'Since my poor, dear Phoebe has gone I have been beside myself. My health is fragile, you know. I have a delicate constitution and this shock has been quite deranging. My specialist physician has to provide the very latest medicine – so expensive, Mr Bailey! But he has a very exclusive practice in Burlington Arcade, one has to be so well connected even to get on his books, so really what does one expect? I have to remain strong so that I can be ready to help Phoebe when she comes back. You know what they say about the disappearances, Mr Bailey? They perturb the spirit. Shock the soul. My poor, dear Phoebe . . .'

Her voice was replaced by delicate sobs. Ava could hear her father's voice awkwardly muttering something soothing. The door opened and Violet flounced out. Ava could almost feel the eye roll from where she sat and she shrank back out of sight as Violet stomped down to the kitchen, banged around and then returned with a tray holding a jug of cordial and some glasses. Ava heard the tray being put down on the table and then the door was pulled closed. What was the woman even doing here? Violet was thinking along the same uncharitable lines if the set of her jaw was anything to go by.

It seemed the cordial quickly restored Phoebe's mother as her voice boomed on. Ava silently thanked her good fortune – such a voice made information gathering so much easier.

'My physician has seen some of the effects of the vanishings himself. He said that often there are reports of a particular little mechanism that might be connected to the incidents. A small metal clockwork device that resembles a chronometer or pocket watch. He said if such a thing could be examined it could provide some valuable clues as to how to treat, or even prevent, the effects of being taken.'

A pause. 'Did you happen to see such an item, Mr Bailey? Or perhaps your daughter? You were the last people to see my dear Phoebe.' Her voice trembled again.

Ava's mind went back to the scene frozen forever in her head. That cloaked man at Greenwich had been holding something that looked like a gold chronometer. What had happened to it after that? She craned to hear her father's words, much lower and harder to catch than Phoebe's mother.

'. . . have never seen an item such as you . . . certain . . . nothing of the sort near the scene of the incident, Mrs Fortescue.'

Ava frowned. Father's certainty was very strange. Her father must have seen that man and the object he held – or even if by some strange chance he hadn't, he would have heard of it in the days afterwards. Had he not seen it as clearly as she had? His glasses might have played tricks on his eyes.

That, or he was lying to Mrs Fortescue's face.

Absurd. Her father was a stickler for social mores and decent character.

But he has lied to you all your life, Ava. What is one more lie?

The door to the sitting room opened. Mrs Fortescue edged sideways, her crinoline compressing like a spring through the door. It must be three metres in diameter, at least. She squeezed through and Ava could clearly see her sneer of disdain as she glanced around the narrow hall. Her voice kept chattering, bright and cheery and completely at odds with her face.

'Thank you kindly for your time and concern, Mr Bailey. I must rush to my appointment with my specialist physician. Appointments with him are like gold dust, you know.'

The last of the crinoline popped out into the hallway and swayed gently around her. She turned to face Father and Violet, her expression all sweetness now. 'Please do let me know if you remember anything – anything at all – about that awful day. I'm sorry not to talk to your daughter. Please let me know when she is recovered sufficiently for us to meet. We can only pray for Phoebe's swift return, and Ava's full recovery of course.'

The doorbell rang again.

'Excuse me, Mrs Fortescue. If you don't mind.' Violet stood to one side of Mrs Fortescue's skirts, at a loss at how to proceed past them to the door.

'Oh.' Mrs Fortescue looked put out but pulled her skirt slightly to one side, allowing a small gap for Violet to edge along the wall and Ava knew without seeing her face that her eyebrow was almost at her hairline. Violet made it past the skirt barrier and opened the door.

'Ah, Mrs Belville. Please do come in,' Father called, beckoning to the woman on the step. He turned to Mrs Fortescue's enquiring face and explained, 'Mrs Belville is a seller of time. She delivers it without fail all over London in an excellent door-to-door service.' He smiled at the small woman making her way down the hall, chronometer in hand.

Mrs Fortescue's face was a picture. She clutched her chest, pink patches blooming on her cheeks like cordial stains on a tablecloth, and gasped, 'You deliver – time? Where do you get it from?'

Father laughed. 'It's a figure of speech, Mrs Fortescue. Mrs Belville takes the precise time at Greenwich every day and then delivers that time in a most excellent service to homes and businesses all over London. How else are we to know how accurate our timepieces are, not being within sight of the Time Ball at Greenwich?'

'Oh.' Mrs Fortescue fanned her face rapidly and gave a little laugh. Ava craned to glance at Violet, who was watching, eyes narrowed. Mrs Fortescue laughed again.

'A misunderstanding. I thought – silly me, never mind. I have troubled you for long enough. I must hurry now. Goodbye.'

She gathered her skirts, pushing past Violet without a second glance, and bustled unceremoniously out the open door to her waiting carriage.

CHAPTER 11
JACK

Donlon

'I need you. Come back.'

The words burst out of Jack but too late. Ava was gone and his heart ripped out of his chest to follow her.

It left a gaping hole that surely all the world could see. As a kid, he'd thought everyone felt like this, that the world could get inside every soul like it did his. But he'd learned that he wasn't normal. That he saw deeper and felt harder than other people. He'd since learned how to put down his shutters, to put a barrier between him and the world that only he could lift. But this was something new.

He wasn't right without her. He knew that as soon as he watched Malaikah soar into the air, taking her away. He could see the gleam of her fading and everything else faded too.

Was this his particular way of being torn? Or was it more?

He'd been nowhere and numb for so long, and then he'd seen her – really *seen* her, with his sight wide open – but too soon. He wasn't back in the world properly and she seeped into him before he was whole again. She had become part of him, like a stitch became part of fabric. As if she was part of the seam that held his torn edges together.

Jack had taught himself to not need people. To keep them at bay. It was how he'd always got through life. But now he did need someone, and to make things worse it was a girl from London – a place that held only bad associations for him – who he would wager had never been without a meal or a bed or love. Who was from another world, in more than one way – far from the urchin underclass he knew so well.

His need scared him. It made him panicked and claustrophobic, but at the same time all he could think about was being near her. He felt at home with her. As though he'd found a long-lost sister.

He inhaled the sharp furnace smell and welcomed the heat singeing his nostrils. This was home. That should be enough for him. This was where he belonged and life had to go on. But now, because of her coming back, it wasn't enough. Coming *back*? What did that mean? But he knew it was the truth.

Before this, his life had always been his work. His apprenticeship with Hammer was his saviour and he knew it. It was everything to him, his first thought on waking and his last thought before he faded into sleep at night. Now, everything had changed.

He stepped forward towards the open maw of the blazing foundry, which burned and raged twenty-four hours a day. He winced as the movement stabbed sharp needles through his leg, his shoulders, his back. The pain was hot and sickening, as if the ravens had plugged him full of poison from their beaks. He staggered towards the entrance, which suddenly seemed impossibly far away. He'd used every scrap of the scant energy he'd had after the snatching. He had come back half-alive, to be attacked by ravens and then feel the wrench of Ava's leaving.

Jack was empty. It was no good. It was . . .

The acrid tang of disinfectant hit Jack's nostrils, as effective as smelling salts. His eyes flew open. He was in a room with two empty beds next to his. Pain ricocheted all over his body. Moving was agony and his breath hissed sharp between his teeth as he sat up.

A tiny woman whirled around. 'And just what d'yer think yer doing?' she said, glaring at him, one hand on a plump hip and the other holding a vial of something murky. It was Agnes, their housemother, nurse, cook, housekeeper and resident witch all rolled into one. She was terrifying.

Jack sank meekly back onto the bed, his hands pulling the sheet up to cover his half-dressed body. Agnes snorted and rolled her eyes.

'You ain't got anything special there, Jack lad. I can tell you that fer nothing.' She came over to him and put one hand on his forehead before holding each eye open and peering into it. 'Sick bay is fer resting. You ain't good for doing anything but lying still yet, my boy.'

'But I have to –'

'What you have to do is open yer gob. Wide now.' Agnes slipped an expert hand under Jack's head, firm yet deft, and propped his head up. In the other hand she held the vial of dark liquid. Jack obeyed, letting Agnes tip the medicine into his mouth. Ugh! The stuff tasted like rotting, piss-soaked straw. He spluttered and scrubbed at his mouth but Agnes grabbed him by the nose and shoved a sugar lump into his mouth.

'Keep it in, lad! Won't do much good down your front, will it? Crunch that – it'll help it stay down.'

Jack cracked the sugar lump between his teeth and shuddered as the sweetness fought with the rancid medicine. It helped a bit, but the medicine was thick as slime, coating his mouth like mucus. He swallowed and retched. He had to get to the sink – he wasn't going to keep it down.

He swung his legs over the edge of the bed and ran to the sink – and stopped. He could move! He felt strong. And the pain had miraculously disappeared, along with his nausea. He looked at Agnes, who had an expression of morose satisfaction on her face.

'My most powerful painkiller. Not to be messed with, that one. Can knock you out cold as well.' She picked up a packet of powder on her preparation table and put it back in a cupboard on the wall, locking it carefully. 'Should keep you going for the rest of the day and then some.'

She gestured to the bed with her head. 'Up you get. I haven't finished with you yet. Have to treat those little scratches of yours. You can put those trousers on if you like.' She pointed to a neat pile of clothes on a chair at the foot of his bed. His own clothes were nowhere to be seen.

Thank the gods for small mercies. Jack pulled the clothes on gratefully before climbing back onto the bed. Agnes turned back to stirring a purplish mixture in a bowl.

'Reckon I'll be right as rain when you're done, thanks Agnes,' he said casually.

She snorted. 'That's the drugs talking, boy. You got a week in here a'fore you're good to go.'

A week! No, it was unthinkable. His head was full of Ava. He needed to find out who she was to him. What these memories were that she stirred in the depths of his mind. And apart from that, as much as he hated the knowledge, he needed her near him. He was certain about that. Already he could feel twitchings inside him, the start of some withdrawal.

He suddenly remembered the refugees from Mort Lake and shame stained his face hot. He'd been so caught up with his own self – and with Ava, who was like his own self now – that he'd forgotten to get help for them.

'Has Malaikah been?'

'Been and gone, lad. Took a pile of stuff for the Mort Lake mob, and Hammer helped too.' She glanced sharply at him. 'You weren't gonna be much help – let's be real about that.' She turned back to her stirring, shaking her head. 'It ended badly for some of them. Those knights are bad 'uns.'

Jack fell back on his pillow as Agnes deftly tended his wounds. He couldn't just stay here while others did the work that needed doing, both here and in the world outside Hammer's.

'I can't stay here. I have to –'

'Have to do what, Jack?'

The smell of singed hair filled the room and a vast shape blocked the doorway. Hammer ducked his head under the doorjamb and stepped inside. A charred leather apron hung over his bare scarred chest and the ends of his bushy

93

beard smoked. His dark eyes glowered under jutting black eyebrows as he said again, 'Have to do what?'

Jack snapped upright on the bed. His mouth had gone dry. Hammer was looking at him in that steady way he had, like he was on slower time than everyone else whirling around him and could wait forever. He'd look at you, brooding and still as a cliff face, silent, until the sweat was trickling between your shoulder blades.

Jack swallowed. 'I have to find a – girl. I met her after I was snatched. She saved me from the ravens.'

Silence. The black eyes on him. Hammer was waiting for more.

'I, ah, I think I can help her . . .'

Lame as a legless mouse, Jack! *Why* and *how* were the two questions in Hammer's face. How could Jack explain that Ava was connected to him? That he remembered her . . . He couldn't explain it to himself, let alone anyone else.

She'd *said* she wanted to go home to London, but he'd seen what was under those words. She wasn't whole, either. His sight had shown him things that she was hiding from herself. Her need was as great as his, if different – even if she couldn't see it clearly yet.

Jack had always been able to see more than people wanted him to see.

'Help her. You?' Hammer crossed his arms in that slow way he had as his glance flicked over Jack's bloody ankles and torso. The three words spoke volumes. 'And what about the work you have here? You been snatched a long time, Jack. Woulda thought you'd be ready to get stuck in and do your bit now.'

Hammer was right about the work and Jack knew how lucky he was to have his place here. Kids would kill for an apprenticeship at Hammer's. It was the luckiest break he'd ever had in his life.

But he had to make Hammer see that he had to do this before he could settle back down.

'She's a new transient. I can help her find her . . .'

Jack's words trailed away as Hammer's black brows furrowed. He tried again. 'I'll work me guts out soon as I'm back. I'll catch up and more. I, I ain't got no choice about this.' He was pleading now, a pathetic whine in his voice. Gods! He didn't dare meet Hammer's eyes now. Hammer hated a slacker and a whinger and Jack sounded like both those things. He wasn't much good to Ava getting sacked, which is what he'd just done, no question. The silence was endless. He squeezed his eyes shut.

Finally Hammer spoke. 'Oxford Circus is next month. Once every five years it comes round and it's gonna be the biggest one yet. We still got whole sets to build. Cages, weapons, towers. Is helping yer friend worth more than helping us with that, Jack?' Hammer's voice was low, but deadly.

Jack's voice stuck like a walnut in his throat. He looked back at Hammer, silent and miserable.

'She is, eh? All right then. Do what you 'ave to do for her, then get your arse back here.'

Jack's head snapped up and he heard Agnes's sharp intake of breath. So Hammer's words weren't a hallucination from the medicine.

Hammer went on. 'You can take three days. Takes any longer'n that – well . . .' Hammer shook his head with more expression than any words could carry. Any more than that, Jack needn't bother coming back.

Hammer ducked back under the door jamb and strode away. Jack sank back onto the bed.

'Right, lad, you got three days. That's 'til Thursday.' Agnes had pulled herself together and now acted as if she'd expected nothing else. She unlocked her medicine cupboard and took the powder out again. 'You're gonna need yer own supply of this. Listen hard. This stuff can knock you into next week. One small spoon mixed in water, once a day, and not a grain more. Got that?'

Jack grunted. Agnes glared at him. 'What'd I say?'

'Um, one small spoon in water once a day. No more.'

Agnes grunted but seemed satisfied. She carefully tipped a small amount of powder into a separate little bag, twisted it shut and handed it to Jack, who stuck it in his pocket.

'Where you heading to?' she asked.

'Tony's. Where else?' Jack grinned at Agnes, euphoria bubbling through his veins.

A footstep sounded in the corridor and Hammer's singed head reappeared. Had he changed his mind? Jack's heart bumped hard in his chest as another thought struck him. He wouldn't be the first apprentice to get a thrashing at the big hands of Hammer. Jack jumped off the bed before realising Hammer was holding a sling bag.

'An advance on yer pay. You'll need something out there. And something to help you open doors.'

Jack reached to take the bag. 'Thanksgive, Hammer.'

96

The words felt inadequate, but Hammer was a man of few words himself. He gave Jack a nod.

'Three days. Agnes will drive you to Tony's.'

He turned on his heel and was gone.

CHAPTER 12
AVA

London, September 1858

'Did you see Mrs Fortescue's face when you said Mrs
Belville was selling time, Mr Bailey?' Violet had
closed the door and turned to Father, who was coming back
out of his studio after adjusting his clocks. Ava was still
huddled on the stairs and thanked her lucky stars that the
conversation was taking place right below her in the hall.

Violet's arms stuck out like angry wings on her hips.
'There is something fishy about that woman's visit here.
She had a different idea about Mrs Belville delivering
time – she thought Widow Maria was selling actual time.
Not the measurement of it.'

'The trade has been rife in Donlon on the black market
and it has now reached London. But Mrs Fortescue knows
a thing or two about it, mark my words. Which is ironic,
seeing as her daughter is a victim of the snatching – which
feeds the trade, as you well know. Even if you have turned
your back on that world for years.' Violet wagged a finger

at Father. 'You know very well it's come to your door and it's high time you took an interest again, Mr Bailey. And who is this specialist physician of hers? What does he know? He's connected to the trade or I'm not Violet Wisetree.'

Father took off his glasses and cleaned them unhappily, shaking his head. He muttered something under his breath, then turned and went back to his studio. Violet crossed her arms and let out her breath in a loud sigh, before marching down the hall to the kitchen.

What was this trade that Violet was talking about? How was it connected to Phoebe's and Ava's own disappearance – and to Donlon? Ava had the sense that the meaning was there, just beyond her grasp. If she could connect all these loose ends, she would start to understand.

Ava sat on the step for a long moment. The exhausted, shocked child in her wanted nothing more than to climb back to bed to safety. To turn her back on the world she had unleashed and to burrow back into the safe, known world. The other part of her knew it was much too late for that.

Her exhaustion was gone, replaced by the fizz of purpose. She waited until she heard two doors close (one with unnecessary vigour) before cautiously getting to her feet and tiptoeing down the stairs. She slid out the drawer of the hall stand and felt around until she found the coin purse that was always there. She slipped it over her wrist, tiptoed down the hall, avoiding the creaky boards, and soundlessly opened the door.

Ava had to walk to the Bank to catch the omnibus that ran along Piccadilly, where Burlington Arcade was. It was like entering a different world from the twisting, pungent streets of Spitalfields. Burlington Arcade was the shopping centre where high society came to promenade, its curved ceiling and gleaming windows emanating wealth and good taste. Ava stood at the Piccadilly end, where a sentry box contained an immaculate Beadle, resplendent in red suit and buttons that gleamed as brightly as the brasswork around the windows.

Ava wished now she'd taken a bit more time with her toilette, looking around her at the flotilla of fashionable crinolines swaying in and out of the arcade. The Beadles were known for their fierce policing of anyone who broke the rules – no running, no loitering, no whistling – and could stop anyone they decided did not meet the dress standards required. She pulled her bonnet closer over her untidy hair, straightened her gloves and shawl and stood as tall as she could. Nothing for it but to wait until another crinolined lady sailed past and match her step so that the vast dress was between her and the sentry box.

She was in. Now all she had to do was proceed at an elegant pace along the length of the arcade, looking for a physician's sign. The more exclusive the establishment, the more discreet the sign, so she peered carefully at each shopfront as she moved along the left-hand row, glancing up to see if there was a clue in the windows above ground level, which were usually workshops or studios attached to the shops below.

Soap, perfume, pens. Jewellery, hats, scarves, hosiery. Fishing equipment, watches. No sign of any sort of physician. Ava reached the end of the arcade and turned to proceed back along the other side. A window of an exquisite French patisserie roused a gurgle in Ava's stomach. More hats, more jewellery. Shimmering silk scarves, another watch shop. A burst of colour in an expensive florist. Puzzled, Ava reached the front of the arcade again. There were definitely no practice rooms being advertised in Burlington Arcade.

'May I be of assistance, Miss?'

A portly Beadle stood to one side of her, hands clasped behind his back, regarding her with blank courtesy. Did he think she was a thief or other undesirable? That was the main reason for the no loitering rule. She didn't cut a very honest figure, skulking and peering into every window in her drab cotton dress and everyday bonnet.

She straightened her shoulders slightly so she would not look furtive and lowered her chin to look up at the Beadle shyly through her lashes. Men seemed to like such becoming helplessness. The expression on the Beadle's face didn't change but his eyes softened slightly.

'Oh, thank you, sir,' said Ava. 'My father is a master watchmaker and is training me to follow in his footsteps. I like to come to the best shops for inspiration in my own designs.'

The Beadle's eyes narrowed. 'Unusual profession for a young girl, isn't it? Not many lady watchmakers around.'

'Yes, it is. My father always wanted a son but I am an only child.' She dropped her head. 'My mother died of the cholera when I was a baby.'

It was the first time she'd told her life story since she'd known it was a lie, but right now she needed a dead mother. She quelled the pang of guilt.

'Busman's holiday, is it?' The Beadle's tone was almost jovial now. She glanced up through her lashes and saw his smile. It had worked. 'Well, you've come to the right place. One of the most prestigious clock and watch shops in London just over there. Let me take you, young lady.'

The Beadle indicated a shop on the right with BLACKMORE'S in gilt lettering over the door. He fell into step beside Ava. 'Mr Smith will be delighted to meet a future colleague. Although he is not the actual artisan himself, being of the gentleman class, he has a keen scientific mind, as well as being a successful businessman. A most impressive individual.'

The window display was indeed impressive. Several beautiful timepieces sat at a tasteful distance from each other and Ava could see at a glance the fineness of the workmanship. She could feel the Beadle watching her.

'Come inside, young lady. You can ask questions about the pieces. Give your opinion, p'rhaps.'

He gave a short laugh and she glanced at him and saw that his eyes were cold above his smile. She should have known that it would take more than a common sob story to pull the wool over a Burlington Arcade Beadle's eye. He had brought her here to make her prove her story.

The Beadle pushed open the door, which slid silently across thick pile carpet, causing a bell to jingle. A young man with sandy hair, a bright mauve and green embroidered silk waistcoat and a magnificent moustache sat bent over some papers. He looked up with a smile.

'Stevens, how are you? Good afternoon, Miss. May I help you?'

'Afternoon, Mr Shawcross. I have a young lady here who knows a few things about clocks. She was admiring the workmanship on yours. I'm sorry, Miss, I did not ask your name?'

'Miss Ava Bailey,' Ava said without thinking, then immediately regretted it. Why had she given her real name? She still didn't have her London wits back.

'Miss Ava Bailey, allow me to introduce Mr Luke Shawcross.'

Mr Shawcross got up and bowed towards Ava, holding her gaze. She felt herself redden but could not take her eyes off the pair of green eyes flecked with gold smiling in her direction.

Stevens the Beadle went on. 'Do expand on what your apprenticeship tells you about the pieces in this room, Miss Bailey.' His voice was heavy with sarcasm.

After a pause, Ava walked over to the nearest watch housed in a glass case. Mr Shawcross came closer and unlocked the case. 'Would you like to hold it, Miss Bailey?'

'Thank you.' She took the watch from his hand and turned it over in hers, examining it closely before looking up with a smile. 'It is a very pretty piece, indeed.'

Stevens gave Mr Shawcross a knowing look. 'A typical comment from a lady.'

'But one would expect no less from Abraham-Louis Breguet, one of the finest pocket-watch makers in the world,' continued Ava. 'He was Swiss-born but worked in Paris last century and the beginning of this one. A great many important inventions can be credited to him, including the wristwatch itself, the automatic wind, the perpetual calendar, the observation chronometer and of course, the tourbillon.' Ava pointed to the watch face. 'He has an obvious signature style – see the shape of the hand, and the Arabic numerals – and this is a fine example of one of his tactile watches. A beautiful piece indeed, Mr Shawcross.'

She handed the watch back to Mr Shawcross. His smile had deepened into admiration. 'I would say that you have attended well to your studies, Miss Bailey.' Ava inclined her head coolly, hiding the flutter of pleasure his green-eyed smile gave her.

Stevens looked gruff. 'Good as your word, indeed, Miss. You have the freedom of Burlington Arcade – do let me know if you need assistance.' He inclined his head to Ava and Mr Shawcross. 'Good day to you both.'

A familiar voice came booming down the stairs. 'I always feel so much better after a treatment, Mr Smith. I absolutely depend on your attentions, kind sir!'

Mrs Fortescue swished into the room. Phoebe's mother did look transformed. So her magical physician operated without signage above a watch shop. No wonder Ava hadn't been able to find it. She gave silent thanks to Beadle Stevens, who had unwittingly marched her to the very door she had been searching for.

With any luck Mrs Fortescue wouldn't recognise her, but Ava wasn't taking any chances. She kept her back turned while Mrs Fortescue gushed about her improved humours and made another appointment for a month's time. Finally the little bell jingled her goodbye and the door swished shut behind her.

Ava turned. Another man had joined Mr Shawcross at the table – presumably Mrs Fortescue's gifted physician. Who, according to Stevens, was a true Renaissance gentleman, thought Ava sourly. In any case, anyone adored by Mrs Fortescue was an object of deep suspicion to Ava.

Mr Shawcross looked up from the ledger they were both perusing.

'Forgive my rudeness, Miss Bailey.' That devastating smile again. 'Allow me to introduce you to Mr John Smith, the proprietor of this establishment. Mr Smith, this is Miss Ava Bailey. A future colleague in the making, I understand.'

Mr Smith had raised his head with a bland smile, but at the mention of Ava's name, his smile froze. There was something about his intense blue gaze, glossy black hair and the set of his mouth that Ava found positively disturbing.

'It is a pleasure to meet you, Miss Bailey. Did I hear correctly that you are Miss – Ava Bailey?'

'Yes, that is correct.'

Hadn't she just been introduced? This was all very awkward. The silence was broken by the jingle of the bell and the door swooshing its way across the carpet. A tall woman of indeterminate age crossed the threshold, head at the imperious angle required for gazing down one's nose. Mr Shawcross leapt forward to take the grande dame's hand and raise it to his lips, bowing.

Mr Smith spoke quickly to Ava. 'I know the Bailey watchmaking family. You must be related, surely? Please, don't leave just yet. I will be back downstairs shortly.'

He turned to apply a full blast of charm to the imperious dowager. 'Mrs Benedict, what a pleasure to see you again. You look supremely elegant, as always. Allow me to escort you.'

He crooked an elbow and the woman's face softened as she placed her hand on his arm. As they proceeded upstairs, Mr Smith turned to look at Ava over his shoulder, his expression a strange mixture of puzzlement and pleading.

'Do feel at liberty to look around, Miss Bailey,' said Mr Shawcross. She dragged her attention back to him. 'Please excuse me briefly while I attend to something.' Mr Shawcross bent down to look back at the papers on the desk and a faint frown ruffled his forehead.

Ava turned to half-heartedly examine some of the other watches – they were exquisite, but the inner workings of watches was not the most absorbing subject at the moment. What was going on upstairs? Neither Mrs Fortescue nor the terrifying Mrs Benedict had even glanced at a piece of clockwork. They were here for something else Mr Smith could provide – and it was not a standard physician's appointment. She would wager her good silk shoes on it.

A shrill whistle outside cut through her pondering. An answering whistle sounded, and then a blur of children tore the length of the arcade.

'Stop thief! Mind yer pockets, ladies and gents! Pickpockets!' bellowed Stevens. He moved with surprising agility for his portliness as he leapt out to intercept a child dodging and weaving through the crowd. He caught the boy by the arm and dragged him triumphantly to the sentry box.

Mr Shawcross jumped to his feet and ran outside at

the commotion. Ava saw her opportunity. In a flash, she grabbed her skirts and bolted for the staircase, leather boots thumping on the stairs. If only her feet were in those silk slippers she had mentally wagered! But she was on the landing and there was still no reaction from downstairs. Up the next flight and at the top there were three doors – two ajar, and one firmly closed. Ava tried the handle of the closed one and it opened with a suprisingly obedient click.

She swung it open before she lost her nerve. The sight beyond the door made her clap both hands over her mouth in shock.

CHAPTER 13

AVA

London, September 1858

Mrs Benedict was lying on a reclining chair. Her sleeve was pulled up to her elbow, her bare flesh pale as dough in Mr Smith's hand. He was leaning over her as he thrust a long needle into her arm.

At Ava's gasp he jerked his head up sharply. He must have moved his hand as well because Mrs Benedict gave a short cry of pain. She had an eye bag over her eyes to shield her from what Mr Smith was doing, so she didn't see Ava. Mr Smith scowled at Ava and put one finger quickly to his lips in such a way that told her if she made another noise she would live to regret it. He turned his attention back to the metal-and-glass syringe protruding from Mrs Benedict's frail arm. Ava's knees went watery as he slowly compressed the barrel.

'There, there, Mrs Benedict. Nearly finished.'

'The time injection doesn't usually pain me in this way, Mr Smith.' Being horizontal did not soften her imperious tone one iota. 'Is everything satisfactory?'

'Quite satisfactory, dear lady. Sometimes the sensation is different. Just lie quietly for as long as you need. There is absolutely no need to rush.'

Ava's jaw dropped. Time injection? She had heard of these new hypodermic syringes that delivered drugs directly into the body below the skin, but injecting time wasn't possible. Maybe it was a manner of speaking – a phrase that described a technical process? She was not familiar with the latest medical terms, after all.

Mr Smith stood and strode to Ava in a couple of long steps before she could properly examine her thoughts. He grabbed her by the arm and marched her, in absolute silence, into the hall. How dare he? Her squeak of outrage was masked by the door shutting behind them. He still had not spoken a word to her and was looking over her head at Mr Shawcross on the landing. Mr Shawcross had his hands pressed together in front of him, cupped, as if he was bringing her a small butterfly. But somehow, she didn't think he was bringing her a pretty insect to admire, however charming his smile. Without a word, he pulled his hands apart and flicked them towards Ava and Mr Smith, as though he was casting an invisible net over them.

Or a spell. Prickles of primal fear scurried up Ava's spine. She saw then that the net wasn't invisible – that it had a slight sheen in the light from the window behind her. Like the edge of a bubble.

Mr Shawcross gave a strange little hop so that he was in the centre of the invisible net, too. And then everything around them stopped.

A surge of pure energy coursed through Ava's blood and her face flushed with excitement. She looked at Mr Smith and Mr Shawcross and saw their pupils dilate and their cheeks redden. The air around them was charged with a kind of electricity and her blood fizzed as if it were champagne. There was a shout of laughter from someone, maybe herself, and she felt giddy with joy. Every sense was heightened and each of the men standing close to her was enveloped in a golden sheen. They were beautiful, especially Mr Shawcross with his gold-flecked eyes that were so green they threatened to burst out of his luminous skin.

She took a breath and put her hands to her cheeks. What was this madness? These feelings sweeping over her were not appropriate! But then another giggle arose and she was floating again. The feeling was more subtle this time, like being on a gently swaying swing rather than soaring through the stars – and with each swing she started to come back into herself.

'It feels so wonderful, the first time.' Mr Shawcross was still beautiful but his eyes were more normal now as he smiled at her, a touch wistfully. 'I remember that sensation.'

'How long have we got, Luke?' said Mr Smith. His tone was sharp.

'Just ten minutes.'

'That should be enough.' Mr Smith took Ava by the arm again and turned her to face him. She pulled away and frowned at him.

'How dare you touch me, sir?'

The sense of euphoria made it hard for her to give her words the weight they needed. Her eyes went to the window behind Mr Smith and widened. She could see shoppers in the arcade beyond, but it was as though they had all turned to stone. She stepped around Mr Smith so that she could peer out of the window.

Two ragged boys were frozen, mid-stride, as they bolted down the arcade. A man was falling back on one heel, cane in the air and top hat suspended between his head and the ground, rigid at an impossible angle. A woman was pulling her skirt out of the way of the hurtling urchins, its great expanse ballooning to one side and revealing two pretty boots on display beneath her petticoats. Another Beadle was in pursuit, whistle to his mouth, scarlet coat-tails flying behind him and hand in the air. Other shoppers had turned at the commotion in the middle of the elegant arcade.

But the scene below her was absolutely silent and absolutely still. Everyone except herself and the two men next to her were frozen in a human tableau.

She whirled back to face Mr Smith. Her heart was hammering. This was sorcery, something from another realm. The two men were talking in low tones to each other, as though everything was quite normal.

'What is happening? You must tell me. Are we safe?' Her voice was shrill even to her own ears.

'More than safe, Miss Bailey. You are in the privileged position of receiving free time. Do you know how much ten minutes of that precious commodity is worth?' Mr Smith had turned to her. Ava shook her head wordlessly. 'No, you wouldn't. Prices are so vulgar, so we'll just say it's more than your father could earn in several months.'

'But, how –'

'You are in a time bubble, Miss Bailey,' said Mr Shawcross kindly. 'We have had an extra ten minutes inserted in our timelines. The rest of the world seems frozen to us until we reach the end of our bonus time.'

So Violet *had* been talking about time being traded. 'But why does –'

'Enough chitchat.' Smith's voice was abrupt. 'It's time for me to ask the questions, Miss Bailey. What are you doing here and why did you barge in so rudely while I was mid-consultation? It was an abuse of Mr Shawcross's and my hospitality, at best.' He looked at her coolly. 'Does your mother know you are here?'

Ava gaped. Was it possible that he knew her mother?

'Or, indeed, your father? Or is Bill Bailey less conventional than he once was?'

She barely noticed the sharp glance Mr Shawcross gave Mr Smith at this question. She looked from one man to the other. 'You know my father . . . and my mother?'

'I ask the questions, Miss Bailey, if you recall,' snapped Mr Smith. 'Please answer me. It is the least you can do after your behaviour today.'

Absurdly, Ava felt a flush of shame. The desire for social acceptability for a respectable young lady was a very hard thing to repress. Even if these were hardly conventional circumstances.

'My father doesn't know I'm here. And my mother – well, it seems you can answer that question better than I can.'

Mr Smith frowned, perplexed.

'I mean,' said Ava, gaining confidence, 'that you appear

to know who my mother is, whereas I have only just discovered that she exists at all.'

Her boldness must be the effects of the extra time she had ingested. It was a heady drug. Both men were looking at her now, Mr Smith's eyes narrow.

'You don't know who your mother is?'

Ava shook her head, not trusting her voice. The question stirred up both anger and regret and she wasn't sure what would come out of her mouth in her current light-headed state.

'Interesting,' said Smith. He paused. 'I wonder, then, what you truly know about your father?'

Ava remained silent. She wondered the same thing herself, but she wasn't about to give Mr Smith the satisfaction of knowing that.

'You know about Donlon, at least? Surely your father has told you that much.' There was an emphasis on the way he said 'father' that set her teeth on edge. She nodded. No need to mention that she had seen it for herself. Jack's face rose behind her eyes and at the memory of him, she felt her pulse steady.

'Perhaps not everything about Donlon, however. Perhaps not how he left under a dark cloud. How he made a terrible mistake. No? Ah.' He looked sorrowful. 'Then it's not for me to tell you that story. Suffice to say that he did.'

Ava knew she didn't have to believe this man. But there was no reason not to believe him, either. He went on.

'So you have never met your mother? What has your father told you about her?'

Ava flushed. It was humiliating to admit that the answer was absolutely nothing. That she had been starved of all knowledge of her mother her whole life. Mr Smith was watching her closely and his lip curled.

'Aha. What a shame. She is a truly extraordinary woman. Such a loss not to have grown up with her, as her daughter.'

Ava's chest was tight, making it hard to breathe. She had to concentrate on getting air below her ribs or her light-headedness would turn into a faint. She could not let his words stir up murky longing. The loss of motherless years.

'But then, your father would not want you to be close to your mother. He has his own reasons for that. I am sure there are many secrets he has kept from you, Ava.' He sighed. 'It is very hard on you, indeed. Not to know your mother, nor Donlon. Such a wonderful place.'

It had not seemed *altogether* wonderful when Ava had spent time there, but she kept that to herself.

'You have seen that time can be bought and sold, yes? The Time Lady of Donlon has harvested unused time for centuries. Wasted minutes, misspent days. Time wished away. All of this can be caught by her time catchers and recycled at no cost to anyone. This is gold time – the premium currency. The only time we deal in here.' He paused. 'And then there is snatching. A more recent development, which you have seen here in London too. Time is snatched from the midst of people's lives, tearing them out of their own life while their live time is siphoned off. Part of their soul is siphoned off in the process, leaving them damaged and torn.' He shook his head. 'Grey time. The worst of the black-market gangs deal in this.'

It was all suddenly, horribly clear. 'So the disappearances are snatchings, and this is when people have their live time stolen?' Ava spoke slowly as she put the pieces together. 'And they vanish while this is happening?' That's the grey place, she thought with a shudder.

'Three minutes left, John,' said Mr Shawcross, glancing at a clock.

'Thank you, Luke. Yes, that's right, Ava. Your mother is a good woman, whatever your father has told you. She always wanted you to be part of her life. I work with her, in fact.'

Ava felt sick with anger. If it wasn't for Father, she would not be motherless. Mr Smith was watching her thoughtfully.

'Why are you telling me this? What good does it do now?' Ava was close to tears and it took all her effort to keep her voice steady. 'Who are you, anyway?'

Mr Smith came closer and stood by her side and turned Ava around to face the window. 'Can you see our reflections, Ava? Does anything strike you?'

Ava looked at her face, then Mr Smith's. Dark long hair, blue eyes, a certain set to the mouth and jaw. Both of them. She shook her head and he made the same motion. Exactly.

She suddenly knew why she had found his gaze so disconcerting. It had been as if she was looking back at herself.

'You see it, don't you? Why am I telling you this? Because serendipity has brought you to me today. You wanted to find your mother, and you are closer to her than you've ever been. Do you know why you and I look so similiar?'

Could it be true? He smiled. 'Just call me Uncle John.'

'A minute, John,' called Mr Shawcross, who had tactfully retreated to the landing.

Mr Smith took Ava by the shoulders and this time she didn't object. He spoke urgently now. 'Listen to me, Ava. This is the moment your life changes. I will take you to your mother. Can you come back here in an hour?'

Ava's chest was full. Her impulse to come here had been right, after all. Euphoria flooded through her veins, and it was not just the extra time. She was standing next to her mother's brother.

Yes. Yes. She would be here. He let her go.

'And Ava? Tell no one. Especially your father. I will explain later.'

The world rushed back in. The commotion of the arcade was a shock after the total silence. Mrs Benedict's voice was calling from behind the door.

'I'm right here, Mrs Benedict,' called Mr Smith.

Uncle John. She would have to get used to that.

He stood up and went to the door, turning to Ava one more time with a finger to his lips. 'This afternoon, 6pm.'

CHAPTER 14
JACK

Donlon

Agnes was the only person who had a steam car at Hammer's. None of the apprentices could afford such a luxury, of course, and Hammer was too big for any car. He was a horseman, with a deep quiet bond with his two massive shire horses, both giant creatures that dwarfed even Hammer. Agnes started the boiler and Jack waited for the car to build up enough pressure before climbing inside.

'Tony's, then?' said Agnes, starting the silent vehicle.

'Yeah. But can we stop somewhere first? It's not far.'

Agnes pulled the wheel around and grunted. 'Ain't got much time for social calls, Jack. You heard Hammer.'

'I know. It ain't just social, though, and the Foundling Home ain't far.'

Agnes shot Jack a sharp glance. 'Hmm. Might be time for you to cut those apron strings, Jack. You're a man in the world now.'

Jack looked straight ahead. Agnes's words stung, but she didn't understand. The Foundling Home would always be a part of him. It was like telling someone to forget their mother or brother. He'd been dumped there by his no-good father when he was a toddler and had already had more than his fair share of knocks.

He had to see Sister Wisetree. She'd taught him that trust did not always lead to betrayal.

'Ain't there some other nun acting as Head Matron there now?' said Agnes.

'Sister Beatrice,' he muttered.

'Rumour is that Sister Wisetree might not be coming back at all,' she added.

Something twisted hard in Jack's chest. 'No! She would 'ave said something,' he said. 'She never said nothing about leaving last time I saw her.'

Agnes grunted. 'Sometimes life don't go to plan, Jack lad,' she said. 'You should know that as well as anyone.'

Jack stayed silent. He knew better. Sister Wisetree wouldn't leave without getting word to him somehow. She knew what she meant to Jack.

Agnes pulled the car into the circular driveway in front of the Foundling Home and drew to a stop under a great yew tree that overshadowed the entrance.

'White City Foundling Home,' she announced and peered around. 'I'll wait here, Jack. Bloody ravens are thick at this place. All those juicy little kids, innit? This place gives me the heebie-jeebies. Don't be long, lad.'

His feet crunched on the gravel driveway as he approached the imposing wooden door studded with metal. Agnes was right. Ravens sat silent as stones, dotted all over the grounds in front of the building. There were more of them than he remembered from before.

He felt panic rising in him as memories of the attack crowded back. He looked away with a shudder, focusing on the great white bell tower soaring above him. He knew by heart the layout of the white buildings that sprawled behind, linked by flower-filled cobblestone courtyards, and he made himself remember every step of every pathway, until his heart slowed. He climbed the steps and reached for the bell cord hanging above the door.

There was a whisper of feet on stone floors and the door swung open. Sister Beatrice.

'Jacky! Finally. I thought you would never come back.'

He hated being called Jacky but kept the annoyance out of his voice. 'Hello Sister Beatrice. Is Sister Wisetree in?'

'She's gone, Jacky. Did you pass on that message I asked you to?'

Was this some horrible joke? Sister Wisetree gone? And didn't Sister Beatrice know what had happened to Jack and her message?

'But – Sister always takes leave periods. She always comes back.'

'Not this time, Jacky. She's been gone too long. The Foundling Home needs stability and that's what I can give it. The message?'

Her voice was sharp and without him wanting it to, his sight flared open.

Sister Beatrice opened up before him, like an optical

119

trick on a flat piece of paper. That message . . . The message had not been from Sister Wisetree at all.

What if Sister Beatrice had been using her position to – No. It couldn't be.

The shutters slammed down again and his sight went black. What was happening to him? He put a hand out to steady himself against the door frame. With an effort, he found his words.

'I gave the message to Mr Buenaventura. Delivered it to his hand. But that's the last thing I did, Sister Beatrice, 'cause after that he snatched me.' His tone was flat.

'You were *snatched*, Jacky? I didn't know. I'm sorry.' She looked genuinely surprised. 'No reply came to that message and I thought you hadn't delivered it. It seems I've misjudged you. And someone else.' Sister Beatrice sounded bitter. 'And I am surprised that someone of Sister Wisetree's standing did not receive a reply.' She went silent, brow furrowed, then looked back at Jack with a start.

'But where are my manners? The least I can do is offer you some tea.' Her smile was as thin as winter sun.

'No, thank you, Sister. I wanted to see if Sister Wisetree was back. Please tell her I came if you see her.'

He had to get away from this place. This was not the place he'd grown up in anymore. There was misery here, singing from the stones themselves. The ravens were here for a reason. They sensed despair.

These children were being used for something. They were feeding something. They were –

He didn't know what to believe. He had to get away – sort through the jangling in his head.

He returned to the car and climbed silently in. Agnes looked hard at him before pulling out of the driveway without comment, for which he was grateful.

Jack leaned back and closed his eyes. He had to hold himself together, long enough to get to Ava.

Jack adjusted the bag around his shoulders and felt the hard shapes of Hammer's gift – Donlon's master keys. Never in his wildest dreams had he thought he'd be entrusted with not one, but two of his own. These were the keys to the city. No door was shut to him now.

He closed his fist around them and it was as if the iron entered his blood.

CHAPTER 15
AVA

London, September 1858

Ava got to the Piccadilly entrance of Burlington Arcade and felt her legs turn to custard beneath her. The adrenaline had subsided, leaving her drained and limp as an old dishcloth. She stumbled to the wrought-iron gates and clutched at them for support, hoping she was being discreet. She could not fall down in the street and be arrested for disorderliness. How would she ever get back to Burlington Arcade by 6pm if that happened?

The smell of coffee hit her nostrils like bitter nectar. That would revive her. She leaned into her corset and headed towards the coffee seller outside on the pavement, feeling for coins in her purse. The first sharp, hot mouthful was like medicine. She drained the cup and handed it back to the seller, feeling that now she could get through the next hour, which loomed endlessly in front of her.

She had taken two steps when a voice stopped her in her tracks.

'Ava!'

'Father?'

Her father's hat bobbed in the crowd, his anxious furrowed brow beneath it. Her heart hardened against the sight of his drawn, exhausted face. This man was not the father she thought she knew, the one she had always loved and respected. He could never be forgiven for the lies he had told. For keeping Ava's mother from her.

But she remembered Smith's words. She could not reveal any of her new knowledge to him.

'Ava, thank the Lord you are well! I was so worried.' He reached out for her hands in a rare fit of demonstrativeness. 'I guessed you heard our conversation and I hoped you'd be here. Thank goodness I didn't miss you.' He held her hands tightly. 'Ava, I have something terrible to tell you.'

'What?' For a moment she forgot her anger.

'Violet has been snatched. Quickly! There is no time to lose.'

'*Violet*?' The despair was a physical weight in Ava's chest. 'Oh no, not Violet!'

Father grabbed her arm uncharacteristically hard. 'Come with me, Ava. Let us escape these crowds.'

She hesitated. What was she to do? She had to be here in less than an hour to meet her mother, but suddenly her world had turned upside down. Violet. The pang in her heart was savage. Her father pulled her along with him and she scrambled to match his long stride.

'Where are we going?' she said.

Father was practically dragging her, weaving among the crowds, and Ava was glad of her unfashionably narrow skirts as the wide cages of the society ladies swung around them. They reached Green Park and Father slowed his pace and looked around.

'Father! What are you doing?' said Ava.

In answer, her father pulled her off the path towards a quiet clump of trees. Ava scurried over the grass to keep up. 'We're going to Donlon,' said Father. 'It is the only place I know where there is someone who can help Violet.'

Ava gaped at him as he drew her aside, out of sight of the crowds in deckchairs on the lawn. He turned to look at her. 'And besides, I am no fool, Ava. You are more familiar to me than you know. Your stubbornness is not just your own. Whatever else your mother might be, she is no feeble woman.' He looked at her earnestly. 'I wish you were less like her, but you make me afraid. I am close to losing you. You are transient now and you can go there whether I like it or not. Well, when you learn to control your transitions, anyway.'

'Why *have* I become transient?' she asked.

'Only a small proportion of the population of either place has this ability. It's something you're born with. It's usually a family trait, like having red hair or a quick temper. Transience usually comes when a person, ah, matures.' Father cleared his throat uncomfortably and Ava thought of the belt underneath her clothing and flushed. 'Or it can be triggered, perhaps like yours was at the Observatory. I was hoping you would *not* be transient, but it was a vain hope.'

Ava looked at her father. She had the choice of going to Donlon with him – whom she knew but also did *not* know, at all, and could never trust again – or with Mr Smith, her uncle. Whom she also did not know – but at least he had

124

been the one adult to trust her with some real information about her mother. No one else had given her that respect.

'So we will bring back Violet. And I will meet my mother.' It was a statement.

'The latter, never.' Father's voice was sharp. 'She is an unfit mother and she cannot be trusted.'

His words were a slap to her face.

'She caused the death of a friend who was very dear to me.' Father's face was hard. 'The only reason I'm returning to that place is for Violet. There is one person I know who can help. I never wanted to go back, after . . .'

As Father trailed off, Ava remembered Mr Smith's words. He had said Father left Donlon under a cloud. That he had his own reasons for not wanting her to be close to her mother. His own selfish reasons, that had dictated Ava's motherless life.

She shook herself. Violet. They had to focus on getting Violet back.

After that, she would find her mother, whatever her father said.

Father glanced around and seemed satisfied. 'You can transit anywhere, you know, but I prefer a quiet place. It allows one to focus. Hold my hand, Ava, and let us turn our backs on the crowd. We will sit here on the grass. Take this.'

Ava settled her skirts on the grass and took a horse chestnut leaf with yellow edges from Father. Autumn was already here, she realised with surprise. This strange year was galloping away.

'Look at the leaf and let your eyes relax,' said Father. 'Look beyond it, as though you are trying to make out an optical illusion. As though you will suddenly see a horse or a man's face, or something utterly different.'

Ava focused on the leaf. It was the most beautiful shade of amber merging into deep green. She peered at the veins fine as spiderwebs and the two brown spots caused by insect or disease. She focused on the starred edges and tried to see something other than leaf, but nothing appeared.

'Try looking through the leaf,' urged Father. 'Let your eyes go to where you would focus if that was a possibility. As though it is translucent glass.'

Ava looked at the leaf and narrowed her eyes, making it blur. How did one look beyond anything solid? No matter how hard she squinted at it, the leaf remained a leaf. What exactly was she looking for, anyway?

'Relax, Ava. Don't try so hard.'

That was very well for Father to say. If she didn't get to Donlon, they wouldn't be able to bring back Violet. The thought filled her with such horror that cold sweat prickled down her spine.

And Ava would never find her mother. Perhaps that one time was the only chance she had. Maybe she would now be trapped in London, knowing of the existence of her mother in a strange world but having to live her life as if she didn't.

Again, Jack's face rose unbidden. The thought of not seeing that ratty visage again was a sharp, unexpected pang.

No, these things were all unthinkable. This time, she would not come running home so soon.

But she had to get there first. She had to make this leaf do something magical. She glared at it but it remained obstinately leaf-like. It wasn't working. She let it fall and looked up at the other leaves swaying on the branches in the afternoon breeze. Her father pressed her hand and she shut her eyes as tears pricked. She blinked hard. She could not let her father see her tears. She looked up through salt-blurred eyes and saw one of the leaves detach itself from the branch and swirl downwards. She watched its fuzzy progress, a green blur against green grass, and dabbed her eyes with her free hand, but it didn't clear her vision.

Her eyes were dry but the world still looked tear-smeared. Trees were losing their shape, the grass was pouring like sand and the air itself was shattering into tiny squares. Her stomach swooped sickeningly.

She'd had this sensation before. She clung onto her father's hand and groaned.

CHAPTER 16

AVA

Donlon

'We're here, Ava. Open your eyes.'

She hadn't realised she'd closed them. The smell and the sound hit her at the same time. She released Father's hand and looked around. They were sitting by a huge pond filled with a strange, creamy sort of mud. The pond was ringed with high fences all the way around except for one end, where a cluster of buildings sat on the very edge. There was a rich, sweet smell coming from the thick gloop in the pond.

The sound was familiar, a rushing punctuated by heavy clunks, creaks and whirring. Behind them was a fast-flowing river, a smaller version of the one Ava had seen the time she met Jack. Small waterwheels and just a couple of spindly windmills balanced on islands no more than rocks in the rushing water. The river dropped steeply from one level to another, creating cascades that fed into the waterwheels.

She glanced around in apprehension, then relaxed. No sign of ravens here.

'We've done well enough, Ava. I tried to direct us to Tony's and his place is just over there.' Father pointed to the cluster of buildings. 'This is Batter Sea.' He looked around sadly. 'Or what's left of it. It used to be much bigger – hence the name. And those fences were not there.'

'Batter Sea? Is that mud *batter*?' Ava asked. 'How can that be possible?'

Father smiled. 'How is any of this possible? How is it possible that we are on a ball in space hurtling around the sun? We are mere humans grappling with reality, my dear.' He looked over at the buildings and climbed stiffly to his feet, offering a hand to Ava. 'Come, let us go and find Tony.'

Ava got up and as she walked with Father along the sea, he explained, 'This is not batter as we know it, made of eggs and flour, but Donloners discovered many years ago that this clay can produce an exquisite base for baking. There are certain ingredients that need to be added to do so, but only members of the Batter Guild know what they are. The ingredients are a closely guarded secret.'

As they got closer to the buildings, Ava saw that they were coffee and tea shops. More than thirty lined the pond, with customers sitting at tables and chairs out the front. Father pointed to the fat brass pipes flowing from the backs of the kitchens into the sea. 'Those pipes pump the batter directly into the kitchen. Only guild members are allowed to set up business here. Every guild family has their own secret recipe, which they guard like gold and pass down generation to generation. Some of these families have been here for hundreds of years.'

They walked along the front of the coffee houses now, which gleamed with brass and polished wood. Flowers grew around the windows and towering displays of cakes teetered seductively in the window. People sat outside at the tables, shaded by spreading fruit trees. A ring of braziers, burning even in the middle of the day, circled the whole area and guards in dark uniforms stood between the poles, looking out. What were they watching for? It was idyllic, with grass and trees spreading out into a huge park.

Father stopped in front of one cafe and put his hand on the door. Ava wrinkled her nose as she took in the peeling red paint on the door and windows, the lurid yellow walls and the tattered sign hanging askew that announced that this was TONY'S!

'Why don't we go to that one?'

She pointed to the neighbouring cafe, where flowers posed gracefully in neat pots and gleaming windows curved around a mouthwatering display of cakes. An elegant sign informed them that this was HARRINGTON'S.

'Because it's Tony we need to see,' said Father. 'Don't let his decor deter you – he's a genius in the kitchen, and the person everyone comes to with news. He is one of the very few relative newcomers to the Guild – they couldn't refuse him, even if his style is a little, well, unconventional.'

Father pushed on the door and practically fell inside as it was violently yanked open from within. A very wide, very round man with a huge black moustache shoved one foot expertly against the door as he flung out both arms.

'I don't believe it! My old friend, Bill!' He grabbed Father and engulfed him in a bear hug.

Ava blinked. The voice that came out of that burly body was as high-pitched as a young girl's. Father grabbed his glasses just as Tony – presumably this was TONY! – knocked them flying, but he was smiling in a way that Ava had not seen for a very long time. Father patted Tony's broad back with his free hand, holding the glasses out of harm's way with the other.

Tony held Father at arm's length and surveyed him, moustache quivering with emotion. 'Bill Bailey! Let me look at you.' He let go to wipe his eyes with both hands, sniffling loudly, before turning to look at Ava. 'And this beautiful girl! Such eyes of blue! Malaikah told me you had a daughter now. She reminds me so strongly of someone – who is it? Bah, it doesn't matter anyway.'

Tony threw meaty arms around Ava. She tensed, but relaxed at the warm vanilla smell and soft feel of Tony. He held her at arm's length, as he had for Father.

'Ah, what a day. Welcome, welcome, both of you!'

His small dark eyes sank into his cheeks like raisins into cake mix and he ushered them in. Inside the cafe were wooden tables and chairs that had seen better days, and a hissing kettle on the range. Tony pulled out a chair for Ava and Father sat down opposite. He leaned forward on the table, looking closely at Ava and then at Father.

'Hmmm, yes. I see. I will be back in, how you say, a jiffy. We have much to talk about!'

He jumped up and trotted off, surprisingly nimble. He

pushed through a swinging door into the kitchen, where they could hear him happily shouting and clanking. Ava leaned back in her chair and let out her breath cautiously.

'What was all that about?'

Father didn't answer. He was looking around, memories chasing across his face. Ava remembered that this was the first time he'd been back in Donlon for over a decade. He'd lived a whole life here, one she knew nothing about. One that involved her mother. There was so much she still didn't know about what he'd done here, and what happened to make him leave without her mother. Pity and resentment wrestled in her chest. There was pain in her father's life, but the choices he'd made had been his. Ava had not been given any choice in any of this.

Father looked at Ava and blinked. 'Tony? He has a rare ability to read each customer and tailor-make a cake for them. His grandfather was a Ham – circus folk with mind-reading ability, who can –'

'I know who the Hams are.'

'Oh.' Father looked surprised. 'Well, you will see. His skill is quite remarkable.'

'I didn't come here to eat cake,' said Ava. 'What about finding Violet?'

'I know. But I have to talk to Tony first. This cafe is where all of Donlon leave important messages. If you need to know anything, you come to Tony's. Be patient.'

Patience was beyond Ava today, but luckily it was an astonishingly short time before the door of the kitchen flew open again and Tony came out, balancing cakes and tea on a tray. He deposited the tray on their table with a flourish.

Ava's jaw dropped. Rather than slices of cake, two little cake sculptures sat on the table in front of them.

'For you, my old friend, one of your beautiful watches.' Tony's voice squeaked even higher in pleasure as he beamed at Father and pushed a cake in the shape of a gold watch towards him. It was perfect in every detail, right down to the chocolate hands and Roman numerals on the face. Ava recognised it instantly. 'It's the watch you're working on – the one on your work bench!'

Father's broad smile was pure delight. 'Tony, you're a marvel. You haven't lost your touch.'

Tony's face creased with joy and he clapped chubby hands. 'You like it? Excellent! Now, Ava, for you.'

Ava gasped at the creation that Tony pushed gently towards her. It was a delicate macaron coated in gold-leaf in the shape of an intricately carved locket, with twisted gold-leaf for the chain. Tony peered at her.

'I see this, but I don't know why. Do you recognise it?'

'Well, no.'

'Then you soon will. Tony's eye never lies.' He rubbed his hands in glee. 'Now you must eat.'

Eat this exquisite creation? Ava hesitated and looked at Father, who clearly had no such qualms. He was already chewing his first mouthful, eyes closed in appreciation. Well, so be it. There was nothing for it but to stick her cake fork into a miniature work of art. She cut off a tiny crumb and lifted it to her lips. Perfumed nectar flooded her mouth.

'Oh!' Bubbles and light and fragrance burst on her tongue. Tony pulled up a chair to sit down with them, looking at her anxiously.

'It's good, yes?'

'It's extraordinary!' She reverentially put another morsel into her mouth. It was as if all other senses had offered their services to taste.

Tony poured black tea into three cups, taking the most chipped one for himself, and leaned forward confidingly.

'What brings you back, Bill? It is a bad time in Donlon. Did you see my poor old Batter Sea? Shrinking before my eyes! And those foul birds! We have to put fires outside and pay for guards to keep them away. No one will sit outside otherwise.' He leaned back and spread his hands wide. 'It is all because of the snatching, they say. Pushing the world out of balance. The Lady has gone crazy! There is talk of civil war, you know. How else to stop her but attack those machines of hers? Who would have thought it, eh?'

Tony's sigh ruffled his moustache. So that was what the braziers were for, and why there were no signs of ravens here. Ava strained to understand all that Tony had said, trying to put it together with other frustratingly piecemeal parts of the puzzle.

'Is the Lady the one who harvests unused time?'

Tony did not look surprised at her question. 'Yes, yes. Lady Montagu was the time queen. She has always harvested time, but old time. Now she is time-snatching – taking it from people's lives. She is the Green Witch people are speaking of. It is something to do with London, too, no?'

Realisation hit Ava like a starburst. Why had she not put the pieces together until now?

Time Palace. Green Witch. The names had been echoes in Ava's head, strange reflections of something familiar.

She heard Miss Buss's crisp voice describing Greenwich as 'the point from which all time is measured here in England, and also beyond', and now Tony was talking about the Green Witch. The words were like distorted mirrors of each other, throwing back twisted truths just beyond her ability to grasp.

She cursed her soggy brain. Greenwich. Green Witch. The centre of time – and time-snatching. She remembered something Mr Smith had said. 'But is the time-snatching her doing, or black-market gangs?'

Tony spoke emphatically. 'It is the Lady. She has the gangs working for her but she alone has the power to harvest time. Who else could create such monstrous machines, eh? Bill?'

Father leaned forward now. 'I have to talk to the Lady, Tony. It's very, very important that I do. But I will not take Ava to Time Palace. Not at this time. Much too dangerous.'

Ava frowned. 'But you said there was someone here who could help bring back Violet.'

'I did, Ava. And that person is the Lady. I knew her well, once, and I do not understand this change in her.'

Ava's jaw dropped. Would there be any end to the surprises her meek father would present her? 'You knew her?'

Tony laughed. 'But of course! He was one of the greatest Time Keepers here in Donlon. It was his job to keep the time catchers in good order, eh, Bill?' Tony beamed proudly at Father.

Father smiled modestly. 'This time-snatching frenzy does not ring true. She was never a warm woman – she was an intellectual, cool and distant – but she was not evil.

Why does she suddenly need all this time? Something else is going on here. I must get a message to the Lady to meet me.'

Tony shook his head. 'You will have to ask Malaikah to go. Or maybe Hammer. You will not find anyone else to travel to Time Palace these days, apart from the black-market gangs. They are the Lady's bully boys. She pays them in time to do her dirty work. People pay them protection money to keep safe from time-snatching and they take care of the Lady's enemies. Things are different, Bill. The Lady is not our time queen anymore.'

Tony leapt to his feet, making both Ava and Father jump. He shook a fist at the window. 'Hey! Get away! I've warned you before.'

An old tramp was peering in through the open door, grinning. 'Well, well, well. Bill Bailey again! Ain't seen you here for a while, 'ave we?'

CHAPTER 17
AVA

Donlon

The tramp's smile reminded Ava of a snarling terrier. 'And I do believe I recognise the young lady here too.' He looked from Bill to Ava. 'I can surmise all sorts of interestin' reasons you might be here together. Well, well, *well*.'

Tony leapt for the tramp and grabbed him by the shoulders, shoving him back through the door. Tony's smile had gone and his face was furious. 'I have told you before – clear off! Next time you won't get off so lightly.'

The tramp staggered back before regaining his balance. He grinned at them in a very unpleasant way. 'I'll see you around, Bill. Miss Ava.' He spat on the ground before turning and ambling away.

Wait. How did he know Ava's name? She felt a horrible prickling on her skin. Tony came back to the table.

'He's trouble, that one. He's a Ham but they threw him out. Always wanting something, especially information.

137

He sells it to people. He hangs around here, hoping to hear secrets.' He looked at Ava. 'I'm sorry for the rough behaviour, Ava.'

'How does he know my name?' burst out Ava. Bill shook his head warningly at Tony and glanced at Ava. 'Ava, my dear, please excuse us for a minute. There is something I need to discuss with Tony in private.'

Fury surged through Ava. She got to her feet and glared. 'More secrets, Father? Isn't a lifetime of them enough for you?'

'I'm sorry, Ava. All that matters now is Violet. Not your sensibilities.' He looked at her steadily.

Ava clenched her teeth in frustration. She hated being helpless like this but he was right about Violet. She pressed her fingernails into her palms and turned and flounced to the window. 'Very well,' she snapped ungraciously. 'I will wait here for you.'

Father and Tony walked to the back of the cafe, voices low. Ava went to stand in the open doorway, where the sound of the waterwheels was much louder. Not many other people were out at this time, except for the tramp, who had retreated beyond the far brazier. He caught sight of her and beckoned. How dare he? Horrid little man.

She crossed her arms and let out her breath in a gigantic sigh. Yet again, Jack's pale face rose unbidden in her mind. It kept doing that. She hadn't been able to shake off the sense that she'd known him before, which was clearly impossible. She kept wondering how he was faring.

'Lady! Miss Ava?'

She jumped. The voice was right at her elbow. How had

he got so close without her noticing? She turned to scowl at the tramp. His expression was different now. He had dropped that awful leer and his face was open and serious. Respectful, almost.

'I'm sorry to bother you again, Miss Ava.'

'What do you want?'

'I want nothing, Miss. I have something to give to you.'

She frowned at him. What could this ragged little man have that she might want?

'I have information, Miss Ava. I know everyone in Donlon. And I know how they are all connected. If you understand me, Miss.'

Now Ava looked at him properly. He looked like a different man, now, his eyes soft, gentle. Face scored with years of hardship, jacket hanging loose from his gaunt frame, back bent forward. Sudden remorse swept through her. She had dismissed him when he was just an old man who had lived a much harder life than she ever would. Poverty was a terrible thing, she knew. There but for the grace of God go she. She was no Phoebe, surely? Phoebe would not talk to anyone of the incorrect social class, but Ava prided herself on her humanity. Her problems were not the fault of this poor old man.

She had forgotten herself and she was ashamed. And perhaps this old man really could help her.

The old man smiled at her, a proper smile this time. 'You are missing someone who is important to you, who has been snatched. I can help you find that person.'

Violet! This wise little man understood and could help her. Hope swelled in her chest as he went on.

'And you also look very much like someone I know, Miss. Someone I think you are related to. Would you like me to introduce you to that person?'

Ava's throat went dry. He knew her mother. Of course, he would. He had lived here all his life, probably. She hesitated and glanced back at the cafe. The tramp leaned forward.

'Don't be feared, young lady. I will do you no harm. I may not be well-dressed like you, but you can trust me.'

She looked straight into his face and it was as open as the sky. Her trust soared like a summer lark. He held out a trembling hand to her and her heart knocked at his frailty. How had she been so blind to think he was bad-hearted?

'Come, Miss. Just follow me, if you like.'

He turned and walked away. She hesitated, looked at the cafe again, then at the man's retreating back. He was walking away, not caring if she followed. That was proof that he wasn't after something from her, if she still needed it.

She made her decision in that moment. She stepped out in his footsteps.

The world shrank to a tunnel with the old man at its centre. She passed through time and space and neither left a mark on Ava until she was sliding along the cracked leather seat of a vehicle unlike anything she had ever seen. It was not a train, not pulled by horses, but billowed steam in almost silent bursts.

'This steam car belongs to a dear friend of mine. Allow me to keep you safe.' He leaned across her and locked the door, then pulled out onto the road.

Ava looked around her at the unfamiliar carriage. She had no recollection of anything since she'd left the cafe. How long ago had she followed the little man? Had they discussed anything about where they were going? A fog of forgetting lay across her brain and she shook her head to clear it. It didn't budge and a bubble of faint panic rose in her throat.

She looked across at the strange man she had willingly got into a locked vehicle with. He looked over at her and smiled and her heart dropped off a cliff. That smile was not the kind smile of a helpless old man, but of gloating victory. Panic scrabbled at the fog and a sickening realisation dawned. He had her where he wanted her and she had allowed this to happen. She shut her eyes, breathed deep, and turned to look at him with clear eyes.

He was filthy. Matted greasy hair, one yellowing tooth clinging precariously to his top gum, and his stench put the Thames to shame. That in itself was repulsive, but it was the gloating look on his face that woke her. He flicked a glance her way and the eyes were cold and hard.

She shrank away from him, disgust interweaving with growing panic. She tried the door but it was locked tight. How had she thought he was a sweet old man? How could she have been so blind? To go off with a strange man – any strange man, but especially such a hideous one – was not something she would ever do in her right mind.

'I don't believe I've introduced meself, 'ave I? Very remiss of me. My name is Silas.' He looked at her again and bared his gums. 'Lordy! No mistaking whose daughter you are, is there?'

Ava took several deep breaths to subdue her panic into submission. It worked enough for her to speak without shaking. 'So you can help me find Violet?'

'Poor Violet ain't really any concern of mine,' Silas said.

Panic surged inside Ava. What had she done? She had to get out of this man's grasp. She remembered vaguely the rest of their conversation. 'You said –' she gulped, her throat so dry she could hardly speak, 'you also said that you would take me to my mother.'

Silas's smile was slippery as soap. 'Mother? Well, indirectly, my dear. There is someone we 'ave to stop and see first. But you will go to your mother, oh yes, indeedy.' He cackled and the stench of his breath filled the car.

Ava looked around frantically. She had to get out of this car. Where were they? The river running alongside the road was broad, widening around islands big enough to hold several windmills each. The waterwheels here were gigantic wooden giants, majestically creaking as they turned. Bridges and stepping stones linked the islands to the shore.

Silas turned onto a bridge that led to a bigger island. He stopped at a sentry point with a bored-looking guard slouched inside. The guard got up and strolled round the car, peering inside and underneath, before waving them through.

The car bumped along a rocky road towards a sprawling tent city. Tents of all shapes and colours covered the island with one enormous bright blue and yellow tent squatting like a canvas castle in the centre. People were milling around everywhere. Silas pulled to a stop and turned to Ava, his face alight with triumph.

'Here we are, m'dear. Out we get.'

'Where are we? What is this place?' Ava noticed for the first time that the shadows were long on the ground. Night was near, she was Lord knows where and nobody who cared about her had any idea where she was. Silas climbed out of the car and opened Ava's door with mock ceremony. She sat frozen to her seat. He reached in and pulled Ava by the arm.

'Come on, dearie. This is your bed for the night. Too late to meet Mama now.'

Silas's fingers were like iron claws on her arm. Ava stumbled out of the car and looked around. People were everywhere – juggling, practising tumbles, twirling fire-sticks, walking on stilts and on their hands. Others squatted over fires preparing food and still more twanged on banjos and violins while children and chickens weaved in and out between legs and tent poles. It was a riot of colour and movement.

'Meet the West Hams, my dear,' said Silas. 'They will be very happy to take care of you.'

The Hams! That was what was tugging at her memory. They were circus folk, like the Hams who had nearly stolen her mind. And Tony had said that Silas was a Ham before he'd been thrown out. Either way, she was in trouble.

She could not stay here with these people. She looked frantically around. The only way off the island was by the bridge, which was being manned by the laconic guard. Ava had a feeling that he was not as sloppy as he looked. If she made a break for it, he would snap into action.

Silas's fingers gouged deeper into Ava's flesh, as if he

sensed where her thoughts were going. Ouch! She grunted and tried to jerk her arm away but he pulled her closer, turning her to face his tombstone grin. She gagged at the stink of his breath so close.

She kicked out at his shins but he dodged easily, stepping aside and twisting one arm up behind her back. She stumbled forward, tripping over rocks underfoot, pain spearing her shoulder. She bit her lip hard. She would not let him see her cry.

He yanked Ava to a stop. She staggered and looked up. They were in front of the main tent entrance.

A tall woman in a loose white shirt and baggy leather pantaloons stood in the tent opening. The woman was bald, intricate geometric markings covering her scalp. She regarded Ava with slanting golden eyes like a cat. The woman drew herself up and paced towards them, slowly, as tall as the sky. She was barefoot, her brown toes splayed and beautiful. Ava forgot Silas's grip and the pain in her shoulder as she drank in her presence.

The woman stopped before her and turned those golden eyes onto Silas.

'Unseemly, Silas.' Her voice was cadenced. 'Have you forgotten so completely the Ham ways?' She looked at Ava and smiled. 'My name is Tamar. You are welcome here.'

Tamar extended one hand and time hung heavy as velvet around them. There was just Tamar's face, Tamar's hand holding Ava's as she led Ava into the tent.

A long wooden bench. Pale green tea in a small curved cup. People swimming in and out of her vision. Smiles,

144

words, glances. The old man who'd brought her here – she'd forgotten his name – talking, talking, talking. Words whirring like foreign birds. She couldn't catch their meaning.

Ava watched Tamar's every move. She sipped her tea when the woman did, smiled when she smiled. She locked her gaze on her like a rope to a buoy at sea.

Tamar looked straight at Ava and morning sun burst over the hill.

'So, young Ava. You are an interesting young lady, are you not?'

Warm pleasure spilled into a smile on Ava's face. Tamar stood up and took Ava's hand in her own. The touch of her was like warm earth and silk.

'I understand that you wish to meet your mother. I can take you to her tomorrow.'

Her mother? The word nudged at the edge of Ava's memory. The faint memory of something she had wanted before she came here. The impulse floated away like dandelion seeds on the wind. All she wanted was to be with this woman. Tamar leaned forward and laid one hand on Ava's cheek. 'You will stay the night here as my guest. You will want to sleep now.'

Yes, Ava did want to sleep, more than anything. She could not think of anything else but the tiredness lodged like lead in her veins. She gave an enormous yawn and Tamar stood and led Ava outside to a small tent by the water's edge.

Then Ava was lying on a warm, thickly cushioned mat on the ground, covered with a blanket so soft that she could barely feel it as it whispered across her skin. She had never been so comfortable in her life. The rushing water and the soothing *clunk clunk* of the waterwheels lulled her instantly into a deep and dreamless sleep.

CHAPTER 18
JACK

Donlon

Agnes dropped Jack off on the road running alongside Batter Sea. The sweet cloying smell of the sea hit him as soon as he got out of the car and he wrinkled his nose.

'Thanksgive, Agnes,' he said, hand on heart. He leaned down to say his farewells but Agnes jerked her chin and drove off without a word. Small talk was not a prized skill at Hammer's.

Jack glanced around for ravens in the automatic Donlon reflex. There were some black shapes on the far edge of the park but the armed guards and fires seemed to have repelled those brutes. His shoulders relaxed and he swung his bag on his back and headed towards Tony's.

Gods, this was a snooty joint. As he walked past the elegantly dressed customers sitting outside over bone-china-clad tea and delicate cakes, Jack felt them cringe away. It was obvious he didn't belong here. He was suddenly aware that the trousers Agnes had given him were too short and his legs looked a sight, all slashed to pieces. It was a relief to reach Tony's normal-looking place, push open the door and hear the cheery jangle of the bell and the *ssss-ssss* of the kettle on the range.

The heavy dread that had laid over him since the Foundling Home started to evaporate.

The place was empty. Where was Tony? Normally you could hear him clattering around, shouting in that funny little squeaky voice he had, laughing, cracking jokes. Now the place was as still as the grave. No customers at all and it looked like no one was in the kitchen.

He walked inside. 'Hello?'

Silence. Jack frowned. There was an uneasy squirming below his ribs. He lowered his bag onto a table and heard a sound. He walked into the kitchen to see a lone woman out there, scrubbing dishes, her back to him. He spoke louder. '*Hello?*'

Her head swivelled like a pigeon's and she peered at him. 'WHAT?' She was obviously deaf as a nail, shouting like that. He raised his voice further.

'WHERE'S TONY?'

She shrugged. 'DUNNO. HE GO. LOOK FOR LOST GIRL.' She banged dishes in the sink, scowling. 'LEAVE ME TO DO ALL THE WORK, HE DON'T CARE . . .'

Jack left her grumbling at the top of her voice and bolted out of the kitchen. He grabbed his bag and flew out the front door, looking around in every direction. There! Striding towards them were two figures – and one of them was Tony. Jack ran to meet them.

'Jack!' said Tony. 'What are you doing here?'

148

'Ava?' was all Jack could manage. His voice was jammed in his throat. Ava might be in danger and he didn't know where to find her. Both thoughts made him giddy with fear.

The other man looked over the top of his glasses. 'Who are you?'

Tony was flapping at them to go inside, glancing around anxiously at the interest they were attracting from neighbouring tables. They filed like obedient geese in front of him and sat down around a table. They looked at each other appraisingly. Tony's usual smile was gone and his face was pale and worried.

'It is good you are back, Jack. Perhaps you can help us. She –'

The other man cut across Tony. 'You know Ava?'

'Yes. Who are you?'

'I'm Ava's father. Bill Bailey.' He swallowed. 'She's just disappeared. And you are?'

'Jack. I met Ava after I was snatched. I came to help her find her mother.'

'Her mother?' Bill looked incredulous. 'Do you know who she is?'

Jack shook his head. 'No. But I said I would help her. I have some skills. And besides, she helped me when I was in strife.'

'That damned tramp took her. I will wager my cafe on it.' Distress had sent Tony's voice even higher up the scale than usual. Tramp? Jack looked at Tony, a silent question on his face. Tony grimaced. 'I'm sorry, Jack. It was Silas.'

Jack sank into his chair, his mind racing. Silas would take Ava to the Hams and sell her for what he could get.

He knew only too well what that man was capable of. He'd sold his own child for a free meal, pretty much.

'You know Silas?' Bill asked.

Jack snorted. 'You could say that. He's my dad.'

Bill went very still for a long moment. 'Your father?' he whispered. His face was chalk white. 'Good Lord. But . . .' He took an unsteady breath. 'Never mind. So where has he taken her?'

Jack sat up, anger burning in his belly. He wasn't going to let his father hurt Ava. He'd already hurt Jack enough. Did his father know what Ava was to Jack? Gods, he hoped not.

'He'll sell her to the Hams. He thinks she's worth something or he wouldn't 'ave taken her.'

Bill put his face in his hands. 'Ava is a clever girl. She would never go with someone like that. I know she was upset with me, but –'

'Don't matter how clever Ava is. Silas got inside her head. Ava had no choice, believe me.'

Jack stopped. Ava's mother must be the key to all this. Silas would know her, he knew all the Donlon gossip. That was why Silas had taken her. Her mother must be from a wealthy family. Maybe the Richmonds? He turned to Bill.

'Who is Ava's mother?'

Bill and Tony exchanged glances. 'I will tell you in confidence. Ava does not know this yet, so keep the information to yourself. I must have your word.'

Jack put his hand on his chest and leant forward to hear Bill's whisper. And Jack felt his heart surge with unexpected pity.

'I'm going after her,' said Jack. He looked at Bill and added quickly, 'Alone.'

'No, Jack. She is my daughter. You can't do this by yourself.'

'I know these people. I'm half-Ham, remember?'

'You tell us what to do and we'll do it,' said Bill. 'But you can't take such a risk alone.'

'You need help, Jack,' said Tony, spreading plump hands beseechingly. 'No good losing you, too – no?'

Jack regarded soft, round Tony and Bill with his anxious, bespectacled face and pale, delicate hands, and sighed. These were not the allies he needed. Jack would end up looking after them as much as trying to help Ava.

'No. This is my job and I can do this better alone.'

'Jack, she is my daughter,' said Bill. He paused, as if the next words were painful. 'Ava is everything to me. How can you expect me to sit by while you go after her?'

Jack glanced into Bill and saw the sharp shapes of self-loathing. This man was in agonies of regret. Jack chose his words carefully.

'You have someone else to save, don't you? Someone who needs you to act quickly?'

Bill stared at Jack. 'How do –'

Jack cut across him. 'Never mind how. I do know. I can help Ava and you can help the person who needs you. And also, I have another plan that I need your help with.' He leaned forward across the table. 'I'm nearly certain that Ava is at the Hams. But if she isn't – there is one other place she could be. In any case, she will be there by tomorrow. I need you to get as many people there as you can.

We might need to fight. Here is my plan.'

He spoke as quickly as he could. Time was precious now. He finished and got up from the table. 'Got it? I'll meet you there.' He swung his bag over his shoulder as he went out the door. He had a mate on the river who could get him close enough to the West Ham island by water.

'Jack?'

Jack turned to look at Bill. What now? He'd stood up at the table and now came over to Jack and held out his hand towards him.

'It was Ava's lucky day when she met you. You're – well, you're something very special. A true friend. I'll never forget this.' His eyes shone too bright behind his glasses as he took Jack's hand and shook it. 'Thanksgive.'

Bill's hand was a frail bird in Jack's calloused palm. Jack cleared his throat, but his voice was stuck and useless. He squeezed Bill's hand, carefully, then let go and turned quickly on his heel. Heat flamed in his cheeks and the back of his eyes felt hot and prickly as he strode out the door.

It was those words. *You're something very special.*

Jack had never been very special to anyone, unless you counted Sister Wisetree – and even then he had been one among hundreds. Praise had been in short supply in Jack's life, until now.

Ben didn't let him down with the boat. He'd got him down-river as far as the first of the big West Ham waterwheels, where he'd pulled into the bank.

'Can't get you any closer, Jack.' He gestured towards the clanking waterwheels between them and the island. Jack tied his bag firmly across his back and clapped Ben on the shoulder.

'I know it. Thanksgive, mate. I will go from here.'

He wasn't at all sure that he could, but he put his hand on the side of the boat and leapt into the water. The water came to his waist and the current tugged at him eagerly. He turned to wade along the bank to get closer to the island to judge where to cross. Just beyond the island lay three gigantic waterwheels churning the water, waiting to smash unwary heads with their paddles. This was the Hams' energy farm. He swallowed. He wasn't nearly as confident about this as he'd pretended to Ben.

The river ran fast here, rushing between rocks and islands and falling in rapids. Hams were no fools – there was a reason they'd chosen this place. They had a permanent power supply from water, wind and sun – more than enough for them and then some to sell or trade. They had the best power packs in Donlon – small as a wallet but each with enough juice to power the Hams camp for a week.

Waterwheels plugged the gaps where water rushed fastest and fell furthest. The trick was to get across the rocks, close enough to wade – or swim – onto the Hams' island, all without getting knocked off your feet or sucked into the path of the waterwheels. One giant paddle could smash a skull like a snail shell. Jack hugged the shore, the strong current tugging at his legs. He had to keep his footing for as long as possible. He could swim, but he was no fish. More like a thrashing cat.

He peered downstream and saw the spot to go for. There was a cluster of rocks, polished smooth as toffee, that stretched in a wavy line from the shore almost to the edge of Ham Island. Water frothed around them but there were enough above the water to be a bridge – precarious and slippery, but a bridge nevertheless. If he could keep his footing, he could make it. If he didn't . . .

The trouble was that the bridge of stones didn't quite reach the shore. He would have to wade out to it. And if he fell – he gulped, looking at the shiny smooth rocks and then at the nearest waterwheel. He hoped the gods were feeling benevolent today.

There was nothing for it. He waded further down along the bank, near where the end of the bridge started. He took a deep breath and waded into the river. The water clutched at his legs, sucking like a live thing. The cuts on his legs were already starting to throb again, the water stinging them. He would have to take more of Agnes's medicine when he got to land.

Gods, the water got deep quick here. It was already nearly at his chest and the effort just to stay upright took all his concentration. Maybe he'd judged this all wrong. He was going to have to swim for it, after all.

The *thunk-splash* of the paddles filled his head. Don't think about it, Jack. Think of one foot steady after the other. And another. And one more. He was going to make it. Just a few feet more. The water was faster here, deeper again, but there were only a few more steps.

Oh gods, he was under! The water grabbed at his body with vicious glee, slamming him against the rocks – shards of agony in his raven wounds. He flailed and kicked something – a rock, a jammed log? – and lunged for it with every scrap of strength he had. Fingernails scraped against cold rock, smooth as ice, he couldn't find a hold ... and then his fingers caught on something ragged. A crack! He had both hands around the rock now, fingers wedged into a precious ridge. He could feel the muscles tearing in his shoulders, see the blood swirling from his fingernails, the pain in his legs was almost, almost too great to bear – but he was on the rocks.

He lay panting, legs still in the water, and raised his head. He was on the bridge!

Now he just had to make it to the island. *Just.*

CHAPTER 19
AVA

Donlon

'Ava! Wake up!'

Someone was shaking Ava, dragging her out of a deep, peaceful sleep.

'Pssst, AVA!'

She didn't want to wake. She turned and curled tighter under the blanket.

'You have to wake up, Ava! It's me, Jack.'

Cold water dripped on Ava's face. She grunted and rolled away. Why wouldn't he leave her alone? He was pulling the blanket off her, tugging at the waist of her dress. She pushed his hands away. A *thwack* of something cold and wet hit her neck and face. She yelped and sat up, rubbing her face with her sleeve.

Jack was by her bed, wringing his wet shirt out over her. He was criss-crossed all over with raven gashes, like some kind of macabre crossword, and dripping like a water rat. He seemed quite unperturbed. Ava scrambled to her knees and shuffled back. What did he think he was doing? He leaned closer to her and snapped his fingers in her face. All she wanted was for him to let her go back to sleep – to snuggle into the soft blanket, her thick, deep mattress . . .

'Ava, look at me. No, at my eyes. You've been hypnotised by the West Hams. You need to look at me. One, two, three!'

As he said 'three' the world rushed back – cold, harsh, unwanted. She took a shaky breath and looked around her. Her luxurious mattress was no more than a pile of old hessian sacks on damp ground. The soft blanket was a scratchy woollen rug, full of holes and covered in animal hair of some kind. She was stiff and itchy, she smelt terrible and her hands and arms were covered with red bites. She ran a hand over her face and felt angry lumps on her cheeks and forehead. She scrambled off the sacks in disgust and scratched herself vigorously. Her memory of everything that had happened after Silas yanked her out of the car was fuzzy. She frowned.

'I don't remember how . . . Where am I?'

Jack reached out and touched her arm in the same strange way he had when Malaikah had taken her away from Donlon. As if he was drawing something from her into himself. She hesitated. It should feel wrong, to have a boy's hand on her skin, but in the same way that Malaikah felt almost part of herself, the feel of Jack's skin roused no protest in her own. Without thinking, she automatically laid one gentle hand on top of his and he seemed to come to himself.

'You're at the West Hams' camp. This is their island. Remember I told yer about the Hams? You've got Peck,

West and East Hams, as well as straight Hams. All different but one thing they got in common is making you think what they want you to think. Mind magic. That's why they didn't bother locking you up. Knew you wouldn't be goin' anywhere. You was easy pickings.'

Was that a note of derision in his voice? She frowned at Jack. 'Why aren't you hypnotised?'

'I know their ways, Ava,' said Jack. 'You might be better schooled than me, but there's things I know you'll never see. I've got Ham blood. I can see inside people. It's a Ham thing.' He dropped his gaze. 'The bloke who captured you? That's me dad.'

'Silas is your *father*?' She hadn't seen that coming. 'So why don't you live here with the Hams?'

Jack gave a short laugh. 'He got kicked out, didn't he? And Ma died when I was a baby. They threw him out for stealing, blabbing Ham secrets for money, that sort of thing. The Hams don't forgive anyone who betrays the clan. He dumped me in the Foundling Home and then – *sssshhh!*'

Shouts and angry voices, loud outside. Silas's voice.

'Tryin' to rip me off! You know the girl's worth every penny I ask and more! Her mother will give you anything you ask for. Tight sods, the lot of you.'

Jack jumped to his feet, pulling on his shirt as he gestured frantically to Ava. 'Quick! We have to leave now. Only way off the island is by river. Let's go!'

Jack stuck his head out of the tent and glanced around. He beckoned to Ava and she followed him outside, heart thudding fit to rival the waterwheels. The tent entrance faced the main camp with the river behind. Jack dropped to the ground and scuttled on hands and feet to avoid the light thrown by the camp fire and the lanterns that bobbed in the darkness. Ava hesitated, then pulled up her skirts and tied them in an ungainly knot to drop to her knees and crawl after Jack.

They headed for the river. Ava's skirts kept catching on sticks and rocks and she soon fell behind Jack. She glanced around. They were far enough away from the lights now so she stood, hoisted her skirts and ran after Jack. He was standing near the riverbank and pointed to the river. The moon glinted silver on the water.

'This is where I crossed. See those rocks? But careful, it's slippery. I went in before.' He looked at Ava sharply. 'You can swim, right?'

'Of course, I can swim,' she replied, too quickly. Luckily it was too dark for Jack to see her expression. 'I have bathed in the sea at Margate several times.'

'Paddling to yer knees ain't swimming. And yer can't wear that lot. You'll drown, fer sure,' said Jack, pointing to her skirts and petticoats. Ava gripped her skirts and weighed them in her hands. So much fabric! Why did fashion demand so many layers and such impractical shapes? The material was already heavy, and once soaked with water they would be almost impossible to carry. She knew that much from helping Violet on wash day, the vilest day of the week.

A stick tumbled in the white rushing river. That would be her, only weighed down with pounds of skirt, huge water-wheels patiently churning immediately downstream.

A human body would be no more than that stick against one of them.

She heard distant shouts. They'd found her empty tent! She made up her mind. This was a different world, after all. And she had no choice.

'I'll take them off,' she said. 'I will wear my bloomers. Can you throw them to the other side?'

'You can't take that off!' said Jack as Ava rolled up the skirt of her dress. Why was he so prudish all of a sudden?

'Of course, I'm not taking my dress off! Just the petticoats. I'll tie the skirt up, like this.'

A few folds and tucks and the skirt sat tight around her waist. She took a deep breath and untied her petticoats and her chemise, stepping out of them in just her long white bloomers. She handed them to Jack, face burning hot in the darkness. 'Throw them across the river, please.'

Jack rolled them into a bundle, backed up and took a run up to the river. He released the white bundle and it flew high in the air, clearing the water and bouncing safely on the opposite bank.

'That's one way of providing motivation to swim,' said Ava.

Jack scrambled down to the water's edge and turned back to Ava, hand outstretched.

'Let's not go in, eh?' he said grimly.

Ava took a deep breath and went down to the bank. She grabbed his hand and stepped into the water, which sucked at her boots with a power she had never felt before. This was nothing like the flat sea at Margate. The smooth soles of her boots slid on the rocks and she teetered, trying to get her balance between the force of the water and the slippery rocks.

One step. Then another. She was grateful for Jack's hand there and she gripped it for support. They were doing it. She was glad it was too dark to see clearly. It meant her focus could shrink to the suck and pull of water around her feet. The only sound in the world was the *clunk* and rush of the river. Another step, gripping hard. And another.

She risked glancing up. They were halfway across the rocks. She couldn't see the last section of rocks to the shore – just water surging between rocks and land. Was that why Jack asked if she could swim? She couldn't swim here or anywhere like it. She hesitated and lost her rhythm, swaying on the spot. She was no match for this current. Fear swelled fat in her throat as the water grabbed at her.

'Come on, Ava!' Jack's voice was faint against the sound of the rushing river. 'Don't stop now.' He tightened his hand around hers and tugged, but she was frozen. If she moved her foot, the current would take her. She had lost momentum. There was nothing to propel her forward.

Jack pulled her hand again and she jerked back in panic. The water was waiting to suck her down, but Jack wouldn't let go. He was saying something through the wet hair plastering his face. She clutched his hand to stay upright. She caught a glimpse of panic in Jack's face as he pulled her back, just before he lost his balance and his feet shot out from underneath him.

CHAPTER 20
AVA

Donlon

There was no time to think. Ava didn't realise she'd leapt after him until they were both in the water, Jack's shirt in her fists as the water whipped them both downstream with terrifying strength.

Ava struggled for air as the river threw her around like a cork. She didn't know which way was up or which way was down. She gulped and swallowed a mouthful of water. She still hung on to Jack with a death grip, possessed by some wild instinct to save him – as if she was in a position to save anyone! – while they whirled around and around in the torrent.

Her skirts unfurled, the weight of them tugging her down. They billowed like a deadly sail and cold terror clutched her. She was going to drown. They both were. She choked, spluttered, flailed in desperation. She needed air. Her lungs were burning.

And then she stopped with a jerk. Her skirt had caught

on something – a fallen log? – and she was stuck fast in the river. She reared her head out of the water and dragged in lungfuls of sweet air. The current raced past her, trying to tug her back in its flow, but whatever had caught her skirt stayed firm. She stayed in the same place in the water, bobbing and swaying in the current like a fishing buoy tied to a rope. She was no longer tumbling out of control.

But what of Jack? She still had hold of him and pulled frantically, terror giving her the strength to yank his wiry body up so that his face was clear of the water. His head flopped back, mouth gaping, eyes staring. He was too still.

'Jack!' screamed Ava.

She grabbed him around the chest with a strength she had never possessed before. He convulsed and water shot out of his mouth. He coughed up more water and dragged in a lungful of air. He was alive! But his eyes were still dull and glazed, and his limbs went floppy again after his breathing spasm.

Raw energy surged through her; the same deep charge that had filled her when the ravens attacked. She had to get them both out of this river. All fear and doubt dissolved. She was fully alive, her mind clear and sharp as she assessed their situation in a split second. A limp, heavy Jack. Her skirts, held – for now – by a snag on a trunk fallen into the river. The riverbank, just there.

It took all her strength to hold onto him. Somehow, she clambered up onto the log, gripping with her thighs as if she was a man on a horse. She grabbed Jack with both hands, one under each armpit, and hauled him face down onto the log in front of her. She yanked at the caught end of her skirts. It came free with a tearing sound.

They were safe. The bright flare of energy left her and she clung to the log, panting, for a few seconds. With her last ounce of strength she leaned forward and pressed hard on Jack's back.

He choked up another spurt of liquid and took a deep, juddering breath. And another, and then another. Thank the Lord! He lifted his head and looked at Ava, glazed but conscious. He was breathing, panting in great, uneven gasps. His chest heaved as he looked around, taking in their situation.

'If your skirts hadn't . . .' he broke off, overcome by a bout of coughing. It was several breaths before he could speak again. 'They – you – saved our lives.'

'I thought my skirts would drown us both,' she said. 'Not save our lives.'

'Are you hurt?' wheezed Jack.

She shook her head. Blood ran strong in her veins and her lungs pumped air that had never tasted so pure and full of life.

'And you, Jack?' She simply couldn't resist it. 'Can you get safely back to shore without my help?' She grinned in the near-darkness and saw an answering flash from his teeth.

'I'll let you have that. This time.'

'Then let's get onto land. Come on.' She started to edge her way along the log.

'Wait. You're getting tangled up. Here, let me help with that life saver of yours. Sit tight and hang on.'

He was right. Her dress was a wet mass around her legs. If only Violet could see her now, half dressed, soaked and alone with a boy in the darkness – even if that boy was just Jack, who felt like the brother she'd never had.

Her grin faded. She was no closer to finding Violet, or her mother. Jack finished fumbling at the back of her skirt where her tiny pocket was, leaving her dress tied like a wet sausage around her waist.

'Ready? Let's go.'

Jack turned and climbed like a monkey along the log, hands and feet gripping. Ava followed, bumping herself along the log like a baby learning to shuffle on its bottom for the first time. The sensation of dry, solid land beneath her was a huge relief. She turned to look at the river. They were no more than a few yards away from one of the biggest waterwheels, which kept on creaking and turning as nonchalantly as if it hadn't been seconds away from smashing both of them into a messy pulp.

They had ended up on the opposite bank, facing the very edge of West Ham Island. Twenty yards beyond them the river dropped and opened out into a deep, fast-flowing current. If by some miracle they had avoided the waterwheel, they would have been whisked out into that. Death would have been delivered by one method or another. Ava shuddered.

Jack looked around. 'I'll get your petticoats – they're over there.' He limped over to a pale bundle near the water's edge and stooped to pick them up. He brought them back and handed them to her. 'We should go just a bit further into the woods. We're too exposed here.'

They moved under cover of the treeline. Jack turned to Ava and looked at her. 'Reckon I owe you a thank you,' said Jack. 'Twice over.'

'I won't tell anyone that a London schoolgirl saved your life, Jack. It could ruin your reputation.'

He was silent and she spoke again, her tone sincere this time. 'I can hardly take credit for my dress getting tangled. I could as easily have sent us to the bottom of the river. And I should thank you, Jack. You got me away from the Hams. Twice over.'

'Thanksgive, Ava,' he said simply and pressed her hand with his. She felt a new strength swelling beneath her own collarbone. It was as if they counter-balanced each other perfectly on either side of some strange fulcrum.

'Well, if that ain't just a beautiful picture.'

Ava whirled. Silas was standing behind them in the woods, leaning against a tree as he regarded them. Something silver glinted in one hand. 'You know those things are forbidden,' said Jack tightly.

Silas shrugged. 'Bein' a transient has its advantages. Nice London piece, this one.' He raised the pistol. 'You know, those Hams could learn a thing from me. Should always listen to an old man's instincts, eh? Here you both are, just as I thought. Over you come. No, not you, Jack. Just Ava.'

Jack had started forward, his face hard with anger, but Silas turned the pistol almost lazily to train it on Ava's head. 'Be sensible now, lad. Neither of us want her to get hurt, do we?'

He gestured for Ava to stand beside him. She glanced at Jack, whose expression was unreadable. She swallowed and stepped to where Silas indicated. The familiar stench of his breath greeted her as he grabbed her arm and put the gun against her head.

'Right we are. You can follow behind, Jack. But mind your step. One false move and –'

He tapped the muzzle of the gun against Ava's head, hard. She closed her eyes and heard Jack step behind them. Silas chuckled.

'Very good. Off we go.'

Silas gripped Ava's arm and led her back along the river in the direction they had come, towards the Hams' camp. The gun kept banging painfully against Ava's temple and Silas's sharp fingers gouged into her arm. She could barely hear Jack's soft footsteps behind them.

Silas glanced behind him. 'Too tricky fer your own good, lad. As usual.' His voice was cold now. 'Time to find a proper lock-up for the pair of you this time.'

They came to the bridge that Ava had driven over with Silas the previous day and her heart sank. After all that, back to where she'd started. They walked over it, waved over by the sentry who gave a laconic grin this time, and headed back towards the main tent. It must be the early hours of the morning, the night still dark and still, but the camp buzzed with low-key activity. Groups huddled by the fire, smoking and drinking, and heads turned as they passed. People emerged from tents to watch them and some fell into step behind them. By the time they reached the great central tent, they had collected a small entourage of insomniac Hams.

Tamar strode out of the main tent and Ava immediately felt that pull, strong as the current she'd just escaped.

167

She looked down. She must not look at Tamar – must not make eye contact, whatever she did. But the woman's gaze was powerful, even indirectly, and before Ava realised what she was doing she had glanced up to see Tamar's great, golden eyes steady on her. Ava sighed and lifted her head. She could feel the warmth of Tamar's presence, the heavy silk of her . . .

But then Jack was beside Ava and his hand held hers, warm and solid. The thread that drew her towards Tamar snapped and Ava blinked. She held onto Jack's hand and dropped her eyes to the ground. She focused on counting the buttons on her wet ankle boots.

Tamar spoke. 'Leave her with us and take your son. If you do, I will agree to your terms.'

Silas gave a hoarse laugh. 'Funny enough, my terms 'ave changed. In fact, there ain't no terms here no more. Second thoughts, see.'

He fired a shot above his head and Ava leapt into the air with shock. He cackled. 'Sorry, my dear. I should be looking after my merchandise, eh?' He pulled her towards his car. Ava stumbled in front of him, glancing up to see a silent ring of watchful faces around them. She almost wished someone would make a move to stop Silas, but nobody was risking getting close to that gun.

Silas opened the door and shoved her inside the car, then pushed Jack in after her. He slammed the door shut and turned back to Tamar.

'Reckon I might get a better offer somewhere else, where people 'ave an appreciation of quality merchandise.'

He gave a final shot in the air before climbing into the car.

Silas must have perfectly assessed how this would all play out, Ava thought.

As they drove towards the bridge, Silas leaned through his window and fired a shot at the guard barring their exit, who threw himself to one side as the car charged straight at him and rattled over the bridge. Silas roared with laughter at the guard sprawling on his back.

'Stupid Hams missed their chance! I know someone else who will be very 'appy to have you, my dear.' He turned back to Ava as the car veered precariously on the road. 'And they'll be sure to take you to see the lovely Lady without any further delay, if I ain't very much mistaken.'

Why would she be taken to see the Time Lady? Jack's hand was on hers again. Silas's eyes met Ava's in the car mirror, the glee in his eyes unmistakeable.

He didn't mean – he couldn't mean?

She looked at Jack wildly. His eyes were sad and without Jack saying a word they told her everything she needed to know.

Silas was giggling like a demented goblin in the front seat. 'You see it now, don't you, my dear? Your dear Ma and our beloved time queen are one and the same! What a meeting that will be, oh my days, yes!'

His laughter ricocheted around the car and there was no stopping the convulsions racking Ava's body. She didn't get to the window in time.

CHAPTER 21
AVA

Donlon

It was as if Ava was watching the scene below from a distance. The car screeching to a halt, the angry man cleaning the seats, the too-still girl and hovering boy.

The three figures got back in the car and drove and she watched them arrive at a Gothic mansion, spiky with spires and wrought iron. It wasn't until they walked inside the mansion and were led by staff into a room with ornate, soaring ceilings and a roaring fire, that Ava's soul came plummeting back into her body.

She was still soaking wet and she stank of vomit – facts that she observed with clear, distant detachment. She looked at Jack, who was watching her with anxious eyes. He was soaking, too, and starting to tremble with cold. There wasn't much flesh on Jack. She looked around at the room's chintzy furnishings, fringed lamps and old leather sofas. The fire crackled invitingly.

'Stand there, Jack. You'll catch your death.' Her voice was

calm and conversational and her words did nothing to fade the worry on Jack's face. 'What time is it?'

Jack glanced at a clock above the mantelpiece. 'One in the morning.'

Ava turned to Silas. 'What a foolish time to bring us visiting, Silas. Do you have no manners at all?'

Silas snarled. 'Shut yer trap, girl. Not another word from you or I'll –'

Silas stopped as the door opened and a servant girl stood to one side to let a tiny old lady pass. She was no more than four and a half feet but she carried herself like a queen, silver hair swept into a chignon and wearing full make-up, despite the hour. Her throat was wrapped with jewels that caught the lamplight and her gown was of purple silk with sleeves that dropped almost to the ground.

She sat down on an ornately carved chair and regarded Silas, who stood with cap in hand, a fawning smile on his face. She sniffed.

'The Time Daughter, you say? Let me see.'

One wrinkled hand, heavy with rings and tipped with long red fingernails, reached out to snap on a lamp on the table beside her. One finger crooked at Ava. Ava approached and the old lady tilted her head and peered over her *pince-nez*. Her mouth puckered in disgust.

'Good gods, she reeks. Yes, there is something of Esmeralda there, in spite of that. But that is not the most striking resemblance, is it?' She laughed, a short bark, before narrowing her eyes at Silas.

'And the boy? What is he good for?'

Silas bobbed his head like a demented pigeon.

'He's a clever lad, m'lady, very good with metal. He's trained by Mr 'Ammer, no less, and is his star apprentice.'

The old lady sniffed. 'I suppose he will have to stay. He'll get in the way if he's roaming around. I won't pay extra for him, though. If anything, he's a liability.'

Silas ducked his head ingratiatingly. 'If you don't mind, m'lady, he's a very useful lad. He's well worth his price and –'

'Shut up, fool.'

Silas shut up. The old woman peered back at the children and wrinkled her nose.

'They look like drowned rats and smell worse.' She glared at Silas. 'They need new clothes. That will come off your fee, too.'

Silas looked sullen but didn't say a word. The door opened and another woman walked in, much younger but with a striking resemblance to the older woman. She stopped mid-step, one foot poised like a cat about to leap, and stared at Ava. She was wearing a silk gown like the older lady's, but in royal blue. She blinked and stepped forward, sinuous as a panther under the rippling silk, her eyes never leaving Ava as she made her way to the drinks trolley. She poured herself a drink and stirred.

'I expected a little more from the Daughter. What a stench!' Her nose crinkled fastidiously, then she yawned theatrically. 'Having the worst night ever, Mimsy. Can't sleep a wink.'

'Why, Sapphira dear? Is Jade still out?' The older woman's words were soft but Sapphira seemed to stiffen ever so slightly. She shrugged. 'She's nearly grown, Mim. I can't keep her locked up.'

'If you don't contain her, someone else will.' The two sisters held each other's eyes and the air was charged with something beyond the simple words.

Sapphira gave a nod, as if in answer to something unheard, then held up her glass. 'Drink?'

'Thank you, Sapphira.' Mim's voice was affectionate now. 'A whisky for me.'

Sapphira poured Mim's drink and brought it over to her, then arranged her long limbs on the chaise longue and took a sip. She let her head drop back on the headrest and sighed.

Mim turned to the maid standing silently by the door. 'Mayhew. Take these children to the basement room. Run them a bath and give them both a set of servant's clothes. Give them a bit of food, too.'

The maid bobbed. 'Yes, ma'am.'

'And Mayhew? I want two guards stationed outside their room at all times. Is that quite clear?'

'Yes, ma'am.'

Mim reached for a bag at her waist. She counted out several gold coins and extended her hand to Silas. He scurried over, grabbed the coins with an oily smile and scuttled out of the room.

The maid beckoned to Jack and Ava and turned to leave the room. They followed her and climbed down a narrow, dark flight of stairs that led into a poky corridor. The maid led them to a door halfway down the corridor and took a key from a chain on her belt. She smirked at Jack.

'Can look all you like, lad, you ain't getting near this key. You a locksmith, ain't ya? A good one, too, they say. No lock too tricky for yer.'

She opened the door and stood back to let them into the room. It was tiny and windowless, a narrow single bed lying against either wall and another door leading to a bathroom the size of a cupboard.

'In yer go. I'll be back with food and clothes. And your guards.' She grinned and slammed the door behind them. The key grated in the lock.

Silence pressed against them. Blood hummed loud in Ava's ears. The weight of her body was more than she could bear. She sat heavily on one bed.

'So, finally, I will meet my mother,' she said. 'Such good news, is it not? It's what I wanted, after all.' She laughed, and suddenly she couldn't stop. The laughter racked her body until her stomach ached, until her breath heaved in sobs that died away, leaving her curled tight and still on the bed.

The same words kept pounding inside her skull. Her mother was the Time Lady. The Green Witch. Her mother did not deal in grey time – she *created* it.

Her mother had created the thing that snatched Violet.

For the first time, she understood what her father had been trying to do all those years. His lies had been the ultimate love and protection. He'd realised that Ava would seek out her mother if she'd known she existed – even if she'd heard all the stories about her.

Especially because of that – because of a perverse fascination, or to show that Ava could be the one to break through to her. She had that in her. Her father knew her inside out – he knew such stories would not keep her away but would have the opposite effect.

Jack crouched in front of her and put his hands on her shoulders.

'We don't 'ave to just stay here and wait for them, Ava. We can get out. Trust me. I'm good at this sort of thing.' A pause. 'Ava?'

She blinked. She had been somewhere else. She shook her head. It was very clear to her what she had to do.

'No. Why keep running? I'm here to meet my mother and meet her I will.'

Footsteps sounded in the corridor and gruff voices mingled with the higher tones of the maid. The key scraped in the lock again and the door swung open. Two burly guards carrying strange-looking crossbows in one hand and buckets in the other flanked the maid, who also had a bucket in each hand. She carried the buckets through to pour into the bath, before coming back to take the other two buckets from the guards.

'Thank you, lads,' she said, then indicated to Jack with her head. 'Her ladyship said to search this one from head to toe. He might 'ave a master key on him if he's from Hammer's.'

She took the buckets through and the guard handed his crossbow to his partner. He stepped into the room and motioned to Jack.

'Stand here. Raise yer arms and spread yer legs.'

The guard crouched with a grunt and patted every inch of Jack, his face expressionless throughout. He stopped at Jack's pocket. 'Take that out.'

Jack pulled out a small sealed packet of powder and held it out. 'It's my medicine.' He rolled up a sleeve and indicated the gashes on his arms. 'These are from the ravens.'

The man grunted again. He reached inside Jack's shirt, pulling out a key hanging on a piece of string.

'This the type of thing you're after, Maisie?'

The maid snatched at the key and waved it tauntingly in Jack's face. 'What 'ave we here, boy? Had your escape all planned, did you?'

She turned to the door and locked it using her own key, then slid Jack's key into the lock. It turned smoothly and the door opened with a click.

'Hammer gave it to me, 'e'll kill me if I lose it.' Jack's voice was tight and pleading. 'Don't take it from me, will yer? You can keep it while I'm in here, but after that –'

The guards and the maid roared with laughter.

'Can keep it tonight, can we?' squeaked Maisie. 'Much obliged, young man. Hand it back to you tomorrow? Course we will! Right as rain, eh boys?'

Maisie doubled over, laughing so hard that she hiccuped. She straightened and wiped her eyes. Slipping the key in her pocket, she smirked at Jack. 'You ain't going anywhere, lad.' She gestured towards the medicine still in Jack's hand. 'How do we know that ain't poison?'

In answer, Jack wet a finger and put it inside the packet, drawing out a powder-encrusted finger. He put it in his mouth and swallowed, grimacing. 'I need it for the raven cuts, to stop them goin' bad.'

Maisie looked dubious, but she nodded. 'Keep it. Don't want to deal with a sick kid.'

The guard motioned to Ava. 'What about her?'

'What, that dozy moo? She look witless. Nah, he's the one

to watch. Anyway, we found what we was looking for.' She patted her pocket.

'Been a long night already, Maisie,' said the bald guard. 'Don't suppose you could bring us a little something to keep us going, eh?'

'On duty? Her upstairs will have me guts for garters.'

'Go on, Maisie. We're big boys. Just a drop won't hurt. And it ain't as if we got our work cut out looking after two kids in a locked room, is it?'

Maisie pursed her lips coquettishly. 'All right. But you owe me one.'

She went outside and the guards followed her. The door thudded shut behind them and thick silence wrapped itself around them.

'Who are these people?' asked Ava. 'They're all terrified of that tiny woman upstairs.'

'That *tiny woman* is the Matriarch and yeah, she terrifies anybody who has any sense. She's the head of the Seven Sisters, Ava. The Family. They're the most ruthless group in Donlon. Mim is one of the most powerful Names there is. The Family have powers that not even other Names fully understand. When the Family bleed – and they always bleed together – all Donlon feels it. You don't go near them at that time. Too much power.'

It took Ava a shocked moment to realise what Jack was talking about, but as soon as she did her cheeks flamed and she looked away. How could a boy even know these things? Let alone talk about them in front of a *girl* as casually as though he was discussing train fares? But Jack went on as if he'd said nothing out of the ordinary.

177

'One of their businesses is doing deals with the Time Lady. People pay the Family for protection against time-snatching and in return the Family do the dirty work for the Lady. They say that the Seven Sisters collect people who won't be missed and give them to the Lady for time-snatching.'

Ava felt her cheeks cool at Jack's matter-of-fact tone and she brought her attention back to what he was saying now. 'So that little lady is the leader of a criminal network?'

'Yeah. Among other things. They've got you because they figure the Lady values you. You're worth something.'

Ava smiled thinly. 'Maybe not. It's clear she abandoned me. Why would she want me now?'

'They've got their finger on the pulse. They ain't usually wrong about their business instincts. She'll want you.'

The key turned in the lock again and Jack put a finger to his lips. Maisie came back in, carrying a bundle of clothes. She put a pile of clothes on each bed, revealing a silver flask hidden between the clothing. She went into the bathroom with two threadbare towels.

Jack leapt in a silent bound to the bed and grabbed the flask. He undid it and shook some of the powder from the little packet into it. By the time Maisie came back into the room he had tightened the lid, given it a quick shake and put it in exactly the same position on the bed. It had taken him seconds and he'd done it in absolute silence.

Ava stared at him. He was a useful lad, indeed.

The maid looked at Ava in distaste. 'Bath's ready. Put your filthy clothes in the corner. You'll have food brought later. And no funny tricks from you, lad, okay?'

Jack grinned gormlessly and Maisie rolled her eyes. She grabbed the flask and went out the door. 'Don't reckon you'll have your work cut out tonight, boys. Them kids ain't as smart as we thought.'

She locked the door behind her. Jack tiptoed forward and put one ear to the door, listening with an intent expression. A muffled cheer came from the corridor and he relaxed visibly. Ava could just make out the words.

'You're a darling, Maisie! This'll help the time to pass.'

'Thank the gods!' whispered Jack. 'They didn't even taste it. Must've burnt off their tastebuds years ago.'

'Why did you put your medicine in the flask?' whispered Ava.

'Agnes told me it's strong stuff,' said Jack. 'It'll knock 'em out within an hour or two. Then we can get out.'

'With what? You lost your master key!'

Jack came over to Ava and put his arms around her waist. She pulled back in alarm. 'What are you doing? This is most –'

He pulled his arms back and smiled. He was holding a key fastened to a pin. He spoke in a low voice. 'This was why I didn't want you to take your dress off. I pinned this in your pocket before you woke up properly on West Ham Island. Don't think I'm daft enough to keep both copies on me, do yer?' He was grinning from ear to ear. 'I had a feeling we would need a spare and that it'd be safer on you. I was right, wasn't I? You were too witless-looking even to get searched.'

Ava couldn't stop herself grinning at Jack's delight.

'Not witless enough to go with you, though. I've had enough adventure for one night.'

Jack frowned at her. 'But, Ava –'

Ava held up her hand. 'No more arguing. I have a bath to attend to. I can't meet my mother smelling like this.' She almost convinced herself with her jovial tone.

She ducked past Jack and pulled the bathroom door shut between them. 'I trust that you are gentlemanly enough to keep that key well away from this door, Master Jack.'

And she locked the door with a loud *click*.

CHAPTER 22
JACK

Donlon

Even when Ava's steady, slow breathing told Jack that she had fallen asleep, he was still wrestling with himself. He looked at the stubborn set of her jaw, just visible in the near-dark room as they lay in parallel beds, and sighed. It seemed that all Jack's efforts since he'd first arrived, dripping, at the Hams' camp had been in vain. He'd nearly drowned himself for nothing. She preferred to remain a prisoner and be taken to Time Palace as a bargaining chip for the Seven Sisters.

Nothing could be more alien to him – even though he could see first-hand why she'd made this choice. Ava needed to understand who she was and look her mother in the eye.

His first instinct was to stay with her, for both their sakes. How could he leave her now? She kept him steady, true, but she also needed him. She was a stranger to Donlon and its ways. He couldn't just leave her in the hands of the

181

most ruthless gang in Donlon, to be delivered on a plate to the Lady, even if that plate was gold-edged. The thought of her being out of his sight made him breathless with panic.

And yet – he knew full well what would happen if he stayed. Ava would be taken to Time Palace and he wouldn't. Jack would be cast aside. He was worth nothing, there or here. He would be separated from Ava *and* be a prisoner.

There was no other option. He had to get them both out of here, under cover of darkness. And there was only one, near-impossible way to do that. He got soundlessly to his feet and stepped over to the door, master key in hand. The lock on the door suddenly looked huge compared to the small key in his hand and doubt gripped Jack, even though he'd just seen Maisie use it. Would it turn again? He held his breath as he put the key in the lock and slowly turned. Nothing happened. He bit his lip while he turned it again.

Click.

He breathed out in relief and pushed the door open a crack. One guard was slumped on the floor, his shoulders against the wall and his head lolling to one side, mouth wide open. The other had abandoned the wall and was spread-eagled flat on the floor, fast asleep. Their snores ripped through the air.

Jack looked back at the bed. Ava lay still, her breathing steady. One arm twitched above the covers as he watched and her face twisted for a moment, then relaxed. She was dreaming. Jack didn't look to see what it was. He watched her with his heart racing as if he was about to jump off a building into an abyss.

Thank the gods, he'd kept some of his medicine in reserve. Enough to numb the throb of his wounds for the journey, with some left over. It would be just enough. He calculated it would take two or three hours to get to Hammer's, which was the only place he could safely take her now – a long, hard walk with Ava unconscious on his shoulders. There was no time to spare.

He knew how to administer unwanted medicine to animals – he'd helped do it to Hammer's horse once – but a sleeping girl was another matter. He took the powder out of his pocket, picked up one of the cups that had come with their stale bread and cheese and poured some water in it. He opened the packet of powder and peered inside.

He paused. How was he going to do this? If he tried to tip liquid down her throat while she slept she would choke, wouldn't she? But if he woke her, she would never do as he wanted.

He looked over at her for a long, struggling moment and then made his decision. He squatted beside Ava's bed, his head close to hers. This would take all his skill. He would have to let his sight overcome her resistance, and then bring her quietly into waking mode. That way, he could control her long enough to make her drink the medicine.

This wasn't how he normally used his sight. The unscrupulous Hams used their power to manipulate the minds of others, but Jack's gift was different. His seeing went much deeper. He operated at a delicate, intense level that the Hams couldn't reach. His was the finest needlework to their rough patchwork. The gentlest touch from him had more power than one of their blows.

He wouldn't normally abuse his power like this, especially with someone he cared about. But he had no choice. He took a deep breath and opened his sight, sending it far into Ava's mindsoul.

There was no resistance. No quiver of defensiveness; no instinctive barrier that he had to break down or worm underneath. He sensed that this wouldn't have been Ava's normal response. It was because – for some reason – she trusted Jack absolutely. An old, deep instinct inside her told her that Jack's presence was not something to fear. She trusted him from the depths of her soul.

Jack paused, shaken. He had never encountered this before. It was as though *he* was the same as *her*, in her unconscious mind.

But what he was doing was a violation. He didn't understand how, or why, but he knew by forcing his will on her now he would undo something profound between them – something that went back further than memory.

He couldn't do it, after all. He had the skill, the strength, but not the will.

He stood up, suddenly sickened with himself. How much of this plan had truly been for Ava's good, anyway? How much for his own? She would be safe here. She was valuable. She would be delivered unharmed to her mother if he walked away from her now, whereas he could not guarantee the same by taking her – against her will and unconscious – halfway across Donlon in the dark of night. And then into the midst of an attack.

By taking her, Jack would be putting her in far greater danger. He knew it was the truth.

He had to leave her, even though the thought of that was a physical wrench. But the alternative was worse. He closed his eyes and took a deep breath. He would see her sooner, this way. If he stayed, she would be taken tomorrow and he would have no chance of finding her again. He had to go, alone.

And he had to reach the army that Bill, Tony and Hammer were assembling. They didn't have the information he had – where Ava was. She would be taken to Time Palace and the troops they were gathering wouldn't know or care that she might get in the way. At least if Jack reached them before they attacked, he could pass on the information he had. And he'd have a chance of getting to Ava – a much better chance than if he stayed prisoner.

He reached down to lay a gentle hand on Ava's head, holding the moment in a single long breath, as blessing, apology and goodbye.

He stood up and walked out of the room without another glance, shutting the door and locking it silently behind him.

It felt a long, teetering way down the corridor, tiptoeing over outstretched limbs and carefully avoiding the discarded flask, but finally Jack crept past the guards. They were dead to the world. He probably could have fallen on them and they'd barely grunt in response. At the end of the hall was a poky flight of stairs leading up to a door and Jack climbed quickly, wincing at every creak. The door was locked and Jack fumbled with his key. Thank the gods, it worked first time.

He came out into another corridor. To the left was darkness, broken only by a faint light at the far end, and to the right was the entrance hall. A grand flight of stairs swept up from the hall to a staircase that rose elegantly above him. Beyond the staircase lay an expanse of gleaming tiled floor, and two guards armed with crossbows at the entrance – and not just any crossbows, but the latest elite model. The battery power on those would have a shaft through his neck before he blinked.

Left it was, then. He turned and tiptoed towards the light, which grew brighter as he approached. It was the kitchen, he realised. He shrank back against the wall as a stout figure bustled out, arms laden high with linen, passing him without a glance. He could hear a rattle of activity from the kitchen and craned his head to see servants standing at the long workbenches chopping, stirring and kneading. Yawning.

He pulled further into the shadows and cursed. Of course, they were up in the early hours. The Family were tough mistresses. But he'd seen a door at the far end of the kitchen, and kitchen doors led into kitchen gardens – so all he had to do was get past.

That was a big *all*.

He peered back into the kitchen. There were two girls preparing food on the bench and an older woman stirring something at the stove, scowling as if it had just insulted her.

'Amy!' she barked. 'Watch this a moment. I need the privy.'

One of the girls went over and took the ladle while the older woman turned and scuttled to the door, groaning.

'Lawks a-mercy! I just went, too. Cup of tea barely touches the sides of me before it's out the other end, these days.' She yanked the door open, leaving it ajar behind her as she ran outside.

It had to be now. Jack let his sight flare wide open and probe the mind of the girl at the bench. She was tired, so tired. She'd been clearing and preparing for the next day until late last night. This was her life and she didn't question it, but with each circle of the sun it ground her down a little more. She got half a day on Sunday and she just wanted to sleep and sleep, but that was the only time she could see her little brother. Here the love surged, warm and pulsing, over everything else and there was the boy in her mind's eye, tiny and sharp-faced with a quick, sweet smile. Charlie, apprenticed to Dave, the driver for the Family.

Jack saw all this in a flash and moved before he could think. He ran into the kitchen with a wide, cheeky smile at the girl at the bench, grabbing a punnet of strawberries. The other girl swung round and both faces registered first shock, then outrage, but Jack's words came quicker than theirs.

'Let it go, darlings, will ya? These are for Charlie. A bet with Dave. Tell yer all about it later, promise.'

He blew a kiss to both girls in turn, put a finger to his lips with a wink, then raced out the open door past the privy, through the cabbages and down to the gate at the bottom of the garden. He vaulted over the fence, still clutching the strawberries, and turned to wave to the two girls in the open doorway.

He was through. Now to get to the river, back to Hammer's – and to eat, rest and prepare for battle.

And then, to Time Palace. To Ava.

CHAPTER 23
AVA

Donlon

Ava woke with a start. *Jack had gone.*

The words rang loud in her head. She looked over at his bed, but no – there he was, still in deep slumber, buried under blankets. She felt a swoop of relief. She must have been dreaming. Thank the Lord she was not alone in this dark, windowless cell.

The iron grate in the door scraped open. Two eyes peered through, then it slammed shut again. The key turned in the lock and Ava braced herself as the door swung open. Maisie came in with water, bread and cheese on a tray. Was that all they ate in this place? The guards were propped up against the wall outside, eyes bleary, and Maisie's face was like thunder.

'If you two lose me my job, I swear to the gods you'll pay!' she growled. She slammed the tray on the small table in the corner. 'Breakfast. Her ladyship wants you ready to go to Time Palace at the end of the day. Just you, not him.'

She gave a nasty smile before picking up the full chamber pot and leaving.

Butterflies swarmed in Ava's belly and she sat up quickly. She swung her legs out of bed. Jack still hadn't stirred. She waited until Maisie had left the room again before getting up and pulling the blankets off him.

She yelped in shock. Jack's head was a pillow and his body was clothes bunched under the blankets.

He *had* gone without her. She couldn't believe it.

She sank back on the bed. Jack had finally given up on her.

The emptiness inside her yawned deep. Jack's calm presence had steadied her when the world around her was flailing out of control. The lack of centre she'd felt ever since finding out her life was built on lies had been filled by Jack's presence.

She couldn't eat the bread and cheese, her dry mouth mumbling uselessly around the crumbs. She pushed the plate aside and waited until the door swung open again and Maisie brought in the emptied chamber pot. Maisie saw Jack's bed and her face blanched the colour of the cheese on Ava's tray.

'Holy damnation, what happened here?' She glared at Ava. 'Where is he?'

Ava shrugged. 'If I knew, wouldn't I be with him?'

Maisie whirled to face the guards still scratching and yawning outside.

'You had one job! One! I would'a thought guarding two useless kids would not be beyond you! Oh sweet gods, I'm finished.' She turned back to Ava and hissed, 'I'm not surprised he left you behind first chance he got. Useless piece of baggage you are.'

She slammed the door shut and shouted at the guards. 'You go upstairs and tell her! Ain't my job to keep him here. *GO!*'

There was much commotion. Ava was dragged upstairs and sat in a room with two different guards flanking her while maids and Family ran around and shouted respectively. Finally, Mim strode over and stood in front of Ava, eye to eye with her even though Ava sat on a chair.

'I did not even want that stupid boy and now he has caused all this trouble. If he gets in the way of our trans- action, then he will be very much the worse for it. Is that understood?'

Ava swallowed and nodded. She could see why burly men were terrified of this woman. She oozed malevolence from every tiny pore.

'I have matters to attend to today. You will come with me to Time Palace later this afternoon, so make yourself presentable. Sapphira will have to see what she can do about that.' Mim gave a sniff, raking Ava up and down with a disdainful glance, and turned on her heel to leave.

A low chuckle came from the staircase. Sapphira ascended the stairs as Mim went down. She leaned languidly on the bannister, looking through the doorway at Ava with her head tilted to one side. 'That won't be quite as terrible a task as my sister makes out. She can be a little harsh sometimes. You look about the same size as Jade.'

Ah yes. Ava had a vague memory of Jade's name from the previous night, when she was still reeling from discovering who her own mother was.

'What about me, Mama?'

Instantly, Sapphira's posture snapped out of languor. She twisted and peered down the stairs. 'Where have you been, girl?'

A dark glossy head appeared above the bannister, and stopped as she caught sight of Ava. The two girls stared at each other for a long moment. Jade kept her eyes fixed on Ava as she ascended the last steps. She was taller than Sapphira with a more brutal grace. She was wearing trousers and a vivid waistcoat, as though dressed like a London man, but her hair was loose and black.

Ava was already on her feet. She gave an involuntary shiver. Jade's presence made her skin prickle and left her tongue thick and silent.

'Who are you?' said Jade. Her eyes were very dark blue.

'She is the Time Daughter. The Lady's child.' Sapphira spoke to Jade's back.

Jade's eyes sharpened. 'I did not know the Lady had a child.'

'It is not common knowledge,' said Sapphira coolly. 'And you have been – where?'

Jade replied without taking her eyes off Ava. 'In London. I saw Father.' The girl said it challengingly.

Sapphira's face tightened almost imperceptibly, then smoothed again. She gave a magnificent shrug. 'You are a fool, then. I have raised you to know better.'

'You chose him first, Mama,' said Jade, softly.

There was the sound of a door opening further along the landing and Sapphira's face changed as she turned to look. She stepped back as a figure appeared in the doorway. At first Ava thought it was a man with cropped grey hair, holding a pipe and dressed in a velvet smoking robe. He moved closer, and she was suddenly unsure. His features were delicate and his long fingernails were painted purple to match the robe, and strands of coloured stones were roped around his neck. His eyes were rimmed with something thick and black and were shot through with red. He drew deep on his pipe and then raised his head to blow perfect, strangely fragrant smoke rings at the ceiling.

'Jade is correct, Sapphira,' he said in a voice as rich as the tobacco, speaking to the ceiling. He looked at Sapphira. 'I warned you against using that one to father one of our girls, did I not?' The black-rimmed gaze flicked between Ava and Jade with a grunt of amusement. 'And now look here. The future stands before us, does it not?'

'Aunt Seer, what does that future hold?' asked Jade.

'Retract that, Jade! Our Sister is not some spiritual weathervane for your personal use!' Sapphira snapped.

Aunt? Sister? Ava could not tear her eyes away from the woman. She was now regarding Ava with those disturbing black and red eyes and a terrible stillness.

'But she might listen to my answer, unlike her mother,' said the Seer softly. There was a long, dense silence until the Seer closed her eyes, as if watching something on the inside. 'One sister's power can save or ruin another sister. Life turns on one choice.'

She opened her eyes and drew deeply on her pipe. Sapphira let out her breath and Jade looked disappointed. The Seer gave a nod as she turned and went back into her room.

'Is that it? She came out to tell us *that*?' muttered Jade. 'I wanted my future, not your past. She was talking about you not doing as she said, all those years ago!'

'Perhaps. But you're lucky our Seer did not decree. You don't ask for the future lightly, girl!' said Sapphira tightly. 'Her words can haunt a lifetime.' She breathed in deeply, then out, as if trying to expel the lingering smoke from her lungs. Her face was hard, all languor gone. 'And Mim wants this girl readied to go to Time Palace. Your green dress will do for her, I think. Bring it to my room and leave it there.'

The words spiralled in the air like the Seer's smoke coils, whose heady aroma still blurred Ava's head. She felt as unsteady as if she'd drunk a flagon of cider. It was not just the Seer's lingering strangeness, but this mother and daughter before her. The daughter, especially. She was distant and brittle and bright as a star, with a sheen that made Ava feel woolly and dull in comparison.

'Go now, Jade,' said Sapphira warningly, and not even this bold girl could disregard that tone. She gave one last lingering look at Ava before turning to go back downstairs. It was both devastating and a relief.

'I will bring something for you to wear shortly,' Sapphira said. 'Ready yourself in the meantime.' She shut Ava's door and the key turned in the lock.

Ava took a deep, loosening breath. She caught sight of

herself in a mirror hanging on the wall and froze. For a long, prickling moment she stared at her reflection as if for the first time. How had she not realised that her face was nearly a reflection of Jade's?

CHAPTER 24
JACK

Donlon

It had taken Jack nearly three hours to walk from the Family's house. Slow for him, but he wasn't in the best shape – his body was on fire and he pushed away the fear that his wounds were festering. He wished now he hadn't put so much of his medicine in that flask. The pain, combined with walking on a belly fed only with a few fragments of hard bread and cheese – and a bonus punnet of strawberries – together with a night of no sleep meant he was drifting.

Walking away from her had been the hardest thing he'd ever done. But he couldn't help her if he let himself remain a prisoner. He had no value in this world – whereas Ava was as high status as it was possible to be. No one would harm her.

No, he had no choice but to stick with the plan he'd come up with. Getting trapped by the Family was definitely not part of that plan.

But first, to Hammer's.

By the time he could feel the heat of the foundry on his skin, it was not far off daybreak. The round moon was sinking towards the horizon and the sky was lightening from black to dark grey. As he trudged towards the longed-for sight of those gates, Jack was swept by a huge wave of exhaustion. It was as if the sight of home – as near as home as anywhere, for Jack – had allowed his defences to drop. The adrenaline that had kept him going, through a rescue attempt, a near drowning, a recapture and then a long, dragging escape from the Seven Sisters – all while injured and sleep-deprived – had reached its end. As had Jack. He barely noticed who opened the gate as he stumbled inside and fell into his small, hard, but never-so-welcome bed.

Jack slept late. He slept through the early morning chatter and clatter in the apprentice dorm, through the lunch bell and into the afternoon. In fact, he didn't wake until a big hand shook him, hard. Even then, it took a long time to drag himself up through the thick treacle of sleep, to see Hammer's huge bearded head leaning over him.

That woke him up properly. He bolted upright, heart thudding. 'Ha – ahem. Hammer.' His voice was thick as treacle, too. Hammer loomed fuzzily while Jack rubbed his eyes clear of deep sleep.

'Back to stay, then, Jack?' said Hammer.

'Yes, um, no. I mean, just for now. I have to –'

'It's all right, Jack. I know,' said Hammer, patiently. Jack peered at him blearily. Had Hammer been making a joke? It was never easy to tell. 'We have a plan, don't we?'

Jack sat up properly, wide awake with a chime of excitement in his chest. 'Yes. Yes, we do.'

'Then let's go and talk about it over food. There's some things we need to get straight.'

Over a three-day stew, which seemed the most delicious thing Jack had ever eaten, Hammer laid out what had happened since Jack left. 'I've been talking with Malaikah. Tony sent us both word from you. This girl, this friend of yours – she's not just anyone. Malaikah's known about her for a while.'

'A while' could be anything from years to centuries with Malaikah. It made some things clearer, anyway. 'Is that why you let me go to her with your blessing?' asked Jack.

'It is. Some of the Names knew she was coming. And she's something personal to Malaikah. He's her guardian here – has been watching her since she was born. The Lady asked him to.'

'The *Lady* did?' said Jack. 'But she abandoned her daughter. Why would she care?'

'There's more to the Lady than the Green Witch,' said Hammer cryptically. 'That story is not all it seems. And there's only one Time Daughter anywhere in history. What's going to happen tonight will go either way – either towards her destiny or against it. We can only hope the former.'

Jack scraped the last thick drops from the bottom of his bowl regretfully. 'But we're going to battle against the Lady.'

'Against the snatching. Not the Lady,' said Hammer impassively. 'We put word out for allies. Lots of damaged souls out there. It ain't been difficult to get support.'

A thought occurred to Jack. 'Where is Mr Bailey? Ava's father?'

Hammer gave an uncharitable snort. 'That one would be a liability in battle. He won't be with us. He's spending the day watching Time Palace for Ava's arrival.' He paused and regarded Jack blackly under thick eyebrows. 'You could go with him, if you wanted.'

'No,' said Jack, without hesitation. 'I'll be with you, Hammer.'

Hammer gave a nod and Jack sensed he'd passed a test. 'Good. But you should check on that little man first. Go ahead and then meet us in the woods at the back of the Palace. We will be waiting by sundown.'

CHAPTER 25
AVA

Donlon

It was nearly sunset by the time Mim finally sent for Ava in the downstairs foyer. Ava was wearing the loveliest dress she had ever worn – a strangely cut but elegant green outfit. Mim looked her up and down and nodded. 'Follow me.'

She turned on her heel and strode out of the room, maids rushing to open doors and curtsy as she passed. Ava followed Mim as she crossed the gleaming expanse of entrance hall.

It wasn't until they were outside that Ava realised it was already full dusk. Tall lamps cast a yellow light on the red carriage with graceful curves and gleaming brasswork. Steam was puffing silently out of the boiler at the back. A liveried driver leapt out of the car and rushed around to open the back door for Mim, who took his hand and climbed aboard. She gestured for Ava to sit opposite her and Ava slid across the gleaming leather seat.

The guards went to follow but Mim waved them away. 'I don't need you. This girl is no match for me.'

The guards hesitated, glancing at each other. Mim turned to glare at them and they melted away, bowing as they backed away from the car. Mim leaned forward to talk to the driver.

'Time Palace, Dave.'

'Yes, ma'am.' Dave was surprisingly young. He started the carriage smoothly and Ava watched the mansion behind them pull away until the road curved along the river and it disappeared from view.

Ava's second steam car ride was a very different experience to the first. This carriage had gleaming curves, soft leather and polished woodwork. Her driving companion was of the criminal class, like Silas, but there the resemblance ended. Here was someone who was mistress of her domain – even if that domain was criminal and ruthless.

Ava stole a look at Mim, who was looking out of the window at the dark grounds outside. Surveying her territory, thought Ava. They were driving along another waterway. The waterwheels and spindly windmills that stood sentinel all over Donlon were grey silhouettes in the dusk, the rising moon glinting on the water. Along the banks of the river were the tall metal poles that Ava had seen before, topped by round studded balls. Dark shapes dotted the landscape. The ravens.

She looked away quickly and tried to settle on what was coming. She had to distract herself if she was going to get through this journey without falling to pieces.

She gathered her courage. 'Er, Miss Mim?'

A slight tilt of the chin seemed to be the only answer she was going to get so she ploughed on. 'Is this how Donlon gets its power?' She gestured to the scene below.

Mim fixed her with a disdainful look. 'How else?'

'Well, in London we use mostly coal and wood. Things that you burn to generate power.'

Mim gave a sniff of disgust. 'Your air must be vile. Why go to such filthy lengths when wind, sun and water are all on hand and free? Do you really not have such basic equipment as this?' She pointed to the river.

Ava shook her head. She had never seen anything like this before.

Mim looked scornful. 'I had no idea your people were quite so backward. I suppose you have never had a mother to provide a decent education, so I will explain. The water powers the wheels, the wind drives the mills and the sun feeds the sun balls on the posts. All that then feeds into power packs that hold energy that you can use later in many ways. Like this car, which also uses steam, as we have for many years. I believe that even London has some steam technology – although very primitive, of course.'

'Oh.' It sounded simple and obvious when put like that. Mim snorted and turned to look out the window again. She clearly didn't think much of Ava's intellectual capabilities.

Ava surreptitiously opened a window a little way to sniff the cool air. Mim was right. The air here was so different to the coal-blackened London smog. Pure and cold and full of life. She remembered Phoebe saying that her aunt in the Cotswolds could always tell when a letter had come from London, just by putting it to her nose. Perhaps Donlon wasn't as threatening and malevolent as she'd first thought. There was a thing or two London could learn from its twisted sibling.

Dave swung the car onto a road leading towards a bridge crossing the river. A guard came sleepily out of a tiny tollbooth at the end of the bridge and held up a hand, one of those strange-looking crossbows in the other. What had Jack said – that guns were forbidden here? When the guard saw Mim he stepped back, waving them across the bridge. Ava thought of the poor Mort Lake people, trapped on one side of the river. The Seven Sisters clearly had no such problems getting wherever they needed to go in Donlon. One thing the two cities did have in common; imbalances in class, power and privilege were universal, it seemed.

Ava hesitated, then blurted before she lost her courage, 'Miss Mim, why are guns forbidden?'

Mim didn't bother to look at Ava, but Ava could still see the curl of her lip. 'Why would we permit them?'

It was clear that Mim did not require an answer. In any case, Ava didn't have one.

She leaned back on the leather seat. The car swayed and bounced, making a soft hissing sound. *Sssss-cachank. Ssssss-cachank.* It would be calming, if this journey were any other. If she wasn't about to meet her mother, the Time Lady of Donlon.

By the time the car stopped, her stomach was tight as a fist. She sat bolt upright. They were on a sweeping gravel drive in front of a pink building surrounded by deep pink stone walls that were instantly familiar. Of course. She'd seen the mansion from the outside of those walls, the first time she'd transited from Greenwich Observatory. So ironic that she'd come straight to her mother's house on her very first visit, and not even realised.

The driver stood by the open door, helping Mim out of the car. He fussed over her until she waved him away, then turned to Ava. No such fussing for her – just a perfunctory hand that he dropped as soon as she was on the ground. He made his way to the imposing entrance to announce their presence.

Mim ascended the steps, Ava an unsteady pace behind her. Ava's mouth was paper dry. The driver had already rung the bell hanging above the glossy black door. Ava's pulse quickened as the door opened. Her stomach flipped but it was just a maid, bobbing as she said something to Mim and the driver. Relief and disappointment coiled together in Ava's stomach. Mim snapped in reply but Ava could hear nothing beyond the high buzzing in her head.

Mim was peering down the hall and the maid shot an anxious glance behind her. Ava could hear the shouting now, above the tinny noise in her head. A woman's voice, deep and sonorous, and a man's, sharp and angry.

Mim smiled a thin-lipped smile. 'One knows how these family discussions can drag on. No point in waiting for it to come to a polite end. No, we will make our own way.'

Mim gripped Ava's arm, pushed past the shocked maid and swept down the corridor, pulling Ava with her with unexpected strength. The maid called out in panic but some curt words from the driver silenced her. The voices got louder as they strode down the hall. The man sounded familiar.

'Do you think I'm a fool?' he shouted.

His vicious tone made Ava's skin skitter. Where had she heard that voice before?

'I suggest you do not make such an error of judgement.'

'You do think me the fool! Do you truly believe I don't know about the lies you spread about me? Or the *joke* you started at the Observatory with that damned Goodwin? *The woman who puts the witch into Greenwich.*' The woman's voice was angry, but deep and musical. It also sounded a familiar note in the midst of all the strangeness – but surely this was Ava's mind playing tricks? 'And don't pretend you weren't behind what happened that day at the Observatory. Lies and more lies, both behind my back and to my face!'

'You're not one to lecture *me* about lies! No, don't you walk away from me!'

A door slammed open and a woman burst out of it into the corridor. Mim stepped in front of Ava. The woman whirled and glared at them. She reminded Ava of one of the more dramatic Hams. A tumble of red-gold hair, the hall lights striking copper sparks from it. She was small but she made up for it with parrot colours – a royal blue coat, ruched and flowing to her knees like a highwayman. Narrow red trousers and bright-yellow ankle boots. The sides of her head were shaved. Delicate tattoos climbed around her ears – flowers, fruit and tendrils of vines.

No, this woman surpassed even the Hams in strangeness. Who was she, yelling at the top of her voice in Time Palace?

'What are you doing here, Mim?' she snapped.

'Greetings to you too, Esmeralda.' Mim's voice was acidly amused. She stepped back to reveal Ava. 'I believe you have already met your daughter?'

CHAPTER 26
AVA

Donlon

This otherworldly woman was Ava's *mother*?

Ava stared at her in shocked silence. It simply wasn't possible. The woman was small, red-haired, with delicate features and sea-green eyes. She could hardly be less like tall, strong-boned Ava with her blue eyes and raven hair. There was no glimpse of herself in her mother's face – nothing. This strange, bright woman was as alien as if she had dropped from the stars.

And yet, there was a tiny chime of recognition. A persistent note at the back of Ava's mind.

'You have to leave. Mim, what have you done – bringing her here unannounced?'

The words bounced around Ava like balls she couldn't catch.

Mim seemed unperturbed. 'I felt that time was of the essence here, Esmeralda, if you will pardon my appropriation of your domain. Is it too late in the day?'

'It is not because of the time, Mim! It is because –'

'Because you want this little bundle of time tricks all to yourself. You want to keep her from me. Yes?'

The man who had stepped out of the room and now leaned languidly against the door frame, as though this was all an amusing performance put on for his benefit, was Uncle John Smith from Burlington Arcade.

It was absurd, in the depths of all this strangeness, but Ava suddenly remembered that she had not kept their appointment and felt a pang of guilt. Oh, how ridiculous! At a time like this – her first thought was *etiquette*?

But Mr Smith did not seem angry. In fact he was smiling at her with something that looked like admiration. Almost affection. 'You made it without me, my dear. Well done indeed. Did you come alone?'

'Don't answer him! Say nothing, girl.' Her mother's voice was sharp 'This moment is not yours, Rupert. You have nothing to do with this.'

Rupert? Hadn't he said his name was John? But Ava had no time to puzzle that out now. One dark eyebrow was quivering querulously on his forehead.

'*Nothing*? Oh, Esmeralda! I really don't think you can level that charge at me, do you?'

Well, he was her uncle, after all. Why didn't her mother want her brother to have anything to do with his niece? It must be to do with whatever they'd been arguing about. But right now, the brother seemed much more warmly disposed to his niece than her own mother was. He was smiling at Ava while the Lady's face was hard. She looked at Ava and Mim.

'You should not have brought her, Mim, but since you have she will have to stay now, for her own safety. I assume you want remuneration? Name your price.'

This moment could not be less like the scenes Ava had secretly imagined. The moment of soul recognition, the bonding, the joy. She looked at the stony face of her mother, waiting impatiently to hear the price she had to pay for her own daughter.

Mim laughed. 'I am rich, Esmeralda. I don't need even your sunstone. I would prefer that you remain in my debt until I need to call it in. If you agree, I will leave your daughter with you. Otherwise . . .' She tilted her head.

Esmeralda hesitated. 'An unnamed debt to the Matriarch of the Seven Sisters? That's a very high price, Mim. Especially when I haven't requested what you sell. Quite the opposite, in fact.' Her deep voice was harsh now. 'You have presented me with an impossible situation. Your timing could not be worse, damn you!'

Her mother threw up both hands in frustration, then reached out to grab Ava by the arm. A sudden memory jolted Ava, of a red-haired young man offering his arm at the Observatory. Surely not? Her mother went on. 'But you leave me no choice. I agree to your terms.'

'Then let us shake on it.' Mim's voice was brisk now. She reached out one bejewelled hand and Esmeralda extended her free hand to clasp it.

'Done,' purred Mim. 'Pleasure doing business with you, my dear Lady.' She turned and made her imperious way back down the hall to where her driver waited.

'I need to speak to the girl privately,' snapped Esmeralda.

She glared at Rupert. 'You will wait outside the room until I give you permission to enter.'

'Your daughter's name is Ava,' said Rupert quietly.

'I know who she is, damn you. Do not play games with me!' Her mother's grip tightened painfully on Ava's arm.

'I don't know what you need to discuss with Ava that could not include me, Esmeralda.'

Rupert's voice was soft and his eyes were dangerous. Ava gave an involuntary shiver. She was glad the look was not for her.

But Esmeralda gave an impatient snort. 'You are both Londoners, with the silly London coyness about bodily functions. I need to find out whether she has started to bleed, what other physical symptoms she has. Do you wish to subject her to your presence during that process?'

Rupert cleared his throat. 'Very well. I will wait in the study. Don't be long.'

Heat flushed Ava's cheeks as Rupert made his rapid way to another door along the hall. She wondered how the brother was a Londoner, while the sister was from Donlon. There must be yet another strange story behind these siblings. Another puzzle she would have to shelve until later.

Her mother pulled Ava with her into the room Rupert had just left. She slammed the door shut behind them and only then did she release her daughter. Ava rubbed her arm. Her mother's touch had left red welts on her skin.

Esmeralda went to a huge mahogany desk in the corner of the room and unlocked one of its drawers. Watching the precise, elegant way her mother moved, Ava was certain. Her mother and the charming young Samuel Timeward from the Greenwich Observatory were one and the same person. How? *Why*?

Esmeralda drew out a bulky velvet bag. 'It is a shock to see you here like this. You have left me no time to explain. I suppose you came to Donlon to find me?'

A sudden image of Violet's warm, smiling face floated in front of Ava, and the pang of grief made Ava wince. She was here to bring back Violet, too. The longer Violet was gone, the more torn she would become. It did not bear thinking about.

Her mother. The words had been spooling meaninglessly in her head but now their full weight slammed home. Ava had been harbouring a hope – one so secret and shameful that she had not let herself properly examine it – that the rumours would be wrong, that there would be a chink of humanity in the Lady's armour, and that Ava would be the one to find it.

Ava squirmed with shame. No. Her mother was a heartless woman and Ava's presence could as much change that fact as a discarded clay pipe could stop the flow of the Thames.

Esmeralda loosened the drawstring of the velvet bag and looked up at Ava. 'So, you are transient now. That's good news. It means that phase one of your time triggers has been activated.'

Her mother's eyes had brightened. What was she talking about? She looked beyond Ava, as if at some marvellous vision, and her words galloped as though keeping up with what she was seeing.

'We are both uncommon, you and I. I have lived for two hundred and seventy-four years and have evolved far

211

beyond any human ever has before. I have seen what true beauty is – it is in the eternal symmetry of the stars and the perfect poise of the universe. And it came to me that I had to see how I – my particular self – could intersect with these eternal truths of science.'

There was a faint flush on her cheeks now. Her skin was smooth as new porcelain after centuries in the world.

Her mother went on. 'I need you to understand the purity of my project – to see that you are a true child of this age of science and possibility. That there can be no one else like you, Ava.'

Ava's heart skipped. Was this it, after all? The great moment of connection between them?

Esmeralda looked at Ava and smiled. 'You are the ultimate expression of my genetic experimentation,' she said. 'The crowning achievement of my scientific ambition. My aim was to produce a child with certain time triggers within her development. I am the Time Lady and your father is an intellectually evolved man. This parentage will produce offspring with unique capabilities. That is you, Ava.'

The words struck Ava like blows. Her birth had been a scientific experiment. She was a Frankenstein's monster. And her own father must have been part of this.

No. It wasn't *possible*. There was no way . . . Her knees were jelly as her mother went on.

'Perhaps it is for the best that you arrived now. You should be at a critical stage of your development, a very exciting phase. Now that you're here I can check for myself. You remember that day in Greenwich, when the other girl was snatched – what happened to you then?'

She paused, evidently expecting Ava to answer, as if this was all part of a reasonable discussion.

'Um,' said Ava, squeezing her thoughts around the question. She could not think clearly.

'Well?' said Esmeralda. 'Did you go to the Void?'

Ava remembered the grey, soul-sucking nothingness she had experienced. Was that the Void? She gave an involuntary shudder and Esmeralda's eyes narrowed.

'I see. That means your immunity to time-snatching was only partly developed. That means your immunity to time-snatching was only partly developed – or worse, perhaps my theory is incorrect.' She paused. 'But no, I can't believe that. The timing is the critical thing. You are on the threshold of womanhood and by my calculations that will be an active phase for your time essence. Have you started to bleed yet?'

'What?' Ava's cheeks flushed again.

Esmeralda tutted impatiently. 'It is a biological process and nothing to be ashamed of. Quite the opposite – you must learn about its power, Ava. I have never understood why your society builds such complication into basic functions. A simple yes or no will suffice.'

A long silence, then an almost inaudible, 'Yes. A little.'

'You're just starting? Perfect. Your development should be changing almost daily at this time. There is only one way to be certain, however.'

Her mother drew an object out of the little bag. It looked like a gold chronometer with a little funnel on the top. Ava was jolted back to that day at the Observatory with Phoebe. This was a time snatcher.

She jumped back, stumbling against the sofa. Her mother couldn't mean . . . No, not that – not again.

'No. Please. No!'

She adjusted the funnel. 'It's just a test. Nothing more, don't worry.' Esmeralda raised the time snatcher to point at Ava, as focused as a cat ready to spring. The machine started to buzz.

The blow hit Ava squarely just below the chest. The breath slammed out of her lungs. She fell backwards and landed on the sofa, gasping for air. She couldn't breathe. Her lungs wouldn't work.

She was so dizzy.

The room was spinning.

Breaking up into little pieces around her.

Not again. There was a metallic shriek and a sharp, acrid smell. The room swung back into focus.

Ava took a breath, and then another, gasping like a fish on the slab at Billingsgate Market.

A cool hand rested on her forehead. Esmeralda crouched beside Ava as she sprawled on the sofa. She was very close and she smelt of gardenia.

'Ava. Ava! Speak to me.'

Ava gasped. It was hard to breathe, let alone speak.

Esmeralda pressed her other hand on Ava's chest, as though willing air to fill her lungs. Her voice shook. 'I thought you had gone, for a moment. I thought I had misjudged it.'

Were those tears in her eyes? Ava couldn't trust her own vision enough yet to be sure. Her mother was looking at Ava with a strangely intense expression. 'Thank the gods. You did not go to the Void this time?'

Ava tried again. 'No. I couldn't breathe but – no.'

Esmeralda shook her head, as if clearing it, as if remembering where she was. She stood up quickly and stepped away from Ava. 'This is good news, Ava. It means my theory is sound. You are immune to snatching!'

Her mother had not known for certain that Ava would not go to the Void, and yet she had snatched her. The joy on her face was due to her precious theory being safe, not her daughter.

'Ava, this is very important – you must not tell your father about your immunity. Tell him nothing about your triggers. Do you understand?'

Ava looked at her exultant mother and felt a deep, dragging exhaustion. She didn't even understand the secrets she was meant to keep. She couldn't sort truth from lies.

If only she had listened to Violet and Father. They had protected her with their lies, after all. Although Violet seemed ready to judge the Lady less harshly. Why was that? Had the Lady become more monstrous as time passed? Or was it just Violet's nature; her tendency to see good in people? But deep down Ava knew that wasn't the case. Violet's eyes were as sharp as a hawk's when it came to humans and their ways. There was no pulling the wool over her eyes.

Usually. Perhaps this one time was the exception that proved the rule.

But Violet was gone. The spasm of grief that gripped her whenever she thought of Violet was still as violent as that first shock. Ava might be immune to time-snatching, but what was life worth in a world without Violet?

If only she could have her drab, dull, frustrating London life back again.

A furious banging rattled the front door. A familiar voice rang out, raised in a very unfamiliar way.

Father!

CHAPTER 27

JACK

Donlon

The moon was just peeping above the horizon by the time Jack reached the woodland that sat like a dense, dark belt behind Time Palace's walls. Once upon a time, when the Montagu family were newly powerful, the woods had been cleared, far beyond the walls. Over many peaceful years nature had taken its course and the woods had regrown to almost touch the back wall of the Palace. After years of calm, Time Palace would pay for its laxness over security.

He reached the woods and paused, one foot raised like a listening deer. They were already here and they were too loud.

He cursed under his breath. They were meant to keep hidden in the woods, not proclaim their presence far and wide. He had to quieten them. How many of them were there? He'd known they would be people from all walks of life – radical political groups against the established system of Names, activists protesting the time-snatching, damaged souls who had been snatched, or whose loved ones had been. People hated the snatching and had come to fear their once-beloved time queen – the Green Witch. Hammer and Malaikah would have had no problem getting support.

Still, they had only had one full day to gather. Jack didn't expect more than fifty people at such short notice. Enough to overpower the guards outside the Palace so that Jack could get inside and find Ava. Then they would be free to attack the Observatory where the time snatchers were guarded. They didn't care about Ava, of course – it was the promise of destroying the hated time snatchers that had brought them here.

They couldn't be far away, judging by the din coming from near the outer wall of the Palace. He ducked through the trees and picked his way over roots and brambles, glancing up until he caught sight of Hammer. The smith towered above the crowd. How many were there? It was hard to tell in the forest night. Bodies blocked the gaps between the trees, making a solid dark mass. He could see the sharp angles of weapons jutting above heads and tall ladders reaching into the trees. They'd come well prepared, it seemed.

He stepped around a vast oak trunk into the clearing, and stopped dead. People stretched as far as his eye could see. He couldn't judge how many were here. The air was taut and hummed with anger.

Hammer turned his head and saw Jack. He raised one hand and the noise was extinguished like a suddenly stilled wind. Heads craned towards the big smith, anxious not to miss his words. Jack marvelled at the power Hammer had – more natural authority in one finger than most kings. It had nothing to do with size or status. It was a power that came from within.

Hammer hoisted the huge clawed hammer he had brought as his weapon high in the air. His voice was low but it carried to the edge of the crowd. 'Thanksgive for answering our summons. We have come together for a common purpose – to end the time-snatching.' A roar rumbled in the crowd and Hammer raised a hand for silence. 'We have the advantage of surprise and we must keep that. Silence is the only way we can destroy the time snatchers.'

And just like that, Hammer quelled the vast crowd again. They rustled and murmured, but not much louder than the dense forest around them.

Hammer went on. 'But our aim is twofold. One is to break into the Observatory, where the time snatchers are kept. The other is to free the kidnapped girl – my apprentice here is honour-bound to free her.' He held out an arm towards Jack and every head swivelled towards him.

Jack smelt the hostility like a brewing storm. His gift reached out without him wanting it to and he saw the pain manifest in the stories around him.

A younger brother who went mad after being snatched and hung himself. A mother of five who was snatched and was still gone, little ones crying for her each day. A father who returned after months and brutalised his own family. An adored sister, once the life and heart of the family, who now sat each day, rocking and staring into the corner.

Stories upon stories, meshing into a collective silent anguish. He pulled himself back with an effort.

'We don't care about the girl. Why's she so special, anyway?'

A man with a shaved head and a knife tattooed across his scalp regarded Jack with the flat eyes of the long-snatched. He held a real knife loosely in one hand but the laconic stance didn't fool Jack. This one was a street fighter, fast and ruthless. Jack chose his words carefully.

'She ain't any more special than you or your kin. And no less,' said Jack softly. 'She is as my sister. And I do as you would for yours.'

Something stirred in the flat eyes, like the flash of a carp in a dark pond, but then it was gone. The man sneered. 'My kin are no more to me. They don't need a torn soul in their midst. So your kin are dead to me, too.' He looked around, mouth hard. 'We're here to destroy the things that destroyed us. That's it.' A rumble of assent.

'Allies, I know you all suffer.' Hammer's voice unfurled amongst the rumbling. 'You want vengeance and you will have it. The time snatchers will be destroyed. But the girl is important. We need her alive.'

'Why? Who says?' said a voice from the crowd.

'Malaikah asks it. And I follow his words.'

The rumble dropped. If Malaikah decreed it, that was enough for most Donloners if they weren't too far gone. Malaikah was so far beyond the everyday world that it wasn't possible to side against him. It was like shouting against the wind, or resenting the sun for rising.

A girl called out, 'So where is Malaikah when we need him?'

Good question. Jack had expected Malaikah to be here with Hammer. Hammer raised his chin and his eyes were stern. 'Malaikah is coming. There is trouble that draws him away.'

The girl scowled, but was silent.

Hammer continued. 'I will answer for the girl and the Lady. It is your job to destroy the devices. Listen now, in silence. This is the plan.'

He held up one hand and waited for the murmurs to drop. When he had every eye on him he went on.

'We attack at dawn. We put the ladders against that wall. The first people up the ladder are the sharpshooters. They will scale the walls and shoot the guards patrolling the back of the Palace. They will do this quickly and in silence. We use the best markspeople for this job. Understood?'

A rumble of assent. Hammer went on. 'Once the sharp-shooters are over and the guards are taken, the rest of us storm the wall. I will lead this charge. We get over as quickly as we can, in an orderly fashion. We are an army at this moment and we will act with discipline. Understood?'

He waited for the murmur of agreement before continuing. 'Once we are over, we rush the Observatory. That is where the time snatchers will be. If there are any more guards, we take them out quickly. The Observatory has thick wooden doors with metal studs, so people with hammers and heavy weapons – focus on smashing that open. The most important thing, after surprise, is speed.

The Lady will call for help as soon as she hears the attack. We have to act quickly to get inside before they arrive.'

Hammer looked across the crowd waiting to attack. 'Surprise, speed, discipline. These are the three words that matter most. This is your day, Donlon. This is your time to take back what you have lost.'

He held up a warning hand to stop the rumble of excitement before it became a roar. 'Those with weapons and shooting skill, hands up. In *silence*.'

A rustle of hands and crossbows were raised. Hammer looked at the man with the knife. 'You have experience, I think.' Hammer pointed to four more – a woman, a girl not much older than Jack and two men who already had bows at the ready. 'Come with me.'

They walked over to stand beside Hammer. 'Those with ladders, raise them against the wall,' said Hammer.

The crowd surged and he held up a hand, hissing, '*Quietly!*'

The crowd parted to let those carrying the spindly ladders through. One by one, they rested them against the wall until there were ten ladders tilted in readiness. Hammer went to each one and tested its stability, adjusting here and there. 'Good. Sharpshooters, come forward.'

Jack moved forward as the others did, his heart thudding fast now. Hammer crouched down to address the shooters at their level. 'Three armed guards patrol beyond this wall. Further down, there are two guards stationed in front of the Observatory door and also at the back and front of the Palace.' Hammer pointed to the girl and the woman. 'You two go first and take the guards patrolling nearest the wall.

The ones closest to us. You two take the Observatory guards.' Here Hammer pointed to the man with the knife and a young man next to him. 'And the others will take care of the guards on the Palace. Is that clear?'

They all nodded in silence. 'Good. This will all happen inside one minute. Not a second longer.'

More nods, sombre this time. The weight of their task was sinking in.

Hammer grunted. 'Good. You two, take the ladders there, nearest the Observatory. You two, take the other end. The others take the middle. Go to your positions.'

They moved towards their ladders. The crowd watched them in tense silence. Jack wiped his damp palms on his trousers and waited for Hammer's word. Each second now seemed to last a century. But the light between the trees now was grey, not black. Dawn was here.

'When I say "go" the sharpshooters scale the ladder and take out their targets,' said Hammer. 'When I say "take the wall" the rest of the crowd climb the ladders and get over the wall as quickly and as cleanly as you can. Your target is the Observatory. Be ready.'

There was a long pause in which it felt as though the whole world held its breath.

Hammer only needed to whisper his next command. '*Go!*'

They were up the ladder before the word had died on the air.

CHAPTER 28
AVA

Donlon

'I must see the Lady. No, she is not expecting me! I would say I am most unexpected, but there is no time to delay.'

Father's voice was different. Gone was the deference of an artisan knowing his rung on the social ladder and in its place was something more resonant. Authoritative.

'Yes, she knows who I am. I was her Head Time Keeper, girl! Quickly, now.'

Esmeralda was on her feet and opening the door as Father's footsteps rang down the wooden hallway. She gestured frantically, glancing at the door that Rupert had disappeared behind.

'Bill! In here!' Her voice was a hiss. She reached out and grabbed him unceremoniously by the sleeve and pulled him inside. 'Quietly!' She shut the door carefully behind him.

'Father!' Ava struggled to sit up on the sofa.

At the sight of Ava, Father practically pushed the Lady aside. The man who rushed over to her was not the self-contained, courteous Father she knew. She almost shrank back as he gripped her arms above the elbows, bloodshot eyes searching hers.

'Are you hurt, Ava?' His eyes narrowed into a frown. He turned his head to snap, 'What happened here, Lady?'

His harsh tone belied the respectful mode of address. It was a strangely formal way for her father to speak to her mother. She had not given much thought to how her parents' reunion would look, but this was a very distant greeting indeed.

He bent down to peer into Ava's face. 'Ava, my dear, can you walk? I must take you from here immediately. It's not safe.'

'Bill, what are you doing here?' Esmeralda's voice was furious. 'Why is Ava here when you flouted all our agreements for a respectable transfer?'

Father whirled to glare at her. 'Agreements? As if you care one jot about agreements! What have you become since I left here? The very reason I took her to London was to remove her from the dangers of this place, which you've multiplied a thousandfold with your snatching. I barely need to remind you what happened here thirteen years ago.' He looked back at Ava. 'My dear, you look deranged. Has something happened?'

Ava swallowed. Esmeralda's glance flicked towards the rug. There was a burn mark and a twisted curl of metal from the broken snatcher lying next to it.

Father's eyes followed theirs. He let go of Ava and in two strides was next to the scar on the rug. He crouched and picked up the metal. He turned it over in his hands two times, breathed out one long breath, and stood slowly.

'Sunstone. The metal we used for the time catchers. I have only recently seen it in one other application, in time snatchers.' He raised his head to fix a cold gaze on Esmeralda. 'Which leads me to ask – what is *this* doing *here*?'

There was a long, humming silence. Ava couldn't bear it.

'It's from a time snatcher, Father. It broke when she tested it on me.'

'You used a time snatcher on Ava?' The icy fury in Father's voice was awful.

'Be calm, Bill. She is unharmed, as I knew she would be. Ava has immunity to snatching! Do you not see the enormity of that?'

But hadn't her mother told Ava not to tell her father about her immunity to snatching, just moments before? Why was she telling him herself?

'She is not unharmed,' snapped Father. 'You know better than I the damage it does to the soul. Look at her eyes!'

'It is merely shock, Bill. She didn't go to the Void and she will recover fully. But she needs to stay here and rest for a while.'

'You forfeited your right over Ava years ago, and you have just proven your unfitness as a mother again. Your meddling with time sent my dearest friend to a horrible death and here you are, doing it again with your own daughter. And if that was not enough, Lady, your time trade has taken Violet.' Father paused for breath, the colour high in his cheeks. 'You must bring her back without further delay.'

He slipped the coil of metal into his waistcoat pocket and

shrugged off his coat. He came round past Ava and draped it over her shoulders.

'Wear this, my dear – you are shivering. Now take my arm. You must lean all your weight on me. We just need to get down the stairs, where a vehicle is waiting.' He turned back to Esmeralda, reaching into his pocket.

'Violet Wisetree?' Esmeralda's voice was sharp. 'How?'

Father drew something out of his pocket. It wasn't until he reached to hand it to Esmeralda that Ava realised it was a time snatcher. 'Where did you get that?' she said, appalled.

Father ignored her, his eyes on Esmeralda. 'Violet was snatched with this. I have no experience with this contraption and Violet walked in as I was trying to work out its functions.' He furrowed his face in anguish.

'Wait. You snatched Violet?' said Ava in disbelief. She pressed a hand to her head. 'Oh!' With a sudden flash of clarity she saw the cloaked figure again at the Observatory, holding the device.

Father seemed to read her thoughts. 'Yes, the attacker dropped the snatcher when he turned to run. I took it and brought it home.' His voice dropped in anguish. 'If Violet is badly torn, I will never forgive myself.'

'Give me that.' Her mother's voice was angry. She took the snatcher from Father's outstretched hand and turned away from them, raising the snatcher to her chest.

She turned back. 'It is done. Violet will return, along with the other one taken by this snatcher. There were two active snatchings on this, which I hadn't thought possible. Something else to address with –'

She checked herself. Glancing at Father, she put the

device in a pocket at the side of her dress. It took Ava a moment to realise that the other snatching was Phoebe. She was not vindictive enough to be sorry that her school nemesis would be returned from that place.

Esmeralda went to the door and turned the key in the lock. She turned back to face them.

'I cannot allow Ava to go now. I need her here.' She raised a chin defiantly. 'After all, Bill, she is my blood.'

Yes, but it took two to produce a child. Why didn't Father make the obvious retort? Instead, he took a deep breath and tightened his arm around Ava's shoulders.

'She means more to me than the world. You have no moral claim over Ava or anybody, Lady. Your time-snatching has caused misery in both cities. I did well to leave and take Ava away from you. She comes home with me.'

Lady. There it was again. There was a note chiming wrong in all this.

'She is my blood, Bill,' said Esmeralda again. 'She is becoming a woman and this is my time with her. I cannot expect you to understand.'

Father's voice was tight. 'I understand that you are a killer. That a human life means less to you than a whim. That you discarded your own child years ago. That you sow misery among multitudes so you can have more time, for the Lord only knows what. What more should I understand, Lady?'

Her mother closed her eyes for a long moment. 'I did not discard my child. I sent her away for her own safety.'

'Why should I believe more of your lies, Esmeralda?'

Esmeralda looked straight at Father. 'You of all people

should understand that sometimes lies are the only choice. Has it ever occurred to you that what you perceive may be false?'

Silence. Father's chest heaved so hard that Ava swayed as he clutched her to him. The only answer to Esmeralda's questions was the sound of a door opening and loud footsteps coming in their direction in the hall.

Her mother's head snapped around as the doorknob rattled. 'Go away! What are you doing?' she hissed.

'Open the door, Esmeralda. Face it. Your cover is blown.'

Father's arm had dropped woodenly from Ava's shoulders at the sound of the voice outside. A strange noise escaped him. Ava had never seen that chalky green shade on human skin before.

The door rattled even more violently and Esmeralda shouted, 'Go away, Rupert! I have not sent for you.'

Father stumbled backwards and now it was Ava's turn to grab his arm in support.

'Rupert?' Father's voice was a croak.

So Mr John Smith/Rupert was also part of her father's mysterious past. Somehow it was no surprise.

Rupert spoke through the door. 'This must come as a shock, Bill.' Pity chilled his voice. 'But the surprise is not all yours. I see we have a cosy family gathering here. Surely I should have been invited, as the official head of the family?'

His words were cryptic, but Ava's main concern was getting Father settled on the sofa. His breathing had become laboured and his arm under hers trembled. He looked on the verge of apoplexy. Suddenly he struggled upright and shouted at the door.

'You were dead! The Lady told me your atoms had been scattered across time.'

Mr Smith – Rupert – had been the dear friend Father had talked about?

'We needed you out of the way, old chap.' Rupert's voice behind the door was a drawl. 'It was for your own good, really. And you got to take our child, which worked well for all concerned, I think.' The bored amusement in his voice chilled her to the bone. Was this just fun to him?

But – what had he said? Why was she their child, when –

Oh. No. Realisations came slamming one after the other, like carriages behind a train braking to a sudden halt, just behind her ribs.

It simply wasn't possible.

But as she thought of that supercilious face with its thick dark hair, deep blue eyes and strong jaw, she knew it was the truth. The one remaining certainty in her life had just crumbled into nothing.

Rupert was not her uncle. He had lied to her face, back there in Burlington Arcade.

He was her father.

That was why Esmeralda had told her not to tell her father. She had meant Rupert. Had she forgotten one of her own lies for a moment?

Esmeralda turned and unlocked the door. 'You might as well come in now,' she said calmly.

Rupert walked in and Father looked up at him, his face tight with pain. 'You are a monster,' he said. He looked at Esmeralda. 'Both of you are monsters. You have toyed with our lives as though they are pieces on a checker board.' His voice rose. 'I will tell everyone what you really are, Rupert. I will destroy you!'

Rupert smiled. 'Bill, old man, you're being melodramatic. However will you do such a thing?'

'I'm still well connected in London, if not here. People respect me.' Father looked at Rupert with an expression that Ava could not decipher.

Something shifted in Rupert's face. The supercilious sneer dropped and Rupert cleared his throat. 'Bill, don't be difficult. I know this must all come as a shock.'

Rupert's face was now open and sincere, his brow furrowed earnestly. He held out both hands to Father. It was an extraordinary transformation, one worthy of the Hams.

'Look, perhaps we can come to an understanding. There's been a lot of water under the bridge. Let's not have harsh words after all this time.' He lowered his voice and stepped closer to Father. 'It was the only way I could think of to let you go free, without the pain of knowing the truth. It was better that you believed me dead. I'm not a good man like you, Bill.'

Father was silent, his face still and expressionless. He sat down suddenly on the sofa. Rupert came another step closer and smiled sadly. 'It's much too late but I now understand the pain I've caused. We're already taking steps to stop it, Esmeralda and I. The time snatchers have all been deactivated.'

'The ones I banished from Time Palace? Is this true, Rupert?' Her mother's voice was sharp.

Rupert's smile didn't falter. 'Yes. Not one of the snatchers that were here are still in operation. I swear it on my life.'

Ava watched all this as if there was a pane of glass between her and the rest of the room. She could not connect the words she was hearing with herself in any way. They were meaningless sounds, like a word repeated over and over until it loses all sense. She watched numbly as Rupert dropped to one knee so that he could look Father levelly in the eye.

But he was not her father. Never had been her father.

Rupert had taken Father's hand in both of his. 'Bill, I'm so sorry for the way things have happened. But it means you have a daughter. She will always be your daughter, really. And we are starting a new era. The bad old days are gone. I would like it if we could be part of the new world together. Friends again. What do you say?'

Father took a deep breath and opened his mouth as if to say something but, before he could, Rupert stood in one smooth movement. He turned a dazzling smile on Ava, even as he grabbed her by one arm and yanked her almost off her feet. Esmeralda cried out and Father leapt to his feet. Ava gasped and nearly fell as Rupert dragged her to the doorway. A second later he was in the corridor, one arm around Ava's neck, the other fumbling in his pocket.

It had all happened with dizzying speed.

The scene buzzed with unnatural clarity. Ava squirmed and kicked but Rupert held her easily with one arm. Rupert was a head taller than Father and twice as broad, but Father didn't hesitate. He lunged towards Rupert, and the look on his face was raw rage.

'No, Father!' shouted Ava.

It was too late. Rupert raised his hand and pointed a

time snatcher at Father. Father was not even halfway across the floor before the fury on his face changed to fear. Ava screamed as Father broke up into thousands of little pieces, his expression sliding into terror as he left this world and entered the Void.

CHAPTER 29
JACK

Donlon

The girl reached the top first; the woman a second behind. They took aim and shot almost too quickly to see, with two muffled thuds in the silence before the others had even taken aim. They were over in the next second and before Jack knew what he was doing, he was up the ladder behind them and scanning the scene.

Two bodies near the wall. Two stocky guards flanking the Observatory door. He glanced at the sharpshooter nearby, aiming straight at the stocky guard on the far side of the door. He couldn't miss. Jack held his breath as he fixed his eyes on the guard. The guard had a little girl. A dark-haired, solemn child of three. He was due time off after today. He'd been on duty all fortnight and had whittled her a wooden cat. He was thinking about the little girl's grave brown eyes sparking with delight when she saw the cat.

Gods, no. Jack couldn't afford to see now. But he was losing control over his gift. And then an arrow flew and thudded home. The guard dropped where he stood.

The little girl would never see her wooden cat.

Jack clung to the ladder in horror as more arrows flew. He had never been part of a planned battle. He'd knocked boys out in fights, in anger, but never been part of an army that aimed and picked off humans like tin cans on a post.

But there was no time to think. The girl and the woman were on the ground examining their work. Two guards, two arrows in the neck. These were skilled markswomen. Other targets lay sprawled in the distance near the Palace. They all scanned the grounds, weapons poised, ready for more guards. None just yet.

The Observatory sat high and silent above them; the Palace just below it. In between was an expanse of grass dotted with trees and at the bottom of the hill on the far side of the Palace, a river rushed through waterwheels.

'Take the wall!'

At Hammer's hissed cry, Jack clambered over the top and dropped to the ground. A rumble of eager feet followed behind. Hammer landed beside Jack, then more and more of their number appeared until the ground was thick with them. Hammer stood with one finger to his lips, beckoning them, faster and faster. The crowd poured over, reminding Jack of a swarm of insects. Hammer picked out a few individuals, gesturing them over to him.

'You five, bring up the rear. Make sure everyone is over. Keep them tight.'

He turned, held his huge hammer aloft and let out a yell, shocking after the whispers. 'With me, Donlon!'

He galloped down the hill and, with a roar, the crowd unleashed behind him.

Jack ran, heart pounding with fear and excitement. Fear that he wouldn't get to Ava in time; fear that his great plan would fail. Excitement at the energy, the heat of the crowd.

He veered to the right. His destination wasn't the Observatory – he had to get to Ava in the Palace. He hoped to the gods she would be there.

Nobody noticed him breaking away, or they didn't care. They had something bigger in their sights. Some were already at the entrance to the Observatory, slamming into the wooden doors with judders that shook the ground. They would be inside in seconds. There was no more time.

Jack whirled and ran for the Palace.

Then there was a swoop of great wings above and Malaikah was soaring alongside him. At last!

His words flapped like strange flags in Jack's ear. 'Windspeed to Ava, Jackbrave. Clingtight to her and I will fallback to swoophigh you both. But first, this crowd I must changemake.' He swept high and turned, soaring over to where the crowd was ready to break.

No time to wonder at Malaikah's always strange words. Changemake? For what? Did Malaikah not want the snatchers destroyed – the terror ended?

Jack pushed everything except Ava out of his head. He felt for his knife, and ran.

CHAPTER 30

Donlon

Ava's screams tore her throat. 'Father! No, bring him back!' She struggled and kicked and this time her strength was huge. Her nails, teeth and heels all gouged deep into Rupert's flesh.

Rupert released her suddenly and she stumbled before regaining her balance and whirling to face him. Rupert's time snatcher was a different one, bigger, with a rigid funnel that sat flat and faced upright – but even the sight of that didn't cut through the red mist in front of her eyes. The vicious slap to the side of her head did, though, and, as she reeled, one hand to her flaming cheek, Rupert caught her arm, and yanked her close again. His arm pressed hard around her throat, crushing her windpipe. She stopped struggling.

Her mother had shouted 'Rupert!' as the slap connected and now she stood facing them, another time snatcher in her hand, her face alert.

'I regret that ungentlemanly response, Esmeralda,' said Rupert, his breathing ragged. 'But she was hysterical. I had to calm her.'

Ava's blood thrummed in her ears.

Rupert gave a snort behind her. 'So you banned all time snatchers in the palace, but still keep one for personal use? Different standards for the Time Lady, I see.' His voice was scornful. 'Is that one for father or daughter?'

Ava's eyes met her mother's in a brief spasm of understanding. He didn't know that Ava was immune.

Esmeralda looked back at Rupert. 'As you well know, your time print is too close to Ava's, so I can't snatch you without snatching her. It would be a shame to lose her, having just met her again.'

Her eyes met Ava's again. Ava understood. Her mother didn't want Rupert to know Ava's capabilities. And she definitely didn't want him to know that she couldn't properly snatch him while he was holding Ava, because Ava would break the time snatcher.

At that moment, Ava knew what she had to do. She had to get away from Rupert, long enough for her mother to snatch him. As if reading her mind, he tightened his grip.

Esmeralda smiled mirthlessly. 'And I see that your vow that you had destroyed all the time snatchers was only technically correct. You've simply created a new one to replace them.'

'New and much improved. The old ones are weaklings compared to the capabilities of this version,' said Rupert. He held it easily out of Ava's reach but she could just see its squat, toad-like appearance if she looked sideways. It had a brutal, functional look about it, unlike the delicate craftsmanship of the first model. 'And yes, I have done as you demanded, before you ask. I reset the old ones.'

'I can't see why you need our daughter.' Her mother's voice was sharp. 'This is the first time you've ever shown any desire to have anything to do with her.'

'Esmeralda, you really think I'm so foolish? This girl will have undreamed-of powers over time! I have ambitions of my own and she will be a great ally.'

'You overestimate the time triggers I've set. She'll have minor skills, nothing more.'

'I don't care!' he said with a snarl of rage. 'You and Bill have played me for a fool all these years, hiding Ava from me. Years of mocking me behind my back, sneaking visits to London and ridiculous charades at the Royal Observatory. If I did not have my own connections in Greenwich I would still be none the wiser. No, you *will* not have what you want!'

He reminded Ava of a petulant child whose will had been thwarted. Ava felt a chill in her belly as she realised what Rupert's anger was really about. It wasn't about Ava's skills helping Rupert in his time trade – as if she ever would. This was about a hurt ego and revenge – pure and simple. There was no reasoning with that and Ava saw the realisation in her mother's eyes. She also saw the flicker of fear, gone as quickly as it appeared.

Fear? Of what? She had made it clear she didn't have normal maternal feelings towards Ava. Her fear must be that she would lose her precious experiment.

Or was her mother as much of a monster as Ava's genetic father? Was all this no more than a smokescreen for her own cold ambition? Perhaps she also wanted Ava so she could keep her away from the time snatchers, which Ava could destroy. Perhaps she wanted what Rupert wanted; maybe even more than he did. How could Ava believe what either of them said? It was like watching two twisted gods warring on Mount Olympus, far beyond human comprehension.

As if on cue, thunder rumbled through the air. Ava glanced out the high windows, but the skies were clear and pricked by stars – not a storm cloud to be seen. The sound came again, moving the ground beneath her. This was more than a storm. Something was shaking the very earth.

'What's that?' her mother said, sharply.

She ran past Rupert, towards the front door. Rupert let go of Ava's neck and followed, pulling Ava beside him by her arm so she had to run to keep up. Ava's mother ran outside, turning towards the thundering sound on the hill. She stopped and cried out. 'They're attacking!'

Rupert and Ava were beside her in a second. Rupert clutched Ava's arm at the sight of the huge dark shape of a crowd, some of them pouring down the hill, others headed towards the Observatory. The noise was gut-chilling – a roar of anger and also a kind of violent joy. They brandished weapons of all kinds – spears, clubs, hammers, even pitchforks.

'The tunnel! Quickly, Rupert!' She turned and ran back inside.

'What the hell are you doing?' shouted Rupert. 'They will kill us all.'

'They think the snatchers are there!' she shouted as she ran. 'They will destroy my catchers instead. You have to tell them, come on!'

'What do I care about your damned catchers?' yelled Rupert.

Ava's mother whirled in the corridor, her hand on a low door. 'You will care when I tell them the truth about snatching! Tell them that you've run scared, run to protect your precious snatchers which you've hidden at the Foundling Home!' She opened the door and crouched down to climb through it. 'Don't follow then. I'll make sure they come after you next!'

And with that, she disappeared into the mouth of the hidden tunnel.

Rupert cursed, took another look at the crowd outside the entrance, dragging Ava behind him, and cursed again. Ava's skin prickled in an ancient fear. They were getting too close. Ava jumped as a small figure rounded the corner and barrelled towards them, coming to a halt at the sight of Rupert and the time snatcher still in his hand.

Jack! His eyes were wild and bright in his pinched face. He didn't take them off Rupert. 'Ava! We have to get away! The crowd is out of control.'

'You!' said Rupert. 'Back for more, rat?'

'Ava's in danger. We have to leave!' Jack was unblinking with fear.

'Not as much danger as you, snipe. She's with me.'

'You ain't taking her.' Jack's hand went to his pocket and drew out a glinting blade. Had he lost his mind? Jack's eyes reflected the cold gleam of the blade. He was going to use it.

'No, Jack! It's not worth it. Don't!'

Jack hurled himself towards Rupert and a deep whirring sound filled the air. Jack's eyes widened, panic flooding his features. Despair darkened his face. Ava reached towards him, her own soul twisting as he dropped the knife and reached forward. They touched hands for a split second, his eyes pleading with her to do something – but what could she do?

And then Jack faded into shattered pieces in front of her and the pain that filled her was too much to bear.

Rupert gave a snarl of satisfaction. 'That guttersnipe is a fool.'

He yanked Ava back down the hallway towards the door Ava's mother had disappeared down. Ava was numb with shock. Not Jack! She remembered his words, 'wouldn't wish that place on yer worst enemy', and felt a sickening thud as she realised he was back there, in his personal, grey, drifting hell.

CHAPTER 31

JACK

Donlon

As Jack plummeted into nothingness, a nightmare reached for him. A bright, screaming nightmare, as if terror tried to snag him with it to keep him in this world.

But this was no nightmare. This was a memory.

Jack is a child, with other children. They are at the Foundling Home. One of them is Ava. Another is a curly-headed boy.
The scariness happens and then Jack does the terrible thing.
The screaming.
And all the people disappear.

The memory was gone almost as soon as it came, and then he saw something else. Not a memory. A face, looking out at him from the Void. Someone who was there before him.

Someone who loves them, who hurts.

It's Ava's father and he is in so much pain.

He fades.

And then Jack is beyond memory, or sight, or recognition, in the Void.

CHAPTER 32

AVA

Donlon

Esmeralda's voice bounced back along the tunnel as she shouted for guards. A tilting sense of unreality gripped Ava. The shock of losing Jack cut through each moment. Everything else was distant, meaningless. It was as though Ava was watching Rupert drag someone else along, feet pounding the earth, bent forward in the low tunnel.

Her mother's voice cut off abruptly.

'She's inside,' panted Rupert, tightening his grip on Ava's arm. 'She's crazy if she thinks she can control that crowd.'

But still he ran faster, as though afraid he was wrong. Afraid that he knew Ava's mother would turn the mob against him.

It was a long, stumbling way under the earth from the Palace to the Observatory. Ava pushed away the thought of what this tunnel may have been used for in its time. That both her blood parents trod it like a well-known path.

They could hear the crowd above them, shaking the earth over their heads. There was a deep, dull thudding.

'They're breaking the door,' grunted Rupert. 'Got to get there before they do.'

A huge, splintering crash, followed by a roar. Ava realised they were right below the Observatory now. The crowd must have breached the great wooden door and begun surging into the stone building. She could feel it quiver under the onslaught, trembling through the earth. Feet hammered down the halls and the air tore with shouts, crashing glass, splintering doors. Every moment it seemed that the earth above their heads would collapse under the weight and fury of the crowd.

They reached the end of the tunnel. A metal ladder clung to the wall, leading to a trapdoor above their head. Rupert pushed Ava up the ladder ahead of him – no chivalrous gentleman, her blood father. She had to cling awkwardly, pressed to the rungs as he reached up behind and above her to shove at the trapdoor. It swung open with a creak.

He pushed her again, roughly. 'Go! Quietly,' he hissed.

She hesitated. The crashing sounds had died and a strange silence had descended. It was unnerving. What awaited her up there? Rupert shoved her again, rougher. She had no choice but to find out.

She pulled herself up the rungs – luckily, her dress was shorter than the usual London style and her legs moved freely enough. Her heart thudded as she poked her head above the opening. The trapdoor opened into a vast, soaring space, filled as far as she could see with people. If Rupert hadn't been right behind her, she would have ducked straight back down. The crowd was just there, mere feet in front of her. Thank the Lord it was the back of the crowd – the trapdoor was against the back wall and the crowd were standing still now, silent, watching something at the front. Whatever it was held them rapt, so they didn't notice Ava and Rupert crawling out like rats from a drainpipe.

Ava stood up and saw what held the crowd in place. It was her mother.

Esmeralda stood atop a raised platform at the very end of the room. It was like a sacrificial altar, with steps leading up to it. On it was a magnificent, soaring structure. A swelling brass belly swept up into a long neck, which in turn flared into a flower mouth, raking the sky like a hungry baby bird. The ceiling above it rose into a glass dome, open to the sky, and the light of a full moon poured down in shafts, bathing the machine in a silvery halo.

Malaikah stood below her mother, a few steps down, a sword raised above his head.

This was the sight that had stilled the crowd, but the moment had already passed. The rumble was rising again and the crowd was starting to shift.

Ava's mother stood with her back to the beautiful structure, arms raised as if blessing or pleading, and she lowered them over the crowd.

The light fell differently in the room. A shimmering veil, almost invisible, like the skin of a bubble that just catches the light here and there, floated down over the people in front of Esmeralda. It was as if they shifted into another world, right there in the same room.

Ava watched in awe as they transformed into skittering, light versions of themselves. Not solid, not transparent, but not quite there either. No longer still, they flashed and jittered so fast they looked like streams of movement, limbs blurred; here one microsecond, there the next. It was impossible to focus on them, as though her eyes were built for another, slower realm.

'Damn her! She's used all the catcher time stores,' said Rupert.

Ava looked at him, not understanding. He gestured angrily at the crowd.

'This is a time bubble. A *massive* time bubble. It takes vast energy to put an entire crowd into something this big.'

With a flash, Ava realised she was outside a time bubble looking in, whereas in Burlington Arcade that day she had been in a time bubble looking out. The rest of the world had stopped for her then, but this time she was part of that frozen world. Inside the bubble, everyone had sped up beyond measure in the extra time her mother had bestowed.

Ava looked back at her mother. That lovely thing behind her must be a time catcher. The Lady had fallen back against the belly of the structure, as if supported by invisible arms. Ava had the strangest sense that they were one and the same being.

'How long have we got?' Rupert's voice was rough. Ava looked at him. He was sweating, his skin pale. 'Esmeralda! Answer me.'

'The Lady is timedrained,' called Malaikah. 'She must timefill in peace.'

'She should've thought of that before, shouldn't she?' snapped Rupert. 'This is not a moment to rest, in case you hadn't noticed.' He glanced around the room. 'This is not the whole crowd. The others are out there. When they've finished wrecking and pillaging like the scum they are, they'll be in here. She's used all the time stores for nothing!'

'She did it to save her Mother Catcher,' said Malaikah. 'To hold the crowd. Her timegift will calm them, like violence sates the ones outside. You will see.'

'I don't give a rat's arse about the Mother Catcher!' shouted Rupert. 'They can smash them all to pieces. They can rip her to pieces too – they hate her enough.'

'Then why are you here?' asked Malaikah. 'If you carenot for her or the catchers.'

'It's called survival,' snarled Rupert. 'To make sure the crowd take her before she can ruin me! I'll see her die before she blows my cover.'

The words hung, raw and shocking, in the air. A ruthless, vicious mind, laid out for all to see. Ava's blood father was ready to throw her mother to the wolves to save his reputation. A life together meant nothing.

'You carenot for your daughter, her mother, the tornsouls. Not even your Billman. You care only to save your paleskin. It covers a rottenheart.' Malaikah's words were a calm but harsh decree.

Rupert's grip tightened painfully on Ava's arm as Malaikah spoke, but his snort was dismissive.

'Your precious Time Lady is no better. She abandoned her daughter to save a machine.'

'Those are foolwords. Our timequeen knows what steers your greysoul. She ran, knowing her daughter waited ahead,' replied Malaikah.

'Enough of this nonsense talk!' shouted Rupert. A fleck of spit landed on Ava's cheek. 'We waste time, which we no longer have, as the Lady has just thrown it all to this filthy mob! It's wasted on this scum! My snatchers will be hardworked to make this up, damn her.'

Rupert spat the last words in fury. He yanked Ava with him and strode towards the platform where Malaikah stood, sword ready. Ava stumbled and collided with a man in the crowd. He made a grab for Rupert.

'Who you calling scum?' the man growled.

It took Ava a moment to realise that the crowd had changed. They were no longer flittering. They were right here with them – solid, steady, humming with anger. How long had they been back?

Rupert pulled free from the man's grip. Another man stepped in his path, blocking his way. A tall woman swung to the side, hemming Rupert and Ava in against the crowd. More people crowded around them both. Ava was on the inside, pressed tight against the crowd. She could smell their fury like a brewing storm. The acrid smell was her own fear.

'Filthy, are we?' A sharp elbow gouged Rupert's ribs. He grunted.

'Time wasted on us types, is it?' Another man pushed Rupert's shoulder so hard he spun around.

'Throw a woman to her death to save yeself, would ye?' The tall woman gave Rupert a shove. He grabbed at Ava for support.

The crowd were tight around Ava and Rupert. She could feel hot breath on her cheek. More hands than Rupert's gripped her now.

'I don't reckon you'll make it back to your snatchers, do you?' A man with long hair flicked Rupert's face with one finger, almost jokingly.

Tears filled Rupert's eyes. 'Please. I didn't mean, I was – please, let me go,' he begged.

'Why should we let you go, scum?'

Rupert gave Ava a sudden shove so she fell backwards into the crowd. The crowd shifted to regain its balance and in that moment Rupert lashed out wildly with both arms. He slammed the time snatcher into the side of the tall woman's head and she stumbled sideways with a groan.

Rupert whirled and ran. He pushed at arms grabbing at him, panting and sobbing. 'Get off! Don't touch me!'

The crowd enveloped him. He wasn't going to make it.

'Stop! Step back.' Ava's mother's voice rang out. She stood upright now, standing tall on the dais. Ava had regained her feet with the help of the crowd and she stared at her mother, along with everyone else. The tiny, vivid figure seemed suddenly huge before them.

'I said, step back!' she shouted.

Arms released Rupert. The crowd shifted away from him. He stood alone at the edge of the room, looking around wildly. Relief and disbelief fought on his face.

'The Lady is wise,' he panted. 'You do well to listen.' He gave an unbelieving, mocking laugh, then whirled to run.

Ava's mother raised her time snatcher and took careful aim at Rupert's fleeing back. Buzzing filled the room,

251

building to a high crescendo. Rupert turned too late, the snarl dissolving on his face even as it formed, and then he melted away into thin air in front of everyone.

His time snatcher fell to the ground. He had raised it too late.

'Don't touch it!' cried Ava's mother. 'Not yet. Malaikah, please.'

The crowd hesitated. Ava saw their hatred, their fear of the metal device lying so innocently on the ground. They wanted to smash it, grind it under their feet, destroy it as it had destroyed so many of them.

But their tiny hesitation was just long enough for Malaikah to swoop across their heads, drop to the ground and pick it up. He held it almost tenderly in both hands.

'This monster holds soulsloved,' he said gravely. The crowd watched, the atmosphere tense. 'The Lady will release them, before the monster is grindsmashed.'

He put the snatcher in one hand and reached across for Ava with the other. He held her close in his now-familiar way as he rose into the air, making those nearby duck instinctively. He landed just below Ava's mother on the dais. He put Ava down beside him and handed Esmeralda the snatcher, like an acolyte handing an offering to a priest.

She took it with one hand. With the other she pulled out a gold-coloured pendant that hung on a chain around her neck. It was strangely familiar and Ava struggled to remember where she'd seen it before. Her mother pressed the pendant to the snatcher for a long moment, eyes focused on something midair, until she gave a nod. She released the pendant and held the snatcher above her head.

'It is done. The snatched ones are back. Do as you will now.'

She hurled the snatcher down in front of the crowd. It had barely struck the ground with a dull clang before it disappeared under a surge of stamping feet.

Ava hardly registered their vicious, focused fury as her mother's words rang in her head. Which snatched ones? That was Rupert's snatcher, the one he had taken both Father and Jack with. Did she really mean . . .

Esmeralda met Ava's eyes, one hand clutching her pendant. She gave a small nod. The pendant swung on her chest and as she looked at it again, Ava had two realisations.

The first was so glorious it filled her with warm, bubbling joy. Before hurling the snatcher into the crowd, the Lady had reset it. She had used that strange yet familiar pendant around her neck to release Father and Jack from the grey zone. The crowd had splintered the snatcher into smithereens now, but it didn't matter. Jack's and Father's souls were back in their bodies, here in Donlon, safe.

The barbed loss tearing Ava inside out was gone, just like that. Relief so intense it was almost painful swamped her and had to be released in hot, fierce sobs.

She doubled over, hands on knees, and let the blurring tears fall. As her breath steadied, an image rose in her mind's eye. She saw the exquisite cake that Tony had served to her in his cafe by the Batter Sea. The second realisation was that the perfect little gold macaron on her plate had been a replica of the locket that hung around her mother's neck.

What did it mean? Before Ava could puzzle out the answer, Esmeralda took something from her pocket and threw it down like a sacrifice. Another dull clang and a surge of eager feet below, crushing the second time snatcher.

Her mother watched the crowd like a fisherman scanning storm clouds.

Hammer appeared in the entrance, cradling the body of a young man in his arms. He looked at Esmeralda and Malaikah and a glance passed between them like words. Hammer bowed his head and then turned to leave, all in silence.

The crowd tempo had changed. Even Ava could feel that. The vicious edge was gone. Was it because of the time bubble her mother had cast? Or was it to do with Malaikah's serene presence or Esmeralda snatching Rupert, or the crushed snatchers in shards on the floor beneath them?

Or was it all of those things together?

Whatever it was, there was a precious moment to breathe. And in that moment Ava searched her mother for clues to tell her what would happen next.

Whose side was she really on? Or was she beyond being on anyone's side?

CHAPTER 33

Donlon

Shouts of anger echoed from the Observatory entrance, jerking Ava back to the present.

'Where are the snatchers?' shouted a voice. 'That's what we're here for.'

The crowd in the Observatory shifted restlessly in front of them. Ava could glimpse bodies jostling at the doorway, flashes of weapons still being brandished and hard-edged faces. More people from outside were coming in.

Ava could feel her mother's tension beside her.

'I banned them all. They're not here,' called her mother.

'So where are they?' demanded a woman's voice. She stood tall at the back, shaven-headed with a tattooed nest of thorns on her bald head. She was wiry but exuded a power and solidity that Ava was not used to seeing in a woman. She looked nothing like Ava's mother, but they shared the same steady gaze and tough grace, as though they stood firmer on the earth than the women

Ava knew. As though they didn't care how the world saw them.

'We hold the Mother safe, Donlonsmalls. This room is peacekept,' said Malaikah.

'I have banished the snatchers, and their creator, as well,' said Esmeralda, quickly. 'I snatched him and destroyed the snatcher I used. He will not return. This crowd were witness to that.' She gestured across the heads of the people in front of her.

'Aye,' said the tall woman Rupert had struck on the head, unexpectedly. 'That pig threw the girl to save his neck, too. He's best gone.' A bruise was already blooming on her cheekbone. 'But you, Lady? You too were part of all this.'

'My part started with the Mother and ends with the Daughter,' said Esmeralda, reaching for Ava's hand and clasping it firmly. 'There was a time in between when I lost my way, because of the man I banished. He was the true time snatcher. Not the Green Witch, which he conjured up and spread stories about around Donlon. I was not blameless either, but I was mostly blind. Now that he's gone, Donlon can turn back from the darkness.'

The woman with the thorns on her skull snorted. 'Those are just pretty words. They ain't enough.'

'You're right. Words aren't enough. And so I will act.' Esmeralda laid her other hand on the belly of the Mother. 'The only things of value to me are my Mother Catcher – who I have shared time with for over two centuries – and my daughter,' she said. 'You can smash everything else, destroy it all. Even the other catchers, but know that you gain nothing by that. They feed only on unused time. Wasted minutes, unoccupied hours, empty days. They recycle old time and are harmless.'

She looked back at the woman. 'But I've had enough time. It hasn't served me well, in many ways, and now it is yours. The Mother Catcher will make time for Donloners but no longer for me.'

The crowd murmured. The moonlight from above bathed her mother's pale skin and there were lines that were not there before. She was showing signs of age. If she took no more time, there could surely be only one possible outcome, even in Donlon.

But the woman was shouting over the crowd. 'And the snatchers?'

'The ones I know about are dead. Deactivated. There are others I can't speak for.' Esmeralda raised Ava's hand in the air. 'But my daughter here will be my successor. She is the Time Daughter, and my greatest legacy to you, Donlon.'

'But,' blurted Ava in panic, but her mother squeezed Ava's hand as she brought it back down, as if to say, we're doing this together. Nevertheless, Ava felt very, very alone as all eyes swivelled to regard her. Did she have any say in this legacy?

The woman and Esmeralda locked eyes over the heads of the crowd.

'So those are my actions,' said Ava's mother. 'I give you my time and I give you my blood. I cannot offer more than that.'

And with that, she dropped Ava's hand and turned to the Catcher. Ava watched with the whole room as Esmeralda peered into a glass chamber just below the base of the flower stem. Inside, greyish flabby shapes jostled against each other, like half-dead jellyfish. She murmured almost under her breath, but she was speaking to Ava.

'These are the wasted time bubbles. Half dead, neither fully used nor alive. This machine takes the time left and recycles it, turning it into new time bubbles. Look closely, daughter. Only you and I are able to extract time from the Mother.'

Ava watched as Esmeralda stepped to the other side of the belly, where another glass chamber shone with a silvery translucence. It looked like soft light held in honeycomb sections, the cell walls so fine as to be almost invisible.

'New time bubbles, ready to be used. They can either be used straight away or stored for later.' Esmeralda pointed to the first brass cylinder. 'This one is for immediate use. A person steps inside and seals the chamber and time is released from the supply. This other chamber stores the time for future use – like drying it. Watch.'

Esmeralda opened the door of the second brass cylinder and reached inside, drawing out something almost invisible. It looked like a flat piece of air that caught the light differently to the air around it.

'A time leaf. This is pure gold time, the most precious time of all – unlike the grey time from the snatchers. That time is tainted with pain.' Her mother's voice was hard now. 'It must all be banished. That will be your role soon, when you are ready.'

She spoke as if there was no alternative to this legacy and Ava wavered between protest and pride. She was someone in her own right who no one else could be. Even if that role was a birthright, not earned.

Esmeralda turned back to the crowd and gestured to the woman.

'Join me here, if you will.'

The woman looked back at Esmeralda for a long second, before stepping forward. The crowd parted to let her through. She ascended the steps, not taking her eyes off Esmeralda for a moment. Ava's mother waited until the other woman stood, taller than her, on the platform. The woman's eyes darted round the room and she crackled with an energy that Ava could almost smell.

Esmeralda raised the time leaf. 'I give you this time from the Mother Catcher as a symbol of the time I pass now to Donlon.'

The woman reached up to take the time leaf, carefully. She looked at it, turning it over in her hands.

'The time is now yours,' said Ava's mother. 'Let me show you how to use it. Hold it between your hands, to warm it and let it feel you. When it's ready – and you will know – open your hands slowly, and step forward.'

The woman did as she said, and as she stepped forward a jolt ran across her skin, like the faintest ripple of light. Her eyes widened, her breath quickened and her face softened in a smile. Ava remembered the coursing energy of that time bubble in Burlington Arcade and watched enviously. The woman was not in a time bubble, like Ava had been, but had absorbed the time straight into her bloodstream.

Esmeralda turned back to the Mother Catcher and now drew out sheet after sheet of time. She handed it all to Ava, a shimmering bundle that rustled and shifted. It was hard to hold and Ava was afraid to be rough with it.

'This is all the time the Mother has ready now. Take this, Ava, and share it with Donlon.'

Ava hesitated, glancing at the crowd. Where to start?

'Go, Ava,' said her mother. 'This woman –' she looked at the woman and paused.

'Kett. My name is Kett.' The woman's voice was gruff but she offered her name like a gift. Ava's mother bowed her head in acknowledgement.

'Kett will help you.' Esmeralda raised her voice to the crowd. 'There will be more, tomorrow and every day. I give you this and ask for your peace in return.'

She looked at Kett and waited for her reply. The moment hung long in the air. Somehow, these two women and the words that passed between them stood for something much bigger.

Kett looked at Esmeralda and Ava before her voice rang out. 'We accept your offer.'

A collective sigh rustled through the room and excited chatter broke out. Something big had been released in those few sentences and Ava felt the relief slacken her own shoulders, even though she hadn't quite understood what was happening.

Kett met Ava's eyes and Ava struggled to keep her own gaze steady in return. This woman did nothing to hide her strength.

'Come with me, Ava.'

She turned and descended the steps and the crowd parted before her. Ava followed as Kett made her way to the back, to the entrance. Ava's heart thumped hard under her ribs as she walked past men and women stinking of battle sweat, weapons held easily as kindling in their hands, eyes trained on her as she passed. She dared not read their expressions.

'Give time to these people first, Ava.' Kett was gesturing to certain people to come forward. Ava couldn't see what it was that gave these people priority – they were a ragtag collection of women and men, some almost children – but she passed out the time leaves, one by one, as instructed.

'Hold onto it for now,' Kett told each person. 'I'll show you how to use it in a bit.' She watched as Ava passed out the last time leaves. 'Thank you,' she said, and Ava flushed with unexpected pleasure as they shared a smile.

Ava felt her whole body slump in relief as Kett and the crowd started to leave. She watched Malaikah go to her mother and lay a hand across hers.

'It is done, Lady,' he said. 'I will Motherstay now. You must take Ava humbling to the Palace. Without your timefill, you must not delay.'

Ava's mother nodded. Exhaustion dragged at her face, the porcelain skin like old parchment. 'Yes.'

She turned and her eyes found Ava. 'Let us go, Ava. There are people waiting for us at the Palace.' She looked back at Malaikah. 'Thanksgive, Malaikah.'

It wasn't until her mother had descended the steps that joy struck Ava with a welcome blow. Jack and Father would be at the Palace. Any twinge of doubt that she might feel differently about Father, now that she knew he wasn't her own blood, dissolved once and for all. She realised this fact of biology could not matter less. If anything, there was an extra sheen on the love she felt for him, knowing he had chosen to raise her himself.

Her heart skittered, bright as sunlight, as she took her mother's arm. Together they walked out, through the crowd.

CHAPTER 34
JACK

Donlon

Jack was back and shame clung as close as his damp trousers. The stink that came off them! And they stung where they touched his wounds. That wasn't water soaking them through. He lay slumped on the ground, wet and filthy in this grand soaring room, a stinking, worthless rat that had escaped from the sewers.

He'd been snatched.

The realisation was both a sickening thump and a jolt of relief. That was why he was filled with self-loathing. Snatching left this humiliation in its wake. This was the worst thing about coming back – the almost overwhelming shame rushing to fill the emptiness inside. Anything was better than this feeling of dark, squirming disgrace – and that was when people turned to other things, to deaden this feeling that wouldn't go away.

He closed his eyes and breathed deep, as if that could draw his soul back together. It was in tattered shreds within him. He had to find Ava, now, for his own sake.

It was as if Jack had needed to sink this low, to finally see how Ava was tied to him and always had been.

A groan. Jack's eyes flew open and saw Ava's father sinking slowly to his knees on the thick rug. He collapsed forward on his hands.

'Mr Bailey! Are you ill?'

Another groan. Ava's father was the colour of old chalk and his eyes were closed. He was breathing deeply as if trying to quell nausea. He spoke without moving. 'I – believe I am. Oh, dear Lord.'

Snatching hit people in different ways, Jack knew. Ava's father was a sensitive man, gentle of soul. Those people fared worst of all. He struggled to his knees and crawled across to him. Mortified at his own reek, he paused, but then put a hand on the cowed man's shoulders. Jack knew the power of human contact when your soul centre was spinning off kilter.

Another groan, but this time more like a sigh. Ava's father raised his head and his eyelids opened slowly, as though they were made of lead. Jack swallowed. His eyes . . . ah, the poor man had been hit hard. You could always tell by the eyes.

Jack had to get them both up off the floor. It weren't right to have him slumped here, so undignified.

'Mr Bailey, I'm going to help you up now. We'll sit you up against that sofa.' Jack sounded more confident than he felt. His own limbs felt like wet bread, limp and useless. He pushed himself upright on his knees and put his hands behind Mr Bailey's back. 'Ready? One, two, *three*.'

Ava's father was not a big man but it felt like lifting lead to Jack. It took all his effort and the man barely moved an inch. Jack let him slump gently to the ground again and breathed deeply, his arms trembling.

'Jack. It is Jack?' Mr Bailey looked up at the ceiling, brow furrowed. 'We are in Time Palace, are we not? It's coming back to me now . . . Oh, my Lord.'

Mr Bailey's face blanched a shade even paler and a look of agony crossed his face.

'Are you in pain? Where?' said Jack, looking for injury.

'No. At least, nothing physical. I have remembered . . .' His voice trailed off and he squeezed his eyes shut. Jack's own heart ached with Mr Bailey's pain. He was too close not to see that Ava's father had been badly hurt by someone he trusted. That was all Jack needed to know – he did not use his sight to see more.

'Ava!' Mr Bailey struggled upright. 'Where is she?' He tried to get to his feet. 'How long was I gone? She was in this room.' He got as far as his knees and swayed, unsteady as a newborn foal.

Jack had shot to his feet. It was all coming back to him in firework flashes. Rupert's sneering face as he held Ava in one hand, snatcher in the other. The panic squirming in his belly at the sight of that humming machine. The feel of the knife in Jack's hand. The last thing he remembered was forcing himself forward, in spite of his fear.

There was the knife. He stumbled towards it and his legs nearly gave way. Gods! He was useless, and he had to find Ava. Another thought hit him. The crowd! They had been just behind him as he bolted down the hill and he'd heard them shaking the very earth just before he was snatched. Gods, if only he knew how long he'd been gone! How much had happened?

Mr Bailey was on his feet now, clutching the back of the sofa, face pale but determined. 'Go, Jack!' He flapped a hand at Jack. 'Go! Find Ava.'

Jack had to go. There was nobody else to do it. The effort nearly killed him but he forced himself to crawl to the door and use it to pull himself to his feet, where he hung for a moment, waves of nausea sweeping over him. His legs were barely holding his weight. He bunched up all his determination and lurched down the hallway towards the front door.

He only just made it to the entrance. He gripped the door frame hard and looked out. It felt like a storm had broken. Some of the crowd was still there, milling around the entrance, while others were rushing off in all directions. What was going on? Dread clawed his heart. Something had happened. There was no sign of her or the Lady. Or Rupert, for that matter, but all he cared about was Ava. In the crowd's mind, she was now linked to the Lady. Their fate would have been the same.

Broken glass glinted in the moonlight and someone kicked a piece of wood out of the way. Every window Jack could see was smashed. The crowd walked with weapons lowered. Their rage was spent but there was still a hum of uncertainty amidst the new mood. Jack watched, every cell tingling with watchfulness and also fear of what he would see. He had to know what had happened in that building but he also knew that these last seconds of ignorance might be blessed – that whatever had happened, had happened. Jack was too late to change anything.

There was no sign of Malaikah, and where was Hammer? He had been going to carry the rear of the attack, watching the flanks with arrows ready. Jack's heart was thumping so hard that his neck pulsed with each beat. He scanned the hill behind and saw Hammer helping a wounded young man. Thank the gods. No time to wonder what had happened – it was enough to know Hammer was there.

His eyes flicked back on the Observatory and he drew in his breath sharply. They were there! The crowd was milling around them with suspicion but also acceptance. Jack groaned in relief. He had been bracing himself for the worst and to see Ava walking, unharmed, gave him a jolt of relief almost painful in its intensity.

But perhaps she was a prisoner of the crowd? He tensed again, every sense alert as he judged the situation, and then relaxed again. No. They were breaking away to walk up to the Palace and no one challenged them. Whatever had happened in there, whatever destruction had been wrought, Ava and Esmeralda had walked free, and at this moment Jack had no wish for anything more in life.

The relief made his knees give way beneath him, but now he didn't care. He stumbled onto the front step and let himself collapse to the ground. He called back down the hallway. 'Mr Bailey, Ava is there!'

'Oh my word. Thank the Lord!'

Mr Bailey emerged into the hallway, leaning heavily on the wall, as if exhausted by the weight of good news.

Bright relief coursed through Jack and he knew the only thing sustaining him now was that, and adrenaline. The emptiness would strike soon, but it didn't matter, now that Ava was safe and found.

Ava saw him. 'Jack!' She pulled free of her mother's arm and ran towards him, face lighting with joy. His own joy thudded to meet her. Without moving a muscle – because he couldn't – he surged towards Ava with the whole of his being as she ran to him.

With a smile huge on his face he glanced beyond Ava to her mother. Just for a second, but what he saw was enough to blind him. It knocked him back on the step. He threw one arm up to shield his face, the other flailing behind him to keep his balance. Dark spots bounced before his eyes and he squinted, trying to see past them. And the noise! The sky was alive with it, like giant birds on a summer morning, squawking, chirruping, deafening. Through it he could just hear Ava's voice, just there, calling him. 'Jack? Jack, are you hurt? Jack!'

Ava's bright face was close as she crouched next to him on the step. He kept his head turned away from the Lady.

'No, just, you know, the –' He couldn't bring himself to say the word. 'I have to go, Ava. I need to –'

'He needs to rest. There are rooms at the Palace.' The Lady spoke and stayed outside Jack, to his relief. 'We all need to rest. Come, follow me.'

The Lady walked up and stepped around Jack and Ava without a backward glance. She knew, Jack realised. She knew that Jack could see through her like coloured glass and she was keeping herself from him, for whatever reason.

'Father!' cried Ava. Jack looked around to see Bill inching slowly down the hallway towards the front door. 'Oh, Father!' She burst into tears and ran ahead, pulling herself free from Jack as she did so.

Jack watched Ava fling her arms around Mr Bailey and cling to him. Jack waited until the Lady had walked down the hall – until both Ava and her father had followed. Ava threw an anxious glance back at Jack and paused, but then grabbed Mr Bailey's arm as he staggered and nearly fell again.

Jack felt almost dead with exhaustion. He leaned his head forward on his knees to gather his strength for one last effort, to get to his feet and follow the others . . .

That was the last thing he remembered.

CHAPTER 35
AVA

Donlon

The grand longcase clock in the drawing room of Time Palace claimed, ludicrously, that it was before midnight on the same day that Ava had first met her mother. Surely lifetimes had been crammed into that space? It was impossible that she had left the Family's place with Mim just hours before. How could only half a day have passed?

But the clock told the truth, and the stars pricked the sky and the round moon rode high, making its turn as calmly as if this night were like any other. Perhaps it wasn't surprising, after all. Ava was becoming accustomed to having basic certainties explode into tiny shards. Her most fundamental assumptions about her life had all toppled like badly stacked books.

She was both wrung out like an old rag and strung tight as a violin string. She helped her mother settle Father on a chaise longue in the drawing room before running back to poor Jack, who had collapsed in the entrance. A Palace guard carried him to a room, and her heart broke as she stroked his hair. His pale face looked faded, as if he hadn't properly returned. How was it that she could almost *feel* the pain of this scrawny boy, like no one else? Perhaps it was the knowledge that he had gone back to the Void because he had tried to save her from Rupert. She felt guilt, remorse and protective anger all at once. She sat with him for a while, waiting for him to open his eyes, but her mother came and pulled her away.

'Leave him now, Ava,' she said gently. 'He needs rest more than anything else at the moment.'

Ava walked with her mother back to where Father lay on a sofa. He had rejected the notion of going to a bedroom, a hunted look in his eye.

'I cannot be alone,' he had said simply. 'I need to have life around me.'

Now Father lay with his head back on the arm of the chaise longue. He looked up at Ava. 'It's good to have you near me, my dear,' he said. His voice was soft but Ava heard the sadness behind the plain words. 'I made you live a lie for nothing. I thought I was doing it for your own good, but I was wrong.' His voice broke. 'Can you ever forgive me?'

Ava ran to Father and threw her arms around him. 'Father, stop it. There is nothing to forgive.'

Her father held her. 'Whatever Rupert was, whatever he did . . .' Father's voice wobbled and he went on with obvious effort. 'Because of him, there is you. And you are the centre of my world.'

Now Ava's own eyes were pricking with tears. She pressed her other hand on top of his. 'We'll go home, soon, Father. You have to get strong again.'

Ava's mother bent to look at Father's face, peering into his eyes. She passed her hands over Father's face and chest, as brisk and sure as if she were patting a horse.

'There is much to talk about. But not now, Bill. You are not recovered and must rest. And besides, I need to speak with Ava.'

She rose and beckoned to Ava to follow her as she walked to another room with windows overlooking the grounds. She gestured to a couple of armchairs and Ava sat in one, her mother sitting opposite. The light caught the copper coils of her mother's hair and brought out the exuberant colour of the tattooed flowers on her neck and head. Some extraordinarily lifelike red berries curled around one delicate ear.

Now that Ava sat so close to her mother, she noticed wrinkles around her eyes, an earlobe that wasn't quite plump and full, a crepe paper quality to the skin on her neck.

Esmeralda's green eyes rested on Ava and it seemed impossible that the force of this woman could be contained within such a tiny frame. She was physically a wisp next to Ava. Perhaps people were smaller when she was born, nearly three centuries ago. A sense of unreality as dense as the velvet curtains hanging in the windows descended over Ava as she sat opposite her mother.

Her mother, who, unlike most mothers, had given birth to her as an experiment. The bitterness rose in her throat.

At least she seemed to be a successful experiment, so far. Perhaps Ava should even be grateful to have such clarity of purpose in her life. She'd been struggling with who she was, where she belonged – well, no need anymore. She knew precisely why she'd been put on this earth. People would give much to have the meaning of their life so clearly laid out.

It wasn't quite what she'd dreamed, was it?

'Ava, there is much I need to speak with you about. So much to explain.'

Her mother leaned forward, suddenly strange and distant after all that had happened.

'You will wonder about the time-snatching. About how it started and what we still need to do to stop it. About Rupert and myself. And you will learn about all this. But first, there are questions I want to ask you.'

Ava looked up, hope flaring in her heart. Perhaps she wanted to know Ava as more than an experiment, after all. Perhaps this would be the moment she reached out to her to say, 'Show me yourself, daughter.'

Ava watched and waited for her mother to speak. Her hands were clammy in her lap.

'I want to know more about Jack. He has a special quality, most unusual. Where did you meet him?'

Jack? Ava took a deep breath before answering.

'He had just returned from being snatched when I met him – in the grounds here.' It was a jolt to remember that she was back where the adventure had started. 'He is an apprentice with Hammer and he –'

'Yes, yes, but who are his parents?' her mother interrupted. She was leaning forward, watching Ava intently.

'Oh – his father is called Silas. He is, ah – well, he was a Ham before he was thrown out. And his mother died when he was little.'

Esmeralda looked thoughtful. 'That explains it, in part. He has a rare ability and one that I will need.' She looked at Ava. 'We don't have a great deal of time. I will need Jack's talent to help me in what I have to do.'

Her mother was smiling and for a brief moment Ava imagined that the smile held warmth for her. But of course, this was just her imagination. There was no warmth for her. Her mother had things to do. With Jack.

So why *was* she looking at Ava like that?

There was a long silence. Ava looked down at her lap. The moment was broken by the door being pushed open.

Jack sidled through. He looked wan, his face grey. His eyes flickered along the ground to their feet but no higher, as if he was afraid to meet their gaze.

She jumped out of her chair to go to him, guilt making her solicitous. 'Jack, how do you feel? Come and sit down.'

He seized her hand and gazed at her with a strange intensity, as if she might float off if he blinked.

'I'm fine. I thought I might find you alone, but . . .' He trailed off.

From her position Ava could see Esmeralda staring at Jack with almost as much intensity as Jack had looked at Ava – what was it with the manners of this world? – but as Ava caught her eye she turned away. At that moment Jack's tension softened visibly. He put a hand on Ava's arm.

'Can we talk? I 'ave to get back to Hammer's and –'

'Why do you have to go back to Hammer's? I need you here, Jack.' Ava's mother cut through Jack's words.

Jack stiffened and clutched Ava's arm, shutting his eyes. He muttered almost inaudibly, 'Got to . . . Can't talk like this.'

Esmeralda stood and faced them both and Jack almost crumpled forward, clamping his hands over his ears. What was going on? Jack looked like he was in terrible pain, as if Ava's mother was emitting a deafening shriek that only Jack could hear.

Instinctively Ava put herself between Jack and her mother. The relief on Jack's face was immediate. He straightened and took his hands down from his ears. His words were clear now, but he directed them at the wall, rather than Esmeralda.

'I made a promise I 'ave to keep, your Lady. I return to Hammer's on Thursday.' His voice was flat, with an odd dignity. Ava's mother made a sound of frustration.

'Jack, you're wasted there. You have much greater talents than mere metalwork. I will give you the freedom of Time Palace, anything you need, if you will stay here as my personal protege.' Her voice took on an almost pleading note. 'There is no one else like you, Jack. You already understand what you are to me, don't you?'

It was too much. Ava was hearing the words she had always dreamed of her mother saying, but they were directed at someone else. It was a brutal slap to her face.

Ava pushed past Jack and ran out of the room, her vision blurring with hot, angry tears. She would never belong here, not in her mother's home or anywhere in Donlon.

She'd been a fool, believing that uncovering her story would give her happiness.

'Ava, wait!' called Jack.

'Let her go, Jack,' said the Lady. 'This is . . .'

Ava didn't catch the rest of the Lady's words as she pelted down the hallway to the Palace entrance, but she didn't need to. She knew what the words would be.

More important. Something that cannot wait. Something only you can do.

Whatever the words, it would be the same clear message. Jack was the only child who mattered to her mother.

CHAPTER 36

AVA

Donlon

Ava slumped down on the top step and pressed the balls of her palms into her wet eyes.

What came next? Was she to stay here for her mother's scientific gratification, to be prodded and measured and assessed? Or was she to go back to London with her father, back to her safe, drab little life, knowing everything she had ever believed there was a sham? Back to Miss Buss and school, and daily drudgery, and Phoebe?

Phoebe! She sat bolt upright, eyes squinting against sudden sun. She had forgotten all about Phoebe. She would be back in London, back from the Void. Ava despised Phoebe but the thought of her drifting in that deadening place all that time made her feel sick with pity. She wouldn't wish that on anyone. And what of Violet?

'You are heartsore, my humbling.' And there was Malaikah, standing with his great stillness at the bottom of the steps. From where she sat, Ava could look him

277

directly in the eye for the first time. It was like having the stars and moon turning their gaze upon you. Somehow, just by standing there he drew some of her turmoil away. She sighed.

'Malaikah. It is good to have you here. Where did you go, before?'

He turned his head and looked to the horizon. 'My bloodhalf is suffering. His loss makes him dark so I went to him.'

'Your bloodhalf?'

'My seedshare.'

'Oh. Your – brother?' guessed Ava.

Malaikah turned back to her and those eyes held her again. 'He is my hearttwin dark.'

That was perhaps a yes. 'I'm sorry your brother is unwell.'

'His winglack peals his angerbell, my humbling. He is my beloved seedshare, but heartdark. You humblings must always keepfar from him.'

The words meant nothing to Ava but dread shivered cold in her heart. Malaikah reached one long arm to rest a hand on her shoulder. 'But fear not, Avaheart. Your soul is furrowed, like your heartguide's. Bill-man must be still to stitchfast his tearing, and I will take you backwards to go forward. We go together to the house of the wimpleones. I have brought the Seedguard and told her truth. Comewith.'

'Well, I –'

'Readyfor?'

'I don't –'

Malaikah leaned forward and scooped her in his arms as if she were a baby. Again, Ava felt no alarm but only deep familiarity at his touch, almost like her own hand on her skin, or like being brushed by the bough of a well-known tree. He was in some profound way not *other* to Ava. His wings beat the air once, twice, faster and faster, and then Malaikah lifted up off the ground, his great wings powerful against the air, wind filling Ava's ears. Ava gripped hard as Time Palace became a toy beneath them and the people in the grounds little tin figures.

She peered around her, the wind whipping her hair across her face and hissing in her ears. She could see all of Donlon sprawled out below, its vastness so still and peaceful from up here. No sign of the ravages within. From here, it was a perfect panorama of snaking river, miniature waterwheels, trees and tiny buildings, the bright moon polishing it all to a magical silver sheen. They were heading west under the moon that hung midway between two horizons.

Minutes later, her teeth were chattering. The wind stripped her body heat away in the night air, so it was a relief when they started to drop down towards a vast sprawl of white buildings, that glowed against the dark earth. Curving roofs snaked along long buildings connected by arches and tiny alleys linked flower-filled squares to each other.

Malaikah dropped down in a courtyard in front of a studded wooden door and let Ava down. The wind dropped instantly, to be replaced by night silence. She looked around, her surroundings almost as bright as in sunlight. 'This looks like a monastery, or . . .'

Her voice choked.

'Yes,' said Malaikah. 'White City. The wimpleones here have a home for the poor parentlacks.'

Malaikah walked up the stone stairs leading to a studded wooden door. He got to the top and looked down at Ava.

She knew this place.

Malaikah held out a hand. 'Come, Avaheart. There is a meetback for you here.'

Ava's feet were rooted into the cobbled stones of the courtyard. Her heart hammered as if she'd just run up a staircase and her mouth was so dry she was having trouble swallowing. Something very strange was going on in her chest, like a Donlon waterwheel was churning her insides. Images and faces flashed through her head, scenes that she didn't recognise but at the same time were deeply, weirdly familiar.

She knew without a doubt that the entrance hall just beyond that door was cool and dark and smelt of a particular mixture of cold stone, wood polish and incense.

'The Foundling Home.' Her voice was a whisper. 'I was here.'

The great door opened at the same instant as Malaikah rang the bell outside. There was a cry, then arms flung wide, a flurry of white and grey pushing past Malaikah and down the steps. Ava was engulfed in a hard, warm hug as rough linen pressed her cheek and lavender and soap filled her nostrils. The churning in her chest spilled over into hot tears and she clutched the familiar body close.

'Welcome home, my sweetling.' Violet's voice was muffled against Ava's head. 'This is where you first came to me.'

Ava clung for a long, long moment to Violet – solid, safe, unchanging Violet – who had been snatched, and might be none of those things anymore. Ava hardly dared let her go and step back, for fear of what she might see.

Violet was wearing a plain grey dress and a stiff white wimple, an enormous clutch of keys at her belt. Ava raised her eyes to Violet's face and drew a sharp breath. She was still Violet, and would always be Violet in every way that mattered to Ava – but there was something else there now. There was a velvet sadness behind her eyes. A grief that had not been there before. Oh, Violet.

Just seeing her standing there with her head tilted in that way, hair flattened into smooth swathes under her wimple, made Ava feel anchored and herself in a way she had not felt since being in Donlon. It didn't matter that here she stood, a nun in a Foundling Home with Lord only knew what story behind her. Nothing could change what she was to Ava.

Violet pressed both hands to her breastbone. 'Thanksgive for bringing her, Malaikah,' she said. She blinked away tears. 'It means much to have her here with me again. Especially as I don't see how I can leave here for some time, with the way things are.'

'You are motherheart to her, Violet seedguard. You grow her wisetree like none other,' said Malaikah. 'And she must truthgather fast now. There is a lifestretch that will snapfast soon.'

Violet frowned. 'Not angelcode, please, Malaikah. English. Are you talking about the Lady?'

'The timequeen has chosen to crowncast. The purenote seeks new harmonies,' replied Malaikah.

Violet tutted in that all-too-familiar way and Ava marvelled that she could treat even this great presence like an unruly child. 'Malaikah, speak clearly. This is no playful matter.'

'I speak deadlygrave, oh Seedguard. The Lady has tired of lovedread and there is only one pathway for her now. It has already started.'

Violet's eyes widened. 'Oh.' She pressed her hands to her face. 'No.'

'Yes, Violetsad. But you must storypass to Ava first. She must knowback.'

Violet shook her head despairingly. 'Oh, my dear. Come inside, quickly.'

She gripped Ava by the hand and trotted up the steps, pulling Ava with her through the doorway.

In the same moment a door slid open in Ava's mind. Memories jostled through it, clamouring for attention amongst the cold waxy smell of the high vaulted corridor and the sounds of feet whispering over stone floors. Violet led them into a long room bright with whitewash and wooden beams. Even without the familiar smoke smell, Ava knew this room led onto the kitchen. Moonlight streamed in through a big arched window, silvering the tiny specks of dust. Ava remembered – so clearly! – stirring flecks of sunlit gold with a finger as a child, imagining they were tiny fairies.

Violet bustled about with cups and a teapot, pouring boiling water from a kettle simmering on the stove and taking the lid off a cake tin, exactly as she did in the kitchen in London. Here, though, her face was tight and unhappy above the familiar movements. She put everything on the table and gestured to a seat opposite as she plumped heavily on a chair, as if suddenly exhausted.

'Sit down, heartlove. Have some cake with your tea. Excellent poppyseed cake. Sister Beatrice is a very good cook, whatever else she – well. Anyway.' She lapsed into silence and gazed into her teacup.

Ava lowered herself onto a wooden chair opposite Violet and looked around her. She was glad of the sudden silence, to let her mind settle around the memories flooding through it. She remembered pushing the woodbox over to the window to climb up so she could look out, but only when the box was empty – even then it was almost too heavy for her toddler arms to move.

Violet sat up and looked directly at Ava. 'I remember the day your mother brought you here like it was yesterday,' she said quietly. 'She was a familiar face here. She is a great scholar, a brilliant brain. Always researching, always learning new things. I didn't understand much of what she studied. Education was everything for her. She would come and see the school – she was a generous benefactor to schools in Donlon – and take a special interest in the gifted ones. She would train them as her research assistants. So we already knew her well.'

Violet paused to sip her tea and Ava watched her, hardly daring to breathe in case she interrupted Violet, but she went on.

'Although we had seen her much less, since you had been born. Not surprisingly, she had been busy with a new child. It was a cold day, I remember that. Both of you bundled up in fur and silk and her shaking like a leaf. Not from the cold, though.'

Ava found her voice. 'What from, then?'

Violet looked up at her. 'Leaving you here tore out her heart,' she said simply. 'But she didn't know grief when it hit her. "I have an ague, Violet," she said to me, but I knew what it was. She was not familiar with human emotions after all her time. The price she pays for living a non-human span.' She held Ava's eye. 'But she adored you. And that scared her.'

She adored you. Ava's cup rattled loud against its saucer when she put it down. She gripped her treacherous hands together in her lap as Violet went on.

'She brought you here because she had reason not to trust your bloodfather. I should say God rest his soul, but that man had no soul. I'm sorry to speak of him like this, Ava, but it is good that he has passed. He did much evil. I never trusted him and after a while, she also saw through him. He used all his charm on her and they say he was like a magician once he got you in his sights. Of course, he never bothered with me.' She gave a dry laugh. 'He saved his charms for those he saw as useful. Or the young and beautiful. But she saw her wrong and tried to make it better. That was the bravest thing she did, you know. Not many people have the courage to look inside themselves and see their own weakness. She knew you would be safe here. Also, and I'm only guessing this, she didn't know how to handle how you made her feel.'

She leaned across and took Ava's hand. 'She asked me to go with you, when she decided you would be safer in

London. It was a big change, and risky, but I took it without hesitating. I loved you too and I had my own reasons for wanting to spend time in London.' She patted Ava's hand and blinked quickly. 'But that's neither here nor there. Have you noticed any change in the Lady?'

Ava shook her head, confused by the sudden switch. It wasn't as if she had known her long enough to notice changes. 'Such as?'

'Signs of ageing, tiredness, that sort of thing?'

Ava paused, remembering the light on her mother's face in the room earlier. 'A few lines in bright light. I hadn't noticed them before.'

Violet took a deep breath. 'Ah. That is new. We don't have much time, Ava. You need to return. But first, come with me.' Violet pushed her chair back and hurried into the corridor. 'Quickly!'

Ava knew that tone. She jumped up and ran after Violet, who was already halfway down the corridor. She made a couple of turns along twisting hallways before arriving at a locked door that reminded Ava of the Observatory. She took one of the keys hanging at her waist and unlocked the door, the grating click loud in the empty hall.

As if the sound was a summons, a nun's footsteps whispered across the stone floors. Where had she materialised from? She was younger than Violet, wisps of dark hair escaping from her wimple and eyes red-rimmed and puffy, as if she'd been crying. Violet glanced at her and sighed impatiently, pushing open the door and beckoning Ava inside.

'Sister Beatrice. I've told you before. You don't need to personally guard this room.'

The nun stepped closer. 'The machines were brought here under my safekeeping. They were assigned to me and I am responsible for them.' She was looking at Ava intently as she spoke. 'This is the girl, I see. I am sorry for your loss, child. I know the words spoken about him are not true. He was a great man, much misunderstood. He only used these snatchers with consent.'

It took Ava a moment to realise who Beatrice was talking about. Word had travelled fast in the night. She must have recognised Rupert in Ava's face – her blue eyes and dark hair – and assumed she was grieving for her father. Before she could reply Violet spoke.

'It is a hard time for her, of course, Sister Beatrice. I have brought her here to see the proof of her father's brilliance.'

Before Ava could make sense of that, Violet pulled her through the door. Ava stepped back in shock. The room was full of time snatchers. Twenty or more lay mounted on individual plinths. Violet put a hand up to stop Sister Beatrice from following.

'If you would give her a private moment. It is much for her to take in.' Sister Beatrice hesitated just long enough for Violet to not-quite-slam the door in her face.

Violet whirled to Ava. 'We have no time. I hope these are all reset – we have only your father's word for it and we all know what that is worth. But I sense no signs of life. Lay your hand on every snatcher.' She pointed to a snatcher and looked at Ava. 'This one first.'

Ava stepped closer, unsure, and Violet tutted. 'Touch it! Malaikah has told me that you are immune to time-snatching. Have you not worked out that your touch can disable the time snatchers? Anywhere, it doesn't matter.'

So that explained why time snatchers kept breaking in her hands. Ava lay her hand gingerly on the metal and jumped back with a squeak as it shifted and went hot under her hand. A glare from Violet encouraged her to try again. She touched it and held her hand there until it started to burn and the metal gave underneath her hand with a crunching sound.

'Good,' said Violet. 'Now the rest. Quickly, girl!'

CHAPTER 37
AVA AND JACK

Donlon

Once Ava established a rhythm, it took her no more than a minute to circle the room, leaving in her wake time snatchers cracked and tilted at odd angles. It made her hands burn but she found she could just bear to keep hold until she heard that final crunch. Violet followed behind, adjusting the more askew machines so that at first glance it would appear that nothing had changed.

'Sister Beatrice will be sniffing around here first chance she gets. This place has become a shrine to your father for her. She was another one he applied his charms to.' Violet's voice was a whisper but her disdain seemed loud. 'She will never believe he did wrong so I humour her, for now. She already had enough reasons to be my enemy.' She stepped away from Ava and said in her normal voice, 'Come now, Ava. Malaikah is waiting.'

Violet bustled to the door and opened it. Sister Beatrice

jumped back and Violet said sardonically, 'Did I startle you, Sister Beatrice?'

Ava didn't like the hungry way Sister Beatrice looked at her, as if searching for something she wanted, or as if Ava were an object to be consumed. Violet locked the door firmly behind them and took Ava by the hand and turned to walk to the entrance.

'She's not so special, Sister Violet.' Sister Beatrice's voice was malicious and Ava turned to see a look of sly satisfaction on her face. 'You know there are others like her.'

'Good day, Sister Beatrice,' said Violet coldly and marched Ava up the corridor.

Ava pulled away to look back at Sister Beatrice. 'What do you mean by that?' she called.

Sister Beatrice smirked. 'You are not the only child of your father!'

Sister Beatrice smiled with a strange, bitter triumph. It took a moment for the meaning to sink in. Ava had a sibling – maybe more than one.

In the next second she realised that she'd already met one of them. Jade.

Ava's hands squeezed tight in sudden, almost painful joy. She was as sure of this as she was of the blood thrumming in her veins. Ava had what she had always wanted – a *sister*. A half-sister, technically, but still, a sister. Another girl, connected to Ava by the blood of their father, but irrefutably connected by blood nevertheless. From a lifetime believing she was an only, motherless child, this new shift in her personal landscape was dizzying.

'But you are the only child of your mother and that is

what matters here,' said Violet sharply, slicing through Ava's thoughts. 'We have little time and if you don't go now you will always regret it.'

The urgency in Violet's voice cut through the seductive strands of Sister Beatrice's. There was an expression in Violet's eyes, a pleading that Ava did not quite understand but which moved her to action. She made herself turn away from Beatrice, away from the dead time snatchers, and ran with Violet down the corridor.

Malaikah was underneath the great yew tree overhanging the entrance of the Foundling Home but standing facing the trunk, as if in conversation with the tree. He turned as Violet and Ava came through the door and clattered down the front steps.

'Malaikah, there is no time to lose. Take Ava to her mother now.'

She flapped both hands at Ava and Malaikah, who swung his arm around Ava's waist. Violet pressed her hands against her eyes briefly but then rose on tiptoe to shout above the noise of Malaikah's beating wings as they started to rise.

'Go straight to your mother, Ava! Don't waste a second.'

Ava waved affirmation to Violet as they hung above her. Violet shouted something else just as Malaikah swept above the rooftops and turned east to go. Ava couldn't quite catch her words but they sounded something like 'Heed you' or possibly 'I'll see you'. She waved again. Probably just motherly Violet telling her to take care.

As Malaikah soared and his wings settled into a steady *whoosh-whoosh* rhythm, Ava's thoughts turned to Violet's three words that changed everything. *She adored you.* They drowned out everything else. Her heart thumped painfully against Malaikah's arm and this time it wasn't just because she was hanging high in the sky.

It was hope, so fierce she could hardly breathe. It was the new possibility that young Ava was *not* a child so unloveable that even her mother didn't want her.

She adored you.

Not a child so impossible to love that false parents and a life of lies had to be invented to disguise the terrible, empty truth.

She adored you.

It was the opposite. She was so wanted, so cared for that she was sent away with good people to safety, and a carefully fabricated life to protect her. Ava's understanding of her own story had been flipped on its head and everything, *everything* had changed, even though not one basic fact had.

She suddenly heard the words that Violet called out, clear as day. 'She needs you.'

Not 'Heed you'.

For once in her life, Violet was not advising restraint or telling her to take care. She was telling Ava to rush headlong into the thing that mattered most in her entire life. Her mother's last moments.

And now Ava allowed herself to face what she had suspected, but had been pushing away, refusing to examine. Her mother's days were finally ending. Her mother was no longer taking time from the Mother Catcher.

What would happen now? Would her ageing be slow as well? Perhaps there was still plenty of time left to get to know her mother. But then perhaps the ageing would be accelerated, like an elastic band snapping back. Ava had no way of knowing and it was almost too bitter to bear. She had only just learned her mother was alive and now was faced with the prospect of her true death.

The moonlit onion domes of Time Palace glinted like a pretty toy in the distance. They gleamed with both hope and foreboding. Ava wanted to hurtle towards them at top speed but also dreaded what she might find there. She realised she was digging her nails deep into Malaikah's arm and let her fingers soften. Malaikah was starting his descent, dropping gradually closer to the earth. They would soon be there.

The Lady had blinded Jack at first. Standing pressed against that wall, with Ava gone, she had pinned him as surely as a stuck butterfly in a glass case. She blazed and roared before him, bright and dark both, centuries of life roiling inside her. He squinted and put up both hands, but could not look away. Something held him there. He was meant to see all this.

Gradually, though, the blinding kaleidoscope settled into shapes he could make sense of. Had she softened before him or was he adjusting, in the way that eyes adapt to sudden changes in light?

'I need you to store me,' she said.

His heart missed a beat. Store *this*? Even if it were possible, there would be no room left for Jack.

'For Ava,' she said. 'For you both. I hold your futures and her past.'

And hearing that, he had no choice. He closed his eyes in assent.

'I will be gone soon,' she said. 'I don't have enough time to tell her everything she needs. You need to see everything, understand everything, so you can pass this information on to her when she needs it.' She paused and the expression on her face was one of longing. 'I want my time with Ava to be only *now*.'

Jack could see something new in her. Something was whirling inside and she was grappling with it, something coiled, soft and glittering all at once. She wanted to hold this thing and yet it terrified her. Her eyes widened and she reached a hand towards him.

'Help me,' she whispered.

She was so close. He stepped away, but too late. She spilled over and the lines between them were gone.

He *was* the Lady and that was . . .

. . . something I have no words for. There are many words I have lost, over time. Words that belong to that dimly remembered place. A place over which I have long hung, cool and distant and perfect as a single, soaring note of music.

Doubt. This is one word. Remorse is another.

Regret. Longing. Anxiety. They are coming back to me now.

Fear. Love.

These two belong together. They were both born with her but I have refused to name them. Until now.

It is a terrible thing, to be human. To feel what others feel. So much cleaner and simpler to be that high, solitary note of music.

My experiment had unexpected outcomes. I didn't predict that the physical fact of birth would stir new sensations. It was merely the pumping of hormones and the awakening of primal instincts, of course, but still – their power disturbed me. I had to send her away, for my sake and for hers.

And also, I had begun to see what her father truly was.

Soon, I could not bear the suffering of other innocents. I could no longer turn a blind eye to what I had become, with Rupert. Could not pretend that what I did was harmless, or worth the price, or not see what he was truly doing, behind my back. The carefully planned birth was a dropped stone that sent ever-widening ripples into my world.

I cannot live this double life any longer. I correct myself – this half life. Because I have to choose. My love for my daughter is a crescendo that drowns out my perfect, solitary note.

And so I choose to forgo eternal life.

Terror and doubt and joy and fear. Yes, I am human again.

But I have forgotten how to be this. How to share love.

Time is running out and I don't know how to be a mother. How to give her my love.

Help me.

'You start by bein' wrong.'

The words were out of Jack's mouth before he was fully back in his body. She was still pouring into him and somehow he had room for her, in deep crevices and pockets he had not known he had. He was pressed to the sides of himself and he knew that he had to get used to that. They could not separate now. Until it was all over, and maybe not then.

The Lady had two spots of bright colour on her cheeks

and her eyes glittered. Grey poured through her copper hair like white ink and her face folded in on her bones as he watched. She was shrivelling in front of him, like the juice being sucked out of an orange.

'What did you say?' Her voice was high and quavering. The voice of an old woman.

'You start by bein' wrong,' he said again. The words came before thought. 'Get it wrong. Make mistakes. Tear it down and start again, and again. Cry, get angry, laugh, *feel*. Keep getting it wrong, learn and keep goin'. That's what bein' human is.'

He was talking to himself as much as the Lady. He, who stood in the shards and debris of his own life. He, who was looking around at everything he'd done wrong, the barriers he'd put up that needed tearing down. He, a boy who had glimpsed a new way of being and still had to find the path there.

She was silent. That thing he could see writhing inside her, the one bouncing around everything else with nowhere to go – that's what she needed to hug close. That tangled, sunbright thing was her humanity, released after being held down for centuries.

That was one thing he could never store for her. He already held lifetimes of knowing inside him, ready to give to Ava, but that part had to come from her mother. He clenched his fists in frustration. She was dying before him and he could see what she had to do, but he couldn't do it for her. Only the Lady could be Ava's mother and give Ava what she craved.

She knew this. That's why the Lady had got Jack to hold her stories, so she could be free to just be with Ava. But now, when the moment was here, she couldn't do it. And it was almost too late.

Jack looked at the two of them, at the eternal woman who had left it too late to become human again, and the boy who was too scared to be, and saw there was no one else. They had to show each other. His heart sank for Ava. After all this, what she wanted most in the world was in the hands of a boy and woman who were not ready. He had spent his life hiding behind his own barriers, and this woman was everything in the world, but not a mother.

He couldn't stand it. He slammed his own hands against his chest.

'You have to do this for Ava! Open up, here.' He bunched his hands hard against his breastbone and felt his own heart swell. He was also teaching himself. 'That thing in your chest? Your heart? Your gut? You *want* that. Stop fighting it!' She shook her head – tiny, slow movements of hopelessness – and a lone tear trickled through the creases forming on her face.

He hesitated, then stepped forward and took both her hands gently in his. He pushed them against her belly just below her breastbone.

'There! It's just there. Let it open.'

Her hand trembled under his. Nothing. The lone tear stood still, trapped now by a deep wrinkle. She was shrinking before him. He closed his eyes and, putting his other hand on his chest, pushed his own strange love for Ava through his hands and into hers.

'This is what you have to give Ava. You owe her this.'

Her hand started to shake underneath his. He opened

his eyes and there it was, roiling through her like a storm across a field. Here it came, swelling under his hand and out of her, centuries of held-down love and anger and joy and sorrow. The force of it pushed him back and she threw back her head and let out a sound he had never heard a human make before.

As Ava touched the ground with Malaikah, an inhuman shriek tore through the Palace. Ava froze to the spot, her spine juddering. 'What is *that*?'

Malaikah smiled. 'Thanksgive that she has humanmade before her happening, Ava. Rushfast to her.'

Jack appeared in the doorway, tumbling down the front steps in his haste.

'Malaikah, it is happening! She has to go to the Mother Catcher. Ava, run to her!'

The roar came again, quavering terribly on the air. 'That is – my *mother*?'

'Speednow, Ava.' Malaikah swooped up the steps, landed at the top and ran through the front door.

Ava looked at Jack, who waved her inside. He looked strange, heightened, in the way people on laudanum looked. 'Go, Ava!'

His urgency spurred her on and she grabbed her skirts and ran after Malaikah.

Jack pressed both hands against his chest again. 'Go well, Ava,' he whispered. He watched as she ran her lolloping run and disappeared inside. He dropped his head. 'Thanksgive.'

Thanksgive that she would have what she needed now.

Thanksgive that he held what she would need, one day in the future. What they both would need.

Thanksgive that he had found her again. That he had finally seen who she was.

And thanksgive that he now had his own truth. His heart was open and the path was before him. Not wide and shining, by a long shot. The way was rocky and steep – but he could see where to go.

He had helped Ava find her mother and now his task was over. He had done it and inside three days, as Hammer had said. It was time to go back where he belonged – to Hammer's. He had promised him, and there was no other life for him here.

He could not think about the pain that would come, when he left Ava behind. But he had no choice. He had to find a way to live with his tearing, for now. To get through each day.

The trembling inside him that would begin. The holes.

It was like cutting out his own heart, to turn and walk away from her. He turned and walked away.

CHAPTER 38

Donlon

Ava ran into the room after Malaikah. He was bent over the chaise longue, next to Father, so that Ava could just see her mother's legs stretched out in their dark blue boots. 'Now is the happening, Esmeralda?' he said.

'Yes. It comes fast now.' Ava's mother's voice was tight, as if she had to guard each breath.

'My Lady – Esmeralda – your daughter is here.' Bill turned to Ava and his eyes were deep with sadness. 'Go, Ava. This is your moment. Speedwell, Esmeralda.'

Malaikah leaned forward and gathered her body in his arms. He stood slowly and turned to face Ava. Ava gasped in shock. Her mother was a tiny, wizened old lady, one wrinkled cheek resting against Malaikah's chest, her wild hair pure white. Malaikah whispered something in her mother's ear, and she smiled. There was a long moment of shimmering light around them and then Malaikah stepped forward.

'Follow us to the Observatory, Ava.'

Malaikah turned and walked out of the room, his wings swooping in a flapping run until there was room to lift them into the sky. Ava clattered down the steps, panic spurring her legs to sprint faster than she thought possible. She weaved though the battle debris still on the ground, feeling each precious second slipping away, each second that she would never get back with her mother. A sob rose in her chest. Faster! There was no time left, already she had wasted too much of it.

She reached the Observatory just a moment after Malaikah landed, her heart hammering as if it would bounce out of her chest. Malaikah pushed open the battered great door with one hand and they stepped into the dark hall. A few curious faces – night workers clearing the aftermath of the crowds – turned to them but Malaikah's voice rumbled with authority. 'Go! The happening wants for peace.'

Nobody argued with Malaikah. They went, and the hall was silent again.

They reached the Mother Catcher. It was impossible not to look up in that room, the gaze drawn up to the open sky, to where the Mother Catcher's open mouth turned slowly, raking the sky for unused minutes drifting by like invisible insects. Malaikah lowered Esmeralda so she could support herself on its curving belly. She leaned forward on the Mother Catcher, her arms spread wide in embrace. The moon bathed both of them as she rested her head on the Mother Catcher and closed her eyes.

Long seconds passed and the room held its breath, hanging in a place where time neither passed nor stopped.

Ava had the strangest feeling that her body was suspended between two heartbeats, time spiralling into this endless, perfect now.

Her mother lifted her head and time moved forward again. She stood with a light movement and smiled at them both. Her hair was still white and her face wrinkled but she stood straight and her eyes were as glass green as ever.

'Thanksgive, Malaikah. You are my heartsoul twin.'

Malaikah put both hands on his heart and bowed deeply. He stood up and his blue eyes shone with tears as he looked at her.

'This happening gives heartpain and souljoy both. I will guardtrue your seedgrow, oh timequeen. Soarwell into forever, my fierceheart.'

Malaikah backed out of the room, his eyes on Ava's mother until the door closed between them. Something slumped in the air around them. It was as if the air had hummed with a deep vibration that Ava had not noticed until it stopped. Her mother's eyes were bright with tears.

'Malaikah is the universe contained, Ava. You can trust him like you can trust the sun to rise. He will always be there for you.'

She held out her arms to Ava and it was the moment Ava's whole life had been turning towards.

They clung to each other, each leaning into the other like two halves of a puzzle put together for the first time, and saw that the gaps within them had always held space for the other. It didn't matter that she had been born as an experiment, or that Jack had been favoured, or that she had been sent away from her mother. Those were just facts tossed on the surface, like sea foam on the ocean. She sank into the deeper currents and knew that the surge of these would anchor her when her doubts drew her to the surface again.

Her mother took the chain from around her neck and held it out to Ava. 'This is for you to wear now.'

Ava bent her head forward and let Esmeralda place the chain around her neck. The locket swung with surprising weight as she straightened. She caught the metal disc and held it out to look at it. It was unexpectedly warm in her hand and on close scrutiny it was almost translucent, like thick gold-coloured glass that held a warm light inside it.

'It is made of sunstone, the most precious metal we have,' said the Lady. 'There was only one place it was ever found and that mine is long empty. It is within the Montagu grounds near Time Palace.'

Ava stroked the metal with one finger. It was not like metal warmed by contact with human skin but rather, generated its own heat. It was almost hot to the touch. 'Why is it warm?'

'It holds energy. In its raw form it absorbs energy from the surroundings and stores it. It can be manipulated to absorb a particular vibration to the exclusion of others. In the time catchers and snatchers, it zones in on time vibrations, which it then stores in the metal. Each person has their own time vibration, which is as unique as a fingerprint. It is tied to their very soul – which is why people get torn.' Her mother sighed. 'If only we had used it all on the time catchers. Time-snatching would never have been possible. Without sunstone, the time snatchers are just a pretty piece of clockwork technology.'

'But why does this not burn me, like the snatchers do when I destroy them?' asked Ava.

'It's the time-snatching you react to, not the metal. You can touch sunstone in any other form. This is a special piece of sunstone as it has been transformed by a strong magnet. If you apply magnetised sunstone to a live time snatcher, it disables its function. Time-snatching does not work with magnetism and when the magnetised metal is sunstone, all you have to do is hold it to the snatcher and it reverses the time that has been snatched.' She looked at Ava. 'Anyone can do this – except you, of course. You would destroy the time snatcher before you can reset it. You need allies to work with you.'

Ava saw her mother's mind leaping ahead to a future when Ava was without her. A future where time-snatching could rise again, even though Rupert had gone. She had been so caught up in the emotion of the moment that she hadn't stepped back to consider what would happen next.

'Whatever else Rupert was, he was careful to control the time-snatching. He always knew exactly where they were and who had access to them. Now that he is gone, I fear for what will happen with the time snatchers still out there. Violet had you disable the snatchers at the Foundling Home, yes?' Ava nodded. 'Good. You must bring them back to the Observatory and have them melted down, and then guard that sunstone. We don't know if anyone else has the knowledge to create time snatchers but we must assume they do. And of course, there are other time snatchers out there now. There can't be many, because sunstone is so rare – but that is all we know.'

Ava remembered the toad-like snatcher Rupert had held. He had boasted of a new improved version – but how many, and where were they? They could be anywhere in Donlon or London. And if they found them – *when* they found them – they had to be able to quickly reset them before destroying them. Ava was the destroyer but if she destroyed without having someone reset them first, she would be locking souls in the grey zone forever.

'Jack could be my ally. And Violet. Not Father,' she said. He had endured enough.

'Not Bill, no. And yes, Jack is your most important ally. You must keep him closer than a brother. Do you know why he is so special to me?' Ava shook her head. 'He holds my stories for you.'

And with those words, Ava's confused resentment towards Jack melted away. 'Jack has your stories? How – but Jack is not a transient. What if the snatchers are in London?'

'That's why you need another London ally. Not Violet – she already has her role. She won't always be where you need her. You need a Londoner who is also a transient, who has a connection to Donlon. Someone who is persuasive and quick thinking; who knows what it is to be snatched and truly understands what is at stake.'

It was hopeless. 'Where can we find someone like that in time?'

Her mother looked at her searchingly. 'We already know where she is. She came back from the Void on the same day as Violet did.'

Ava looked at the Lady for a long, uncomprehending moment.

Wait. No, she couldn't possibly mean that.

'Phoebe?' Ava almost choked on the words. 'You can't possibly mean her?'

'I realise it seems unlikely,' said the Lady.

Unlikely? It was impossible! How could that over-skirted, fluttery-eyed simpleton be the ally Ava needed? And how did her mother even know about the girl? Her mouth dropped open, but she was too flabbergasted to speak.

'I understand, Ava,' said the Lady. 'But I don't want to waste the last of my time justifying Phoebe to you. Suffice to say her father is the illegitimate son of George Richmond, one of the richest families in Donlon. He is the only surviving heir, which makes Phoebe in line for that fortune, if he can prove himself. Phoebe has a direct vested interest in Donlon, especially as it is the rich families that will be held to ransom by time-snatching. Trust me. And Phoebe is much more than what you see. Remove her from the influence of that absurd mother and she will become something else entirely.'

Ava's mother leaned forward and put her hands on her knees. Her breathing was loud in the room.

Ava put the unthinkable idea of making Phoebe her ally out of her head. Time enough to wrestle with that thought later. She went to her mother's side.

'Mother, you're tired. Here, take my arm. Let us sit over there.'

Mother. The word sat as easily on her tongue as if she had used it all her life. She took Esmeralda's bird-weight on herself and led her to the seats in the corner of the room. The seats were old and well-worn, showing where

Esmeralda had spent much of her time over the last two centuries.

Ava helped her mother settle on the sofa, berating herself silently. She should not have allowed her mother to tire herself like this. She had somehow restored herself from contact with the Mother Catcher but she was so close to the end. She had to make sure her mother gathered her strength as much as she could.

'Let us forget Phoebe,' said her mother. 'Violet can explain the details to you. She knows it all, of course.' She smiled. 'Violet is a formidable force.' She drew a deep breath and winced, putting up a hand as Ava jumped forward. 'Don't fret, Ava. Some aches and pains are catching up with me, but they are well overdue. My time is springing back over the years and I am going through my ageing all at once.'

Ava swallowed hard, but the lump in her throat wouldn't dislodge. 'Mother, please take some extra time. Just a little.'

The Lady shook her head. 'I can't, Ava.'

'But you can! Your Mother Catcher is just there. She can give you more time. It won't matter if you use just a little of the stores you promised to Donlon. No one will begrudge you that.' Ava put her hand on her mother's pleadingly.

'No, Ava. I will not take time that is no longer my own. My Mother Catcher restored me just now but I will not take even one time leaf from her. I've made my final choice.'

'What choice?'

'The choice between having eternal life, or love. It's not just about the pledge I made to the Donlon crowd. I've had enough life, Ava.' She pressed Ava's hand in her own. 'Eternal life has made me inhuman, like a dark goddess. I looked at humans from on high and they were other. I had a child as an experiment and the experiment had unexpected outcomes. Outcomes for which I am forever grateful, as they restored my humanity to me. *You* restored my humanity to me.'

'But I have only just found you. It's too soon to lose you.' Ava knew she sounded like a disappointed child, but so be it. She could not deny that in herself any longer. 'And I can't fight the time-snatching without you.'

'Yes, you can. You're the Daughter – *my* daughter – and you have great strength within you. You will see.'

Her mother reached out one hand to Ava's cheek, her eyes bright. 'Ah, Ava. Don't you see? I've had what is rare. I've touched the stars and been as eternal as the moon. But I have never had love. This thing, this common human experience, is the true treasure. This is the exchange I have chosen. Eternal life is not the greatest treasure, after all.'

Her mother smiled at Ava. 'To become fully human, to really love you, I have to die. And thanks to you, I can die with a full heart. This is the greatest gift that you have given me.'

Ava looked at her mother through tear-blurred eyes and finally, *finally*, she understood.

Her mother loved her more than anything. Her mother loved her more than she loved life.

The understanding was so huge that it had to overflow, sweeping into every empty corner and neglected space inside Ava. Every aching little knot finally loosened and dissolved, swept away as easily as salt by warm water.

How could anyone have more from a mother, than this?

When Ava thought of that time afterwards, she could not have said whether it was minutes, or an hour, or a day. Ava sat with her mother and gently combed her hair with her fingers while Esmeralda told her stories from long ago. She had visited London and walked with great men and women, discussed the importance of education for women with Mary Wollstonecraft, heard poetry from William Blake's lips and watched the sky with Caroline Herschel.

'She called it "sweeping the skies" when she took her recordings. What a brilliant woman she was. I kept her with me for as long as I could, but a woman living beyond ninety-seven years was already unheard of.'

'Wait – you gave Caroline Herschel more time?' Ava gazed at her mother in awe.

'Why should such a strong mind be betrayed by a weak body? It was no more than any friend would do.'

And she talked about her long life, and about Donlon, and about people she had known. She mentioned, almost casually, that she was the good friend of another queen.

Was her mother serious? 'Which queen? Not Queen Victoria?'

'Of course. I have known all the London monarchs. It would be disrespectful of me to not acknowledge them. The Palace knows about us, as do the City. But Victoria was easily my favourite. We were queens together, although

I did not require a crown. I regret not saying goodbye in person. Perhaps you can do that for me?'

Ava laughed. Did her mother truly believe she could meet the Queen, just like that?

'And my beloved Observatory. You know that is where we first met, don't you, Ava?'

Ava smiled at the memory of the elegant Mr Timeward. 'Yes, I've worked that out. Why did you do that?'

'I much prefer London men's clothes. I have no idea why the women handicap themselves with those skirts. And I needed to see you, and your father was not willing to allow this. Miss Buss helped me arrange that, in her role within the Order. I told her my problem, and she took care of it all.'

'Miss *Buss*?'

'Oh yes. She is a remarkable woman. You will find out more about the marvellous Miss Buss when you go back to London, I am quite sure. But Ava, you must understand that the Observatory is a sacred space for me. Your father turned me into the Green Witch as a snide joke, but I have chosen to embrace that. I *am* the Green Witch, and Greenwich is my namesake in London. It will be a sanctuary for you, too, if you need it. I have left something very precious there, but I have no time to collect and give it to you. It is yours and you must treasure it. Mrs Airy knows everything about it, and you may always confide in her.'

'Wait – what? The wife of the Astronomer Royal?' Ava pressed a hand to her head. The world was tilting, yet again.

'Yes, my dear. She is another wonderful woman. You will be surrounded by them, which comforts me greatly.

I am leaving you in the best of hands. Now, I must also tell you about my conversations with Mary Somerville. She loves birds, you know, as well as being a brilliant mathematician.'

And Ava followed her mother into yet another story, with a feeling of coming home. She took each story and stored it carefully inside herself, in that space that had always been empty.

And they also talked about nothing. Small things. Trains and buttons and funny things people had said. Not great, or earth shattering, or profound. But it was what she had yearned for, finally.

It was – yes. It was the greatest treasure.

Little by little, Esmeralda's voice slowed and her movements became stiffer, but Ava did not hurry her. When it was all over, she held the light body in her arms, and she could not tell if the tears that came were from an overflow of joy, or loss.

Malaikah had come at the end. She felt his still presence before she saw it, his figure blurring behind tears as she held her mother's shrunken body. He knelt next to Ava, one hand on her head and the other on Esmeralda's heart, and spoke words that hummed just beyond sense, but were full of comfort.

'The happening is done and it was lovemade, Avaheart. This was all told before. She wears the heartshroud to travel back to her own mother. I will carry her, as I swore to her at the storystarting.' He lifted Esmeralda and looked at Ava. 'You standhigh, Avaheart. Now you are warriorstrong.

A comet has called you into power and now you meet it, skybright.'

Ava had forgotten Donati's Comet with its bright tail curving over London. So she had not imagined its beckoning to her. The tightness in her chest dissolved and it felt natural to let Malaikah take the body from her arms. He turned and went outside, where he soared with her mother to the heavens. Ava watched as he became a tiny dot in the pink sky of the east, and afterwards never asked where he had gone with her. It was all as right as the sunrise and the wind in the trees.

Ava sat with the Mother Catcher for a long time before she was ready to leave. She knew that these hours – or days, or aeons, or minutes, she would never know – marked the fulcrum of her life. She sat in the midpoint of her time on earth, knowing that however long she lived, her time would be forever divided into *before this* and *after this*.

Finally she rose and walked into the new day, carrying all of her story with her.

CHAPTER 39
JACK

Donlon

It was two days since Jack had seen Ava. Two days since he'd gone back to Hammer's to take up life as an apprentice again. It felt like lifetimes had passed since he'd stood over an anvil, and so much had changed since then.

He had to see Ava again, before she left for London. He was desperate to see Sister Wisetree too. He hadn't seen his beloved mother figure since before he was snatched the first time, and her long absence was an ache inside him.

Hammer had given Jack permission to go to the Foundling Home after work the next day. He'd sent word to Ava to be there, too. That day felt like a week but finally it ended and he ran to wash, change and eat a quick meal before setting off to the station.

Jack now knew that he and Ava had always saved each other, in different ways. That long-ago day at the Foundling Home played out in his mind's eye as if it had happened yesterday.

312

It was summer. He and Ava were small, maybe he was three, four years old? They were playing near the creek outside the Foundling Home with another little boy called Jeremiah. He was dark skinned, like Sister Wisetree, and Jack remembered wishing he had beautiful skin like that, too. They were under the fierce eye of a nun, who was making sure they didn't try and cross the creek. The three children were throwing sticks into the rushing water and seeing which one tumbled the fastest.

The nun had jumped up and yelled and Jack had thought they were in trouble. But the nun wasn't even looking at them – she was staring up at the Foundling Home and then she started to run towards it. Grown-ups were always doing incomprehensible things, so they didn't think anything of it and turned back to their game. Jack looked longingly at the woods on the other side of the creek. This would be a good time to go exploring.

There were some people in the woods. Jack prodded Ava, who raised her head. Jeremiah looked up, too, and they all stared at the three people in colourful clothes. They waved at the children. Smiled. Held up the best wooden toy boat Jack had ever seen, with full rigging and sails. They had a ball, and some little dolls in dresses.

The three children scrambled to their feet and splashed across the forbidden creek, running to the strangers without hesitation. Without a moment of fear or doubt, which would have been strange, if these strangers had not been Hams. They had sent a kitchen fire into Sister Philomena's head and swept any childish fear away.

Jack and Jeremiah had the precious boat between them and were already carrying it to the water. Ava had wanted the boat too, but one of the Hams pushed the two dolls – which Jack remembered were clad in bright silks and had real hair, one black, one red – towards her. She stopped and reached for them.

Quick words passed between the Hams but all Jack and Jeremiah could see was the wonderful boat. It was the most beautiful thing they had ever seen, sailing majestically on the water. They gazed at it, drinking in its grandeur.

When Ava's cry came, it took a moment to filter through, as though they were surrounded by thick fog.

Jack turned. One of the Hams had Ava by the elbows, gripping her from behind. Her arms were stuck out behind her like broken wings and the dolls were on the ground. The Ham picked her up and bundled her roughly over his shoulder, then turned to run into the woods. The other Hams were beside him, urging him on, glancing around them nervously. Jack could see, looking back with older eyes, that these were weak Hams, maybe outcasts, and young. Their powers were patchy.

The Hams were nearly at the woods when the thing happened. Jack's fear and fury boiled up and flew towards the Ham holding Ava. He remembered a flash and then he was inside the Ham's head and hurting him. Wanting him to let Ava go.

The Ham screamed, an awful, high-pitched sound, and let go of Ava to clutch at his head. Ava fell to the ground and the Ham kept screaming. There was blood coming out of his ears. Blood on his hands. Blood trickling red down his neck.

The rest was a blur – the other Hams shouting, Jeremiah running from the river towards Jack, clutching the boat with wide eyes. The blood-covered Ham staggering away, helped by one friend while the other stopped and turned just as Jeremiah ran past. Jack running to Ava and being inside her head, gently this time, looking to see if she was hurt, and the two of them talking without words.

Then looking up to see the last Ham grab Jeremiah. Jeremiah struggling, the Ham staggering with him to the woods, Ava jumping up to chase him, Jack pulling her back, grown-ups suddenly around them and shouting.

Jeremiah disappearing into the woods with the Hams.

Sister Wisetree making awful, wailing, un-grown-up sounds.

That was the terrible day that Jack's power first came to life. It was a violent birth.

Jack rang the entrance bell at the Foundling Home and took a deep, shaky breath. That day had seared his child's mind so badly that he'd shut it away, squashing the memory deep inside him. He couldn't remember anything for a long time after that – only that both Ava and Jeremiah were not there with Jack at the Foundling Home anymore. Had he thought that he, Jack, had been the reason for them going? That it had all somehow been his fault?

He glanced around him almost fearfully. Last time he'd been here was when he came with Agnes to find Sister Beatrice in Sister Wisetree's place. He had felt the very stones singing their misery to him that day when he had half-glimpsed a terrible truth.

But this time it was Sister Wisetree who answered the front door and joy bubbled up inside him.

'Jack, love! Come in,' she exclaimed, pulling him to her for a bear hug. 'Ava will be so happy that you've come.' Her damp-eyed smile told him much more than the plain words could.

He clung to Sister Wisetree. Much had changed since he'd last seen her. He saw how much he'd needed her, and perhaps she needed him now, too. Just the touch of her returned some of his old steadiness back to him. Reminded him of that pre-snatching Jack, with the sharp clothes and jaunty tread. That old Jack seemed a long way away these days.

But there was something he had to know. He pulled back and cleared his throat, dreading her reply. 'Sister Beatrice was here last time, and –'

Sister Wisetree raised one hand to silence him. 'I will say this, and then we will not speak of it again. Sister Beatrice is guilty of unforgivable crimes. She worked with that man and supplied him with children as time feeders. She abused her position and my name doing so. She has gone and will not return.' Sister Wisetree looked at him steadily and Jack saw a glimpse of a Sister Wisetree that he was glad he would never be on the receiving end of.

He nodded understanding and the moment passed. His sight flickered at the sadness behind her eyes.

'It's all right, Jack,' said Sister Wisetree. 'You can look.

I think you know most of the story yourself now, anyway.'

Jack frowned, not understanding. She smiled, sadly. 'Go on. Use your sight. You will understand more then.'

Jack paused. He had trained himself to hold his sight in check and it seemed wrong to open it on Sister Wisetree now. It felt invasive, as if he was reading her most private letters. But she had invited him and she knew better than anyone what he could do. He let his sight unfurl.

He saw that day again, but this time Sister Wisetree's pain jagged too sharp for him to bear. He shut down his sight and put his arms around her. Her tears were hot on his shoulder.

Jeremiah had been her son.

Jack stayed late at the Foundling Home that night. There was so much to say. Time spent just being in the same room as Ava and Sister Wisetree was essential for him, he realised.

'He was my adopted son. My sister's boy. She died when he was a baby.' Sister Wisetree's voice was soft. 'I've been looking for him ever since, in both London and Donlon. He is transient and even at that age already had incredible circus skills, so he's valuable in either place. His father was a Ham, you see. The Lady asked me to go with you to London, Ava, after that day. She knew you were in danger here – the wrong people knew who you were. I agreed, as long as I could keep my place here open as well. I needed to have a foot in each world, and Jack was still here. The Lady sent a message to Bill, because she knew Bill would raise Rupert's child as his own. She lied about Rupert's

317

death, as we know now, but that's a story for another time.'

Sister Wisetree reached out and took Jack and Ava by the hand. Her grip was almost fierce. 'You two held me to the earth while I was buffeted by grief. You saved me, both of you.' Her eyes were bright and sad. 'And now you know why things are as they are, between you. The horror of that day, and the flowering of Jack's sight, branded your souls. You share a scar that binds you closer than blood siblings.'

Sister Wisetree left them alone in the kitchen to talk soon after that.

'Do you think she'll really find him, after all this time?' Ava's question echoed the one whispering inside Jack. She was leaning on the table, head on her arms, eyes locked on Jack.

'I hope so,' said Jack. 'The snatching stirred up the old pain inside her and made it new. She'll suffer until she finds him. If she ever does.'

'You know about that.' It was a statement.

Jack looked at Ava. 'I know how another person can help a torn soul.'

'But Jack, I won't always be here. I'm also in two worlds.'

'Yeah. I have work to do.'

Which was an understatement. He had to use the moments he did have with Ava to re-weave his self, so he could get through the days without her. There was Sister Wisetree, and there must be other people he could turn to, who could help him and he them, but it was impossible to even imagine that now. He wasn't sure how to do it, but he'd find out. He had no choice.

'There's one way you can help,' he said.

'Tell me.'

Jack closed his eyes. He didn't know if he had the strength for this yet. Whether he could open a pathway in Ava's head for her to see. But it was the only way he could unload the Lady's stories inside him. He had to pass them over, as he had received them.

He hoped to the gods this would work, or he would be trapped behind the Lady forever.

The Lady had said to Jack, afterwards, 'You will know, Jack. You are already enough.'

Know what? Know what to tell Ava? Know when to tell Ava? Know *how* to tell Ava?

But now he did know, all of those things. The stories that were ready to go to Ava pushed at the top of his mind and needed just the gentlest shove to fly to Ava, where they belonged.

Ava's eyes widened and she gazed at something far beyond this kitchen. Her mouth fell open. *'Oh!'*

Jack let out a long breath. Thank the gods, thank the gods. The stories whose time it was were gone from him. He had passed them to Ava. *He could do it*. The relief was vast inside him. He had done what he had to do.

Which meant the time he'd been dreading had arrived. He took both her hands between his, pressed tight and breathed this moment into himself. Tears welled up in Ava's eyes. Her tears might be for the stories she was within, or for Jack, or her dead mother, or for what would come next. Or they might be for all of those things.

There was no need for words. Words could not hold all that was passing between them, in any case.

Jack untwisted his fingers from Ava's and turned his life silently away from hers. Leaving her deep in his soul, and her story.

EPILOGUE – AVA

London, October 1858

Ava stepped onto the leaf-sodden path and made her way through the dark green trees. The familiar mulch smell of damp earth, cold stone, greenery and decaying leaves sat heavy in her nostrils. She had been a regular visitor, to the cemetery since her return from Donlon, feeling a compulsion to bear witness to the grave of the aptly named Elsie Swindleton.

For Elsie had been swindled out of her own story. Swindled out of the legacy she left behind and the memories that others carried of her. It seemed the least that Ava could do was stand at her grave and acknowledge the true story of the woman who lay, forever silent, beneath the earth.

Ava put her flowers down so that she could shake out the rug she was carrying. She laid it on the cold ground before settling herself in front of the grave – she had learnt that much from previous damp-kneed encounters. She leaned forward and ran her fingers over the familiar words. Words that hid the woman lying below.

IN LOVING MEMORY OF ELSIE JUNE SWINDLETON
BELOVED MOTHER OF AVA AND WIFE OF BILL
WE WILL ALWAYS REMEMBER YOU
RIP 1829–1848

'I know this is not who you are, Elsie,' whispered Ava. 'I know that your true story has been buried with you.'

Ava arranged the flowers gently on the foot of the grave. These days, she felt real affection for the seamstress whose story she had been trying to build, block by block – a more solid, true affection than when she'd thought Elsie was her mother.

'You lived with your baby and your husband, who was sometimes there and sometimes not. You worked your fingers to the bone and you often went hungry. You were a tiny woman and hunger made you weak. When the cholera hit, you had no strength to fight it. The last bit of strength you had was sending your baby away to safety with your husband. You never saw your boy again.' Ava paused and blinked hard. 'You would be so proud to see the young man he has grown into, Elsie.'

The shock of her final day in Donlon, when she had sat with Father and Violet in the kitchen at the Foundling Home, still hummed through her. The stories had come then, alongside endless cups of Violet's brew, teasing out the last knots in Ava's understanding of her own life. For Elsie, the woman chosen to be Ava's mother in name, was Jack's true mother.

Ava pressed prickling eyes with her palms as she knelt

on the earth. Jack had lost his real mother so that Ava could have a false one. She missed him with a dull ache and thought of him as often as she thought of her mother. The two were together in her mind. Family. She leaned forward and put a hand on Elsie's gravestone.

A deep groan made Ava jump. She snatched her hand away from the grave but of course it wasn't from there. It was a human groan, not a ghost. She could have sworn she was alone here. She climbed to her feet and looked around. There it was again! And now there was another sound, a higher voice, like a woman's. A prickle ran down her back. Was somebody hurt? In danger? Ill?

The air twisted into shadows around her and the head-stones swooped as if they were at sea. Dizziness clutched her skull and she closed her eyes to stop the swaying. When she opened them again, the graveyard was gone.

She whirled around. It was happening again. She was back in that dark forest where she had first seen Malaikah and his brother, the hunter, what seemed like lifetimes ago. Where was this place? Why had she been brought here, again?

Heart hammering, she peered into the darkness. The groans were louder now and coming from somewhere in the midst of thick trees. Uncertainly, she stepped towards the sounds.

The high voice cried out, 'No, you must not see! Your brother is not whole! Go, go!'

A deep answering voice. 'Fallback, Needlie. I would cleave with my hearttwin.'

Malaikah! At the sound of his voice Ava broke into a

run. She could see a light in the trees coming from a tiny hut. Malaikah's great frame stood in front of the doorway, confronted by a young woman with her arms spread wide. Malaikah pushed her gently to one side before ducking his head to step through the doorway. He made a sound, then dropped to his knees.

'They must yet grow!' cried the woman, clutching a bloodied needle in one hand. 'His blood is still mingling with the bird. Your brother will fly, too, oh winged one, and you will meet in the skies!'

Ava drew close to look inside the hut and let out a cry of horror. A half-dead bird convulsed on the ground with bloodied stumps where its wings should have been. Malaikah's brother lay face down on the ground, eyes shut, with the bird's wings sewn onto his red-streaked shoulders. The new wings twitched feebly. Malaikah knelt, head down, both hands resting on his brother's broad back.

'What happenchance, my hearttwin?' he whispered. 'The sky is not your truehome. You miserymake, my brother.' He looked at the Needlie outside the doorway. 'You monstersew today, oh Stitchdark.'

'The needle stitches light and dark, Malaikah. You know it well.' The girl turned to Ava. 'You, girl! You are part of this stitching. Your future is sewn.'

Ava was frozen with the strange horror of the scene in front of her.

'Avaheart, this is not your place.' Malaikah's clear gaze held an anguish she had never seen before. 'You must stayfar from my twin. Promise me.' He pressed one hand to his heart and his voice dropped so that Ava could hardly hear his last words. 'I can makenot the choice between you and my twin, Avasoul. You must stayfar. Go now; he must not see you.'

Ava clutched at the wall. She wanted nothing more than to leave but her limbs betrayed her. She could not move as the creature's yellow eyes opened and fixed on her. In that endless moment she felt the primal terror of a mouse cowering in grass, with the deadly predator locked in freefall above her. She tried to scream, but the sound froze in her throat.

The next moment Malaikah, his brother and the Needlie blurred, and disappeared.

ACKNOWLEDGEMENTS

So many people to thank:

My parents, for instilling a love of books and reading from the very beginning. Thank you to Mum, for reading me all those stories and for blowing my trumpet at every opportunity to anyone who would listen, and to several who wouldn't. To Dad, for being the fastest reader and proudest supporter of every single edit of this book, and everything else I've ever written. I only now truly appreciate how precious the solid, loving, supportive start in life you both gave me is.

My husband Jon, for being my sounding board for hours of story ideas, plot problems, interesting facts about Victorian London, and most of all for his enthusiastic advice on everything related to battle strategy and historical weapons. Thank you for being my live-in research consultant, for always having my back when I needed an essential writing retreat and for hand-selling my book to random bookshops. Your love and support mean everything.

My two beloved kidlets, Ruby and Gabriel, for whom I started this story in the first place and who make me proud every single day. They were much smaller when this book idea germinated and they've been an essential part of the reading and feeding back process ever since. I still have a very early version of this story with some harsh editorial comment from a young Ruby.

My adored sisters, Fleur (aka Maxx) and Kathryn, for always being publicly and privately supportive of both me and my writing, and for being the best little sisters in the entire world.

Christine Baines, for being the most loving, supportive, generous mother-in-law that I could possibly hope for, and for being constant inspiration for living life to the glamorous full.

The many teachers I've had along the way – too many to list – who have all helped build writer Karen. Special mention must go to Debi Alper and Emma Darwin, for running their superb Self Editing Your Novel course, which was a clear and definite turning point in getting this book publication ready, and to my inspirational high-school English teacher, Margaret Rennick.

My incredible band of beta readers, who have helped me immeasurably in honing this book and steering it in new directions. Lorraine Wilson, whose wise comments are so full of insight, J.A. Ironside, the endlessly incisive Structure Bear, as well as Jane Shufflebotham, K. Laurelle, Rupert Baines, Fiona Erskine, Kate Fryer, Melanie Irwin, Dad, Jon and my kids. You have all been an important part of this book's journey. Thanks also to the Random Writers for years of camaraderie, support and excellent writing, and to all my fellow writer-friends – they are overwhelmingly generous, supportive and positive and it is a joy to be part of the YA/MG and broader writing community.

My wonderful friends have been my loudest cheerleaders and you all know who you are. Particular mention goes to my much-loved Merks – Cazza, Emmanuelle, Laura, Eva, Begoña and Steph, with special thanks to Theresa Parker, couturier extraordinaire. Theresa whipped me up my very own crinoline cage when I couldn't find one to try on for research purposes and casually delivered it to me on a Merk weekend in Amsterdam, where she finished it off with the expert assistance of Cazza and Laura.

Camilla Martindale and Pete Moses, for generously supporting this book and its sequel by making the highest bid in the #AuthorsForFiries online fundraiser auction in January 2020, which helped those affected by the terrible bushfires of that year. Also, my long-time friend Meri Fatin, for appointing herself as my publicist in WA and bombarding her long-suffering extensive network with news of my book.

My agent, Danielle Binks, who I had in the crosshairs as my ideal agent long before the happy day I signed with her. She is passionate, supportive, wise, a fierce advocate for her authors and for writing in general, and a generous fount of publishing and OzYA knowledge.

My razor-sharp editors at Penguin Random House, Amy Thomas and Lisa Riley, who have managed to be kind, positive and supportive while simultaneously homing in with surgical precision on everything that needed attention. I stand in awe of Amy's word-honing skills. Thanks also to Tina Gumnior and Laura Hutchinson, who enthusiastically pushed this book out into the world, and to Tony Palmer, who created its stunning cover. Heartfelt gratitude to Katrina Lehman, who has since left PRH as Senior Editor but who was my very first champion there.

Many thanks to Andrew Pettit and Fergus Forsyth of the Australian Antiquarian Horological Society, and to Anna Rolls, Curator of the Clockmakers' Museum in London, for their generous advice on historical watchmaking.

And last but by no means least, to Victorian-era expert (and great-great-great grand-daughter of Charles Dickens, who was alive at the time this book is set), Lucinda Hawksley, who cast her knowledgeable eye over this book for historical bloopers, and to my friend and history of medicine expert, Natasha McEnroe, who did the same. Any mistakes are entirely my own.

My first book baby has been raised by a village and is all the better for it. Thank you, all.

Karen Ginnane is an Australian author for middle grade and young adult readers. Her debut historical fantasy adventure novels *When Days Tilt* and its sequel *When Souls Tear* are part of the Time Catchers series published by Penguin Random House.

Karen has been variously employed as a freelance copywriter, a marketing director for Paramount Pictures in London, a grain weighbridge operator in rural WA, a swimming teacher, a life model, a deckhand in Chile and an English teacher in Japan. She's also taught creative writing, published short stories and in 2020 received an Invited Residency to Varuna National Writers' House for *When Souls Tear*.

Karen runs a tour operator business with her husband, who is a Londoner, and lives in Melbourne with him and their two children. And two cats.

You can find her online at **karenginnane.com**

Continue the thrilling Time Catchers series in
When Souls Tear. COMING SOON!